Praise for

THE BOY AND THE DOLPHIN

———— •◆• ————

"Dick Schmidt has crafted a charming story of a relationship between a boy and a dolphin. Spanning more than a decade and set against the backdrop of a fictitious Caribbean island, this wonderful story explores the connection between human-kind and the natural world and how it can enrich both.

"This inspiring story reminds us that the world would be a better place if we could all find a way to live in harmony.

"I have known Dick for several years. As a businessman and philanthropist he has demonstrated his deep commitment to conservation. This touching story is another example of his passion for nature and the oceans."

—Philippe Cousteau

"Dick Schmidt's first novel is simply first rate. Fascinating, heartwarming, and absorbing from beginning to end. The characters are finely drawn, the plot ever captivating, and reading this novel, you are completely transported into Toby's world, surrounded by the beauty of the Bahamas and South-east Asia."

—Doris Kearns Goodwin

THE BOY AND THE DOLPHIN

Dick Schmidt

LANDSLIDE
PUBLISHING

Landslide Publishing, Inc.
201 Plaza Real, Suite 140
Boca Raton, Florida 33432

ISBN-13: 978-0-99750-101-8

Illustrations by Dale Raymond

*Dale Raymond, ISDA, HFES, is an industrial designer.
He lives with his wife in the Tampa Bay area.*

Copyedited by
Carol Killman Rosenberg • www.carolkillmanrosenberg.com

Cover and interior design by
Gary A. Rosenberg • www.thebookcouple.com

Printed in the United States of America

To Barbara,
my true north

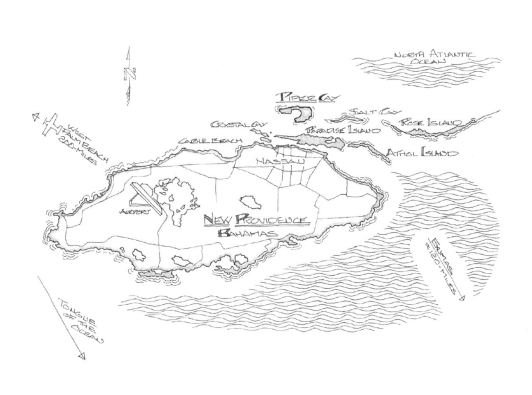

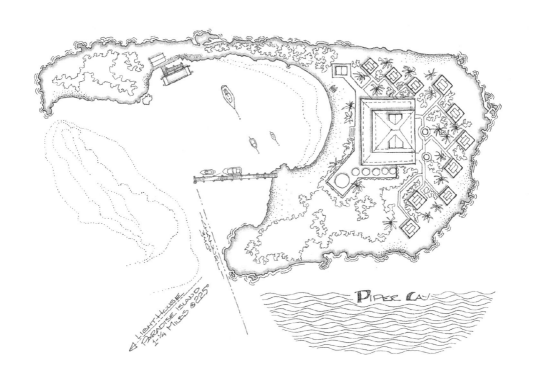

LIGHT HOUSE
PARADISE ISLAND
1¼ MILES @225°

PIPER CAY

PROLOGUE

The sun is high and the incoming tide has cleaned out the refuse-filled waters of Nassau's harbor, revealing a deep blue in the natural channel formed between the island of New Providence and Hog Island, which defines the outer perimeter of the harbor. The edges of the channel lighten to a pristine turquoise near the sandy beaches of the island, contrasted with the garbage and wreck-littered wharf along Potter's Cay on the south side. The tide change means more than pretty water to the ecosystem in the area. The incoming tide also washes through the reef around Rose Island to the east, which pushes the small fish and mullet away from the reef's protection. This makes good hunting for the large pod of bottlenose dolphin that frequents the area.

    The cow forages the down-current side of the reef with her close traveling companion. She is a young female, about six years old and very pregnant with her first calf. Her companion stays close, so she will be able to help with the birth when the time comes, something she is familiar with, as she has had several calves of her own. They hunt well together, often batting small baitfish with their flukes to

1

stun them, making the catch all that much easier. Both are healthy animals with traditional markings, dark bluish gray tops and light gray bottoms. The companion has a notch missing from her dorsal, the result of an overzealous lover some years ago. The pregnant cow is unmarked, unusual for a six-year-old. Younger, she is a little smaller than her companion, weighing in around 500 pounds, yet she eats twice as much, a result of her condition.

The feeding is easy today, as the current brings the easy pickings over and through the reef where the cow patiently waits for an opportunity to grab small fish in her sharp conical teeth. The reef is shallow, and at the turn of the low tide, she can hear the water foaming around the coral where it breaks the surface. The sun is high, the water is clear, and she can see the coral tips jutting above the surface when she comes up for air. The current is pushing her away from the coral as the tide starts its flood.

It is a perfect day, complicated only by the agility the cow has lost because of the calf she is carrying. Although uncomfortable and yearning for the release of her burden, she is prepared for the event, having scouted a suitable location to give birth in the lagoon of the L-shaped island next door. The lagoon is protected from predators and weather, yet filled with mullet and shrimp for her to eat while she prepares to introduce a newborn to her aquatic world of adventure.

With the help of her companion, she will be able to tend to her calf as well as her own needs, which will be considerable. The shallow end of the lagoon will give her a fixed place where she can put the calf, so it will be able to reach the surface for air as it struggles to learn the art of breathing. The newborn will need air every few minutes at first, until it learns how to maximize intake in its tiny lungs. She and her companion will nuzzle the calf into position, so it will not slide off the sand shelf into deeper water, which at nine feet will be too much for it to negotiate while it learns to use its flukes to swim in its first few hours of life. That process will advance quickly, and after a few days, the calf will be comfortable staying at the surface as it learns to breathe more deeply.

The cow and her companion will be in full attendance until the calf is comfortable with the basics. Nursing will also be easier in the shallow water; by rolling on her side, the cow can offer her mammary slits to the calf so they will be more accessible than if they were birthing in deep water. A nudge from the companion will position the calf so it can insert its tongue in the slit to access the thick, sweet milk. This will happen as often as four times an hour while the calf is an immature and cannot feed on solid food by mouth. This will take at least six months, and even then, although the calf will have new teeth and can feed on solid food, it will continue to nurse for another year.

The cow is uncomfortably full from the foraging when she feels the first cramp deep in her belly. Instinct tells her that the time is nigh for her to head for the lagoon. A signal to her companion starts them on the three-mile journey to the island. The tidal current is with them, which helps. The cow stops from time to time as she is overcome by an occasional birthing cramp.

Crossing over the sandbar and moving into the lagoon, the two find a perfect slope of beach to perch for the birth. The beach has a deep hole on one side that is filled with discarded hemp nets and metal debris left there by humans. This is all the better, as they can see countless shrimp and crawfish on the bottom, shielding themselves from the high sun overhead. They won't have to go far to feed themselves in the coming weeks, just an added bonus.

The pains increase in frequency until her last push against the cramp eases the pain somewhat, as it moves lower in her belly. Tiny pliable tail flukes push out from her vagina, and her companion helps with gentle nibbling tugs on the calf's tail. More and more appears with each push, as the lower part of the calf becomes exposed. Being born tail first makes the survival probability better, as the newborn can exit the womb gracefully, without having to worry about breathing until it detaches from the placenta.

During this process the calf is very aware an event is taking place. First at its tail, it feels the cold, chilling water, which is eighteen or so degrees colder than what it has been used to for the last several months. As she comes further and further into this world, it gets colder and colder, and finally the cold wetness around her finds her eyes. The shock opens her eyelids, and she is overcome by brightness, something she has never experienced before. She clamps her jaw and feels the bone around her mouth, but she has no teeth, which won't start to come in for another five or six weeks. She feels her body literally unfold, as her dorsal becomes free of the confines of her mother's womb, and at last, her head pops clear of her mother.

There is some blood, but not much. Quickly the cow's companion pushes the newborn up the sand to fresh air, and the calf takes her first breath. On instinct, she blows out the goop clogging her blowhole with a robust cough-like exhale. Air comes easily to her now, and she lies exhausted in the shallow water on the sand shelf, surrounded by her mother and the companion. They roll the calf side to side, deeper in the water and out, and begin the long and tedious process of introducing this new little girl to the world.

CHAPTER ONE

The quiet of sunset at Piper Cay is profound, the sun setting over the small spit of land that forms the southwest side of the natural lagoon. The evening no-see-ums will be arriving soon to make the pleasant solace of the modest pink on the horizon a place to avoid for a couple of hours. Toby Matthias measures his time alone, as he contemplates returning to the main cottage where his wife and daughter are waiting for him, giving him the space they think he needs. Friends of the family are here for his grandfather's memorial service.

Toby has a lot to think about and many decisions to make in the next several days. His decisions will mark a turning point in his life. It is a sad time for him. He was raised here on this island by his grandparents, who took him in after his parents were killed in the freak air crash of KLM 633 shortly after its departure from Shannon, Ireland, in 1954. They were en route to New York on their way home from a European vacation. Although half of the passengers survived the crash, Toby's parents were not among the fortunate ones. He was only eleven years old, and, young as his parents were,

7

naturally no plans had yet been made for this eventuality. At the time, Toby's grandparents were still reasonably young and recently retired, living out their later years in the Bahamas and running an inn for tourists who wanted an Out Island experience that wasn't too far from civilization and an airport.

Piper Cay is the perfect setting, located outside Nassau harbor, across from what the locals knew as Hog Island. The island forms a natural barrier for the harbor in Nassau, situated west of the chain of small islands that form a protective reef on the north side of New Providence. While Toby was away at college, new owners began development and renamed it Paradise Island to make it more attractive to vacationers. The Commonwealth provides a stable government, banking, and currency, and communications and transportation to South Florida are somewhat reliable.

Toby's grandmother, Irene, passed away while Toby was in high school. He has recently finished a lengthy tour as a Navy fighter pilot aboard the USS *Constellation* in Southeast Asia, where he flew cover operations over Laos and bombing missions in the designated route packs in Vietnam. Now, just as Toby is preparing to decide whether to make the Navy a career choice or to leave the service, his grandfather, Vernon, has passed away.

Although married with a six-year-old daughter to consider, Toby faces a dilemma. The Navy is offering him a career position if he would like it, or he can separate from active duty. His grandparents have left him virtually everything from his childhood, their investments, and the Out Island Inn, run down as it is, but with a good reputation of sun and sand for the following of repeat customers that keeps the place going.

A piece of him remembers the years growing up in an unconventional world of the Bahamas, the private day schools, years at prep school in Florida, and the University of Florida. The memories rekindle his love of the islands and the sea. On the other hand, he lives a dream life as a fighter pilot, but absent that he must spend much of his time thousands of miles away from his wife and his precious little girl, he doesn't know if he wants to give up the adrenaline rush of a cat launch, shacking a rejoin with his flight lead, or the terror of a night trap aboard a carrier.

His only fear is of doing something stupid like inviting a SAM up his tailpipe, but that would go away with his appointment opportunity in the Navy. A new fighter weapons school is being initiated in Miramar, California, to teach Navy fighter pilots the lessons learned from Vietnam, where the U.S.'s initial air combat record is less than stellar. If Toby accepts the new appointment, he will be reassigned to the new "Top Gun" school as an instructor, where the only enemy will be other experienced Navy pilots. He will be able to live in a home, not a bunk, and his family will be able to join him, to normalize him. The best of both worlds, he thinks.

Alternatively, he can leave active duty and return to the islands to manage the cottages, living what many would also consider a dream life. The main house and cottages have become a little neglected over the years since his grandmother died. His grandfather didn't have the motivation to keep the place as manicured as he had when Irene was still alive.

Toby reflects on how common it seems that aging couples often follow each other closely to that last stop on the train. His grandfather was more like a father to Toby in his willingness to share learning experiences with him. He made Toby work hard for his place in the family with chores on the property. Keeping a cheerful attitude for the guests was a constant obligation, so Toby acquired a keen ability to work well with adults at the expense of social development with peers.

This explains why he gets on so well with superiors. He has always been that "nice young man" someone brings home when visiting others' families. He was a devilishly handsome kid growing up, with fierce blue eyes, constantly browned skin, and long, wavy blond hair. This carries through as a young man of twenty-six. His hair, now military short, is still light, and his vision is excellent through his deep blue eyes. He isn't tall or short, about five-ten, very fit, yet he moves with a languid gait one would associate with a taller person.

He sits on the end of the dock, barefoot in slacks and a dress shirt, watching "red ball" drop toward the horizon. The dock extends a hundred feet into the cove on the south end of the island, built on sturdy iron beams hammered into the marl bottom. At the end, the last beam extends eight feet above the planking, wired for a small white light used for finding the dock during approaches at night. Unlit day markers define the narrow channel over the sandbar in front of the cove, but the light can be used with a good compass bearing of 340 degrees to navigate the channel safely on non-moonlit nights. On the other side of the dock, the iron beam is not so high and supports an eight-inch brass ship's bell. Once active, the clapper is now corroded to the point that it can no longer swing freely enough to ring the bell. Toby's thoughts turn to the bell, and he is flooded with memories as he recalls his years as a young teen in this cove with his best friend and companion. He hears the screen porch door slam shut, as his daughter, Jenny, runs out the dock to greet him.

"Daddy, Daddy, Mommy says it's time to come in for dinner and talk to the people who have come to see you." She is a mini Toby, with blond hair and blue eyes, barefoot in a simple sundress. It isn't lost on him how natural she looks in this setting. "Aren't the bugs going to bite you pretty soon?"

She sits next to him and puts her head in his lap, kicking her legs out in front of her and spreading her toes in the disjointed way she makes them look like stubby fingers. She surveys the surroundings and notices the bell, pointing it out with her toes. "Daddy, that bell is dirty! Does it ring? What do you use it for? Are you going to clean it up?" she machine-guns her musings.

"Jenny, that's a very special bell," Toby replies. "You remember the story I told you about when I was a little boy, a little older than you, and I had a very special friend named Phinney."

"You mean the dolphin you saved?"

"Yep. That's the one, but I didn't save her. She was just a little baby at the time; it was her mother I saved."

"I like that story; tell me again, Daddy, please. Please!"

"I can start it a little bit, because we do have to go in. Some of our guests have traveled a long way to pay their respects, and I need to attend to them."

Excited at the prospect of hearing the story again, Jenny sits up and looks at her father with anticipation. . . .

CHAPTER TWO

The calf and her mother cruised the rocks on the inside of Rose Island, as the young dolphin learned how to root small fish out of the reef. She was four and a half months old now, swimming and breathing on her own. For the first few months of her life, she had been sustained by her mother's milk, which she suckled from nipples located inside small slits on her mother's breast below her pectoral fins.

The milk was sweet, thick, and nourishing, but as her little conical teeth started to come in, it was time for her to learn how to hunt. The teeth were not for chewing, as she swallowed small baitfish whole, but she could stun and immobilize them with her bite, something that had come naturally to her. She was comfortable in the water, and her small body, about fifteen pounds, was very agile. Her pectorals, dorsal, and tail flukes had firmed up since her birth, as the cartilage grew and toughened them. She did not have the body length to keep up with her mother, but Mother was patient, staying with her as she moved along the rocks, flushing out small fish and stunning them with her tail so her baby could eat.

With the rich milk to nourish her, the calf had gained more than two pounds a month. By the end of the year, she would be nearly self-sufficient and able to sustain herself, but for the time being, she was dependent on her mother for learning and feeding. They never separated.

The calf had learned to communicate with her mother with clicks, which she could make in rapid succession from vocal chord–like sacs in the back of her throat where her flapper closed the vent that connected her breathing blowhole to her lungs. Open, it enabled her to force air past her vocal sac membranes that emitted high-pitched staccato-like squeaks, clicks, and other sounds. She was also learning to use her instinctive echolocation sonar, which she sensed through her jawbone. She was actually learning to "see" shapes, moving and nonmoving, that presented themselves in conditions where her excellent eyes could not perform. She learned from her mother in a three-step process, beginning with the mother performing alone, mother and calf doing it together, and then the calf doing it by herself.

Mother chased a small baitfish out of the rocks and stunned it with a bite, and the calf copied her, but she was having trouble holding her position on the reef because the tide was starting to ebb at a speed that made it hard for her to stabilize herself, the current pushing her against the reef as it pulled the stunned little fish back under the rocks. Try as she might, the calf was not able to recapture the meal. The tide was dropping rapidly now, and the current was becoming more troublesome. The top of the reef was exposed, and the waves were foaming on the surface, clouding the visibility and making noise, which the dolphins found distracting.

Mother had a better idea, and she signaled the calf to follow her as she headed for the cove at the L-shaped island where the calf was born. The calf was very excited about this because life was a lot simpler in the quiet water of the cove, where there was always some-

thing interesting going on. They began their trek westward; Mother patiently swam alongside her calf. The two resembled an aquatic Madonna and Child moving in tandem at the surface in the brilliant sunshine, mother shortening her thrusts, daughter lengthening hers, so that the two moved and breathed in unison.

As with all laws of fluids, the energies and speeds required and resulting from objects moving through them were directly related to the lengths of the objects. The calf's shorter body length made the effort all the greater for her, but this was how she grew strong, so that she would be able to keep up with the party she had been born into and with whom she would probably spend the rest of her life.

Toby was up early this spring morning. His grandfather, Vernon Matthias, whom he called Pop, had given him a lot of chores to attend to before the end of the weekend, and he wanted to have some good sunlight left at the end of the day to do some spearfishing and sailing before he had to think about heading back to day school on the mainland.

Pop was far more than a grandfather to him. Vern and Toby's grandma, Irene, had taken him in after the sudden loss of his parents. They had left the Chicago area a few years earlier when the family business was sold, using their share of the proceeds to pursue the fantasy of living in the Caribbean in a simple fashion, buying an available island on the north shore of New Providence.

Only a mile from the harbor at Nassau, Piper Cay was an L-shaped piece of land with a natural bar across the front of the cove on the south side. The sand bar was passable at high tide for boats drawing eight feet or less, and provided natural protection to the inn the Matthiases had built on the thick part of the island known as Piper's Landing, while allowing the prevailing trade winds good access to the lodgings for comfort in the evenings and during the high Caribbean sun. The inn offered a unique Out Island experience for vacationers who wanted something more than Miami Beach concrete. The natives were jovial and accommodating, and made natural hoteliers. The fishing was superb, and the operating costs were minimal, since food was abundant from the sea and Nassau had a thriving produce market. Cuban rum and cigars were easily procured, and the colonial commonwealth government was refreshingly proper compared with the laid-back island culture.

Toby's immediate responsibility was to clean up the trash that had been accumulating in the corner of the lagoon. The native population that looked after the inn lived in somewhat makeshift quarters on the northwest corner of the island or on the mainland in Nassau. Almost everything on the island was recycled until it was of no possible use, where it invariably ended up in a trash heap in the far corner of the cove near an old storage shed that housed what little landscaping equipment was required of the operation. Locals spread their handmade fishing nets there to dry and repair them. Rusted buckets filled with refuse littered the surroundings, and the eyesore was becoming visible to the guests.

A short dock stood next to the shack; tied to it was a steel refuse barge for the island trash. Trash was stored there until it was full, then it was transported by dinghy to the southwest point of the island where it was burned. Toby spent the morning picking up rusty buckets of junk and loading it on the barge. Most of the fishing nets that had been spread out were rotted beyond repair. Toby selected the worst and put them on the barge. A couple of good nets were still wet from sitting in the water at high tide, and these he stretched between the dock pilings and the bollards on the barge. He wrapped the edges tightly so there was no slack, keeping them above the water. He was proud of himself for figuring a way to keep them out of the water regardless of the tide, because as the tide ebbed and flowed, the barge rose and fell with it, so the nets would get a good drying.

Satisfied, he cleaned up the rest of the area; when he felt it would pass muster with Pop, he walked the shoreline back to the inn. He found his grandfather on the veranda by the main dock, poring over some post binder accounting books and making entries of the month's receipts and expenses.

"Hey, Pop, I finished cleaning up the dump. Do you want to check it out?"

"I'm sure I'll be satisfied if you are," Vernon replied. "You've got some daylight left; why don't you get your grandma and me some fresh grouper for dinner? We have quite a few guests in residence, and Major is setting up a beachside lobster pit for them. They're going to have a beach party."

Major Hegwood was married to the inn's cook. His ancestors had lived in New Providence since it was settled by Tory plantation owners fleeing the Carolinas in the early 1800s, taking land grants from King George following the Revolutionary War. Nobody knew why he was called Major, but it had stuck with him since he could remember. Probably a descendent of a prize breeding slave, Major was a big fellow who felt it was his prime responsibility to keep the guests entertained with natural island living.

"Can I take the Albury, Pop? I want to get to the outside reef at Salt Cay, and I don't have time for that in the rowboat." The Albury was Vernon's prize runabout; an Albury family–built lapstrake open fishing boat made in the Abacos, powered by a twenty-five horsepower Evinrude. Toby didn't get to use it much.

"You be sure to be back by five o'clock, and don't get fish blood all over the boat. And be careful!"

Toby grinned his excitement as he angled toward the dock and the Albury.

———— •◆• ————

Toby stopped by the dock shed and grabbed his mask, fins, and custom trident-pointed spear, which he'd made from an old shuffleboard court pole and strips of old tire inner-tube rubber. Major had shown him how to make the spear, fashioned after the ones made by local fisherman. Toby didn't have access to surgical tubing to make the launching sling, but he improvised with the old inner-tube rubber, and that proved effective enough.

He ran down the dock and jumped in the runabout. He checked the fuel level in the tank, pumped the priming bulb a few times, set the choke, and yanked on the starting chord. After three tries, the reliable old Evinrude came to life. He let it warm up for a minute and pushed the choke back in. He untied the half hitch at the dock, settled in at the back of the boat, put it in gear, and he was off.

Slowly over the bar, he opened it up, passing the edge of the cove into the open water. There was a gentle breeze out of the southeast, and he headed into a light chop toward Salt Cay. As he passed the edge of the island, he noticed a grown dolphin and a calf making their way toward the cove. Unconsciously, he nodded to them as kindred spirits going about business on the water.

The trade wind freshened as he cleared the island point and entered unprotected water on his way to the reef on the sound side of Salt Cay. It was a favorite place of his, as the reef was shallow in about twelve feet of water, dropping off into the sound abruptly to who-knew-what depth. The wall brought bigger fish up from the deep in search of food. Meal-sized grouper, snapper, hogfish, and all manner of wildlife hid among the rocks and coral in the shallow water, avoiding predators coming up from below. The Albury sliced effortlessly through the chop with occasional spray coming over the port bow.

Toby's long blond curls glued to his forehead as he took the spray. He loved the solace of being alone on the water on a mission. It made him feel less guilty about the sheer joy of being at sea, imagining himself a hunter providing for his family. From his vantage at nearly sea level, Piper was a speck of pine and casuarina behind him, and the sandstone dune of Salt Cay grew steadily as he approached.

After a few minutes of running through increasing swells, Toby rounded the northwest side of the island and ran along the shore, inside the reef. The water was flatter as the Atlantic swells beat themselves against the barrier reef, and Toby took advantage to run harder to the point where he knew it was shallowest. He uncoiled seventy-five feet of braided hemp rope, tied a bowline on the end to a ten-foot length of chain attached to the anchor, and threw it over the bow in fifteen feet of water on a sandy bottom. He payed out the rope and made off the bitter end to the bow post at the front of the boat. Holding some slack in the line, he waited until the wind brought it up tight, gave a tug to make sure he had a bite in the sand, and returned to the motor, turned it off, and tilted it up. He surveyed where he was, about fifty feet from waves still breaking a little on exposed parts of the reef in front of him.

Feeling proud of himself, he turned to his gear, put on his oval U.S. Divers mask and fins from his meshed fish bag, grabbed his spear pole, and rolled over the side. He finned to the anchor line, spit in his mask and rubbed the glass with his fingers to defog it, then donned it and looked around. The Bahamian water was crystal clear, and he could see the edge of the reef in front of him. It started with a few clusters of rocks with fans of red and purple, staghorn, and brain corals, brown and strikingly similar to the pictures of human brains Toby had seen in biology class. He saw dozens of tropicals of all colors and a lone spotted boxfish. He moved toward the darker patch of reef in front of him. The lee edge of the reef rose abruptly with boulder-sized rocks covered with beautiful corals. Here he could already see bigger fish moving in and out of the caverns and crannies of the reef.

He kicked his feet in the air and pushed his weight under, and as his fins got purchase on the water, he kicked his way to the bottom, clearing the increasing pressure in his ears by squeezing his nose with thumb and index finger inside his mask, and then clearing his mask of water by blowing air out through his nose. The mask fogged a little, but not before he spotted a perfectly sized Nassau grouper, light brown with cream stripes on its sides, hiding in the rocks just looking out.

Back to the surface for some fresh air, back down, clearing his ears, Toby stretched the inner tubing on his spear pole halfway down, gripped the pole and lined up with the grouper, and released his grip. The pole shot forward and caught the fish right above the gills. A kill shot! One try. Toby pulled his dinner out of the rocks and carefully twisted the barbs from the fish. He stringed the fish through its gills and put it in his bag. It was bleeding a little, but not enough to attract attention for a while. He looked around the reef for another.

He had more success on the ocean side of the reef, and with two fish in his bag, he swam back over the top of the reef to the boat. Crossing the back side of the reef, he spotted a sizable reef shark and, with a nudge of adrenaline, quickened his pace to the boat, knowing the shark could smell blood in the water. The reef shark followed him to the boat, but abandoned the activity as Toby threw the fish bag into the boat and lifted himself over the gunnel.

He had two four-pounders to show for his effort, one Nassau and one strawberry grouper. Pop would be pleased. The anchor came up easily after he started the Evinrude, and he was on his way back to the inn on Piper Cay.

The trip back was easier, as the quartering waves helped the little Albury surf when Toby caught the wave just right. He liked catching a wave and steering down it to prolong the surfing, just as he did while sailing the seventeen-foot Comet sloop moored at the inn. He liked feeling the power of the sea, and he enjoyed having the ability to use it to his advantage. Pop was a good sailor, and he had shared his experience with Toby—especially in the first few months on the island as Toby was adjusting to a new life and Pop was trying his best to establish a bond with him after the tragic loss of his parents.

The Evinrude drummed along as Toby instinctively surfed the waves home. He was pleased with his hunting efforts, and his mind drifted in contemplation of the year and a half he had been living with Pop and Irene. He drew pleasure from different things. Whereas, before in Illinois he had friends, school, and baseball this time of year, now he had a culture of adults, his grandparents and their guests. He enjoyed the island life; who wouldn't? But it proved a difficult adjustment for him.

He went to school on the big island in Nassau at Queen Vic's Christian. The school was formal so he had to wear a blazer and tie on most occasions, otherwise starched white shirts and slacks, in classes and in all weather. The culture was strict, and very English. Most of the students were children of Nassau merchants and state department officials' kids. At the end of the day, Toby was picked up by the island ferry that brought in the evening workers to the inn at Piper Cay, and he left in the early morning when the launch went in to pick up the day crew.

In a nutshell, Toby didn't have much of a social life, and he was an outsider to the kids his own age when he did interact with them. So, his friends became his grandparents and the guests at the inn. Occasionally, the guests brought children with them, and Toby fulfilled the job of showing them the Out Island experience. He took them sailing, snorkeling, beach combing, and fishing, but the relationships didn't have lasting value. One girl his age, who was rebelling against her parents, got a little frisky with Toby, but he was too inexperienced to know what to do about it. They kissed a couple of times, but when she left the island, he was only confused by what had happened.

As a result, Toby turned inward and learned to get satisfaction from being independent. He read a lot, particularly a Joseph Conrad fan, and his favorite book was *Lord Jim*. It reinforced his sense of island adventure, and his isolation helped him identify with the book's lead character. He found nobility in being alone, confident in making his own decisions and being responsible for their consequences.

———— •◆• ————

Earl Rolle was delayed getting to work at Potter's Cay inside Nassau harbor, and as a result, the mail packet he captained was about fifteen minutes late getting off the dock to deliver his load east to Eleuthera and the Abacos, other remote islands in the Bahamas chain. Ordinarily this would have been of no consequence, but sometimes insignificant events combine to make a difference. The rusted steel World War II landing craft was not particularly efficient in the water, drawing a huge bow and quarter wave behind it as it chugged slowly out the inlet and around the lighthouse on the tip of Hog Island. He paralleled the shore to cut inside Piper Cay and take advantage of the lee of the island. Amphibious LSTs didn't take choppy water well, as the ride got very wet. When Earl cleared the reef off the point of the island, he headed northeast toward Eleuthera and throttled up, drawing a five-foot wake behind him.

Just as Earl was clearing the lighthouse, *Wavedancer,* a forty-five-foot Huckins charter fishing boat was pulling in her baits after a long day of fishing in the sound. As the crew secured the fishing equipment, the guests settled in with some beer for the ride back to Nassau where they would have photos taken of them with their day's catch. The captain increased the speed to a comfortable fifteen knots, just enough to help break the swells that were building as the afternoon wore on. The stern wallowed, and the boat made a sizable wake behind it as it worked southwest back to the harbor.

The two boats passed each other two hundred yards east of the entrance to Piper's cove. As luck would have it, the two wakes, which individually would have been knocked down by the bar across the cove entrance, met just as they crossed the bar. Building on each other, they rolled a sizable swell into the cozy, quiet lagoon.

———— • ◆ • ————

Toby rounded the point of the island and crossed the bar at the entrance to the cove. He steered to the end of the dock where he tied up and brought his grouper to the fish-cleaning stand where Pop complemented him on his catch. Nodding to the fish-cleaning table on the end of the dock, Pop said, "Fillet those, and we'll have them for dinner. Your grandmother will be pleased that we won't have to go to the fish fry at the beach."

"Can't Major clean 'em?" Toby whined.

"You know the rule, son; you caught them, you clean them!" Pop said grumpily.

Toby heard the screen door slam, and his grandmother came out. Walking barefoot down the dock in her sundress, Irene beamed when she saw the fish. "You're right, Vern, but he also gets to choose who eats them! Why don't you let the kitchen staff clean them?"

"No, I'll clean them up," Toby said hastily before Vernon had a chance to add his predictable sarcasm. "Pop's right. I won't have complete satisfaction unless I finish the process. They'll taste better that way, anyway." Toby then noticed his grandmother's shortened butch cut, natural gray over a full face with deep dimples and steely blue eyes. "Grams, did you get a haircut?"

"Yes, sir. Ossie cut it short, said I won't have to mess with it so much. I call it 'wash and wear.'"

Ossie was Major's wife, very fully figured and always wearing a red-and-white checkered bandana, right out of central casting for *Gone with the Wind.*

"Do you like it?" Irene posed, fashion-model style. "Your grandfather isn't so sure; doesn't think it's ladylike."

"I like it. It suits you. I bet I've got the best-looking grandmother in the Bahamas!" Toby replied, thinking it was a compliment.

Noting Irene's frown, he turned to the fish-cleaning table and, using his sharpest knife, started filleting the fish. When he had the fillets separated, he threw the heads and backbones off the edge of the dock, where the nurse sharks milled around, vacuuming up scraps as fast as he tossed them in. The nurse sharks were a permanent fixture at the end of the dock where they lived, sunned, ate scraps, and amused the tourists. A scrap of fish never made it to the bottom; skins and all were devoured.

Toby noticed two freak waves, obviously made by boats, meet and crash over the bar at the entrance to the cove. As it washed under the dock, Toby watched as the skiff tossed violently in the air, straining against the single dock line at the bow. The process repeated itself as subsequent wakes washed under the pier. He saw them recede toward the corner of the lagoon and returned to his fish. Vern and Irene looked on as Toby filleted the fish with the skill of a native, paying no attention to the wake moving across the water.

Toby was interrupted by a commotion in the corner of the cove by the old shed he had cleaned up that morning. Next to the barge, a baby dolphin was jumping and screeching, splashing water.

The noise was very distinctive, reminding Irene of a wounded bear. "What's going on over there?!" she shouted, pointing at the barge.

Toby and Vern looked at the baby dolphin splashing about and screeching in what could best be described as a tantrum.

The calf and her mother covered the distance from the reef to the point of Piper Cay quickly. The following waves helped them conserve energy, and they moved about eight miles an hour toward the cove and their destination. As they rounded the point, they heard the metallic hum of an approaching outboard, slicing through the waves coming from the cove. They knew the sound, and understood these craft were manned by humans. The cow cautioned her calf to stay clear of the metallic-sounding sear of the motors. She had seen the damage they do to sea creatures caught unaware. Some fish were attracted to the sound and associated it with a food supply.

As the skiff approached, the calf saw a human boy sitting at the back of the speeding boat where the noise came from. She recognized the blond hair blowing in the wind as she arched her back on a breathing kick, and remembered she had seen him around the dock at the cove when she'd hunted there with her mother. As the skiff passed, she saw the boy nod and salute her with one of his skinny pectorals, not understanding the significance. She did feel a connection to the boy in spite of this, and she felt that the signal was directed at her and her mother. She would have liked to acknowledge it, but she didn't know how, so she kept her head up on the next several kicks so she could keep sight of him, but then he passed, and she pressed to make up the pace she had lost.

The two glided over the bar and entered the flat water of the cove. They swam the shallow water for fun, enjoying the warmth of the sun penetrating the shallows. As they passed by the dock, they saw the nurse sharks lying still at end of the dock, also enjoying the sun. For giggles, they made a pass by them, which agitated them, and the sharks scattered. The calf knew play. Her mother had taught her which animals dolphins could annoy and which they could not. Sometimes, they would find scraps of food when the sharks scattered, but usually not. Nurse sharks were efficient scavengers and didn't leave much behind.

Mother and calf explored the reaches of the cove. The calf knew this to be her birthplace. She felt a sense of peace here and enjoyed coming with her mother, even when they didn't have a plan. There was a beach in the sweep of the cove on the other side of the dock. They could move in slowly to the shallow water until it bumped their bellies, where they could roll and scratch themselves on the sandy bottom.

The calf knew she had to be careful not to get too far up on the sand because she could get stuck, as she did once. Her mother had to bite her fluke to pull her off. She also knew that the sun could dry out exposed parts of her body, so she had to keep herself immersed. They loitered for quite a while, moving about the cove searching out food. After a time, the skiff returned. The calf could see the boy on the dock throwing fish remnants into the water, as the nurse sharks swarmed for the scraps. Neither dolphin felt like competing in the melee, so they moved on with their exploration.

The cow and her calf found the mother lode in the corner of the lagoon by the stubby dock where the metal barge was tied up. Dozens of crawfish seeking shelter and protection had gathered under the barge. Mullet and other tropicals swam in and out among them. The cow could just get her nose under the barge at this tide and stir the crawfish into moving. As the occasional lobster left the shelter of the barge, it became easy pickings for the two dolphins. They could take their time and stir out their prey as they were ready for it, sort of an all-day buffet with unlimited rights for seconds. The cow had more success at the end of the barge closer to the dock, where there were also tender mullet.

It was at that moment that the rogue wake crossed the bar, building in height as it rolled into the shallower water, heading for the end of the cove where the dolphins were feeding. As the first wake reached the barge, it lifted the rusty hulk over four feet in the air, first the outboard end and then the end moored to the tiny dock.

The first surge snatched the dock line taught and snapped it. As the barge settled, the cow moved between the barge and the dock, her calf, spooked, backed into the lagoon.

The second wave lifted the barge, which was now secured only by the fishing nets stretched across the dock to the barge. They were old but sturdy, and resilient because the tension was spread across the mesh. The metal bollard on the barge snapped at the weld, and it toppled over the side, bringing the net along with it. The cow was stunned by the crashing barge as it landed on her forehead. The weight of the steel bollard sank at the end of the dock, bringing the fishing net with it, pinning the cow four feet under the water at the base of the dock pilings. Lessening surges under the barge served to pull the net tighter as each passed under the barge.

The calf watched with concern. She had never seen anything so violent before, and she could not see her mother pinned under the dock. The water was cloudy with stirred-up silt and sand. The calf moved cautiously closer to survey what had happened. As the silt cleared, she saw her mother lying on her side at the base of the stubby dock, only just beginning to stir. She approached slowly and began to understand that her mother was not responsive; the one eye in view was staring blankly upward, but not seeing.

As the trauma wore off, the cow began to try to move her pectorals and flukes to free herself, but she was bound securely by the fishing net weighted by the heavy bollard. As she struggled, the calf began to realize that this was a dangerous situation. Her mother was trapped, unable to move, and she was not able to reach the surface for precious air that she would soon need.

Panic began to set in, and the cow twisted mightily, thrusting her flukes. She soon realized that she was only using up precious oxygen, and she was trapped. Her calf swam close and, looking, could see the panic in her mother's eye. She bit at the net and tried to pull, but it was of no use. She understood the seriousness of the situation and watched as her mother settled and relaxed to conserve her air, awaiting the inevitable. The calf began to panic, again pulling on the net with little result. She knew her mother had only moments of air left, as she had been active for a while under the barge bringing out crawfish. Then she remembered the boy on the dock. This was human doing; maybe he could be of help. She swam to the big pier and jumped. She could see three humans talking, but paying no attention to the cove.

Options exhausted, the calf resorted to panic. She tore through the water back to her mother, who was lying peacefully on her side with her eye closed. The calf danced on her tail, screeching her grief, jumping, and thrashing above the water. Her cries almost sounded human, as they were piercing to the reaches of the cove. She heard a splash and looked toward the pier, seeing the boy leap into the water.

Strangely splashing, the boy covered the distance slowly. The calf moved toward him, nudged him with her snout, and returned to her mother. The boy was moving slowly, thrashing like a wounded fish, but he was making progress. The calf repeated the process to encourage him along. At last he reached the shallow corner of the cove and stood. The calf continued in her agitated state, moving between the boy and her mother, not screeching anymore.

Irene pointed again, as Toby and Vern surveyed the situation.

"That baby dolphin sure seems upset!" Vern noted. Toby nodded, and they all watched as the small dolphin swam the distance to the pier and stood on her tail, still screeching. "I think that big wake has loosened the mooring on the old garbage barge. Maybe you should check it out, son."

Toby could see the fishnets he had set out to dry had collapsed, and the barge was drifting away from the stubby dock.

"That was some wake that came through here. I saw the barge

lift up pretty high," Irene added. "That small dolphin is acting strangely. Toby, take the skiff over there and see what's going on."

"It'll be faster to just swim, Grandma. By the time I untie the skiff and beach it, I will have gotten there faster by swimming." Toby grabbed his freshly sharpened fish-cleaning knife, put it in its leather scabbard, and tucked it in the waistband of his shorts. With a turn and a wave, he dived into the lagoon and began swimming. After only a few strokes, he felt the baby dolphin nudge him in the ribs. He knew instinctively that something was wrong over there and that this small dolphin was involved. It kept swimming back and forth between him and the barge. He couldn't imagine what it could be. He had never had a dolphin encounter before, but he knew they were not a threat.

He realized that the small dolphin was only a baby, a *calf* he thought it was called, and it was most assuredly trying to lead him to the barge. As he reached the corner of the cove, his foot touched sand and he stood, moving cautiously toward the dock, careful not to step on anything sharp that could have come loose from the barge. The water was still a little cloudy, but he could see the fishing net stretched from the dock to somewhere under the water. As he neared, he saw an incredible sight. A huge dolphin was lying quietly at the base of the dock, pinned under the net, which was weighted down by what looked like the rusty bollard from the barge.

The calf poked him on the shin and moved toward the larger mammal. Toby waded forward, and as he approached, the huge bottlenose remained still. He thought maybe it was dead. It dawned on him the connection of the two mammals, and as he reached out to touch the larger animal, which must have weighed at least 500 pounds, it opened its eye and looked right at him.

In a heartbeat, Toby realized it was pinned by the net. The calf was concerned because this was its mother, and he needed to free her or she would drown. He pulled the fish knife from his shorts and began cutting the net. The sharp blade made fast work of the hemp, and soon the mother could move her pectorals. She kicked to try to get to the surface. Toby began working on the net covering her lower torso, and soon she was able to free herself enough to breach.

With an explosive release of air, she cleared her blowhole and began heaving heavily, replenishing her body of the oxygen she needed. A few minutes more, and Toby had cut her free. She turned and moved to deeper water where she jumped playfully with her calf. As he stood there next to the barge, water up to his waist, the calf returned to him, poking its head out of the water and softly stuttering her clicking sound. As she moved between his legs and nudged close to him, he realized she was trying to acknowledge what he had done.

He noticed the vaginal slit on her lower belly, and realized the calf was female. He decided to call her Phinney. The adult female stayed in the vicinity for a while, as she observed her calf making social contact with the boy, but after a few minutes, she signaled the calf that it was time to go, and they moved slowly toward the lagoon entrance. The calf kept turning back to look at Toby until they crossed the bar to the open water.

Phinney did not know she had been given a name by the young human, but she decided to think of him as Boy. Reflecting on the situation, she had been so scared to see her mother helpless, unable to move freely, unable to breathe. Boy had moved so slowly through the water, and he certainly couldn't swim very well. He thrashed about more like he had been injured, but in his way, he had covered the distance with the encouragement of her prodding. She was concerned when she glimpsed the shiny blade of his knife, but saw immediately the results, as he cut her mother free. When her mother took her first breath, she was so relieved. As her mother became free and swam clear of the wreckage, she leaped out of the water, consumed with happiness.

Then she saw Boy standing in shallow water looking down at her, and she was filled with emotion she had not experienced before; she was grateful. She felt the need to be near him, to touch him. She moved between his legs, nudging him. She lifted her head out of the water and looked him in the eyes, and saw that he had intelligence and awareness, as did she. She didn't know how she knew he was a male; she just knew!

Her mother signaled her it was time to go, and she followed, looking back every so often, as she and her mother crossed the bar and headed out to the reef at Rose Island to rejoin the pod. When they got there, among the others, Phinney felt hungry, and she suckled at her mother's mammary slits. She would not be supplementing her feeding by nursing for much longer, as she was learning to provide for herself. She wished she could share her joy with others in the pod, but bottlenose dolphin do not have real storytelling skills. They communicate with signals, body movements, and sounds, like clicking, screeching, and twilling, limited mostly to commands and warnings. They learn by mimicking and doing. Phinney couldn't wait to learn more about Boy.

CHAPTER THREE

BAHAMAS ⋅→⋅ 1957–1958

Toby endured the remainder of the spring entertaining the guests staying in the cottages. His grandfather paraded him around the dining room in the evenings, showing him off as the boy who saved the bottlenose dolphin from drowning in the lagoon. He enjoyed the time he spent with adults, and he was very comfortable in their company. He continued turning inward, however. His most social experience was the occasional visit to the cove by Phinney and her mother when they came foraging in the calm waters.

If Toby saw Phinney in the lagoon, he immediately jumped in, and the calf swam to him and rubbed up against his legs. The engagements were always supervised by Phinney's mother, who kept a close eye, although she knew Toby was not a threat. As the weeks came and went, Toby noticed that the calf was growing rapidly, nearly ten percent with each visit.

When the term ended at Queen Vic's, Toby's grandparents closed the inn for the summer of 1957, leaving it in the hands of Major and Ossie to look after until the season started up again, and they took Toby on a road trip around the United States, which gave him an opportunity to reconnect with his native country. Toby got to see the Grand Canyon, the San Francisco Bay Bridge, Niagara Falls, and the Museum of Science and Industry in Chicago, where he saw his first submarine, a World War II ship captured from the Germans at the end of the war. After Labor Day, they returned to the island to prepare for a new season and school year.

Phinney spent the warm summer months learning about the ocean, growing, and experiencing her first tropical storm. Still gaining a couple of pounds a month, Phinney was two and a half feet long now, weighing in at about thirty-five pounds. She was capable of hunting and feeding on her own, but she was seldom far from her mother. Her mother's companion was no longer part of their lives, as she had moved on to a new mate and was preparing to give birth herself after the start of the low sun season. She and her mother still foraged around the lagoon at Piper Cay, but she saw no sign of activity during the season of heat and a high overhead sun.

She felt a sense of loss that she might not see Boy again, just as some members of her pod moved on or joined other pods from time to time. She still enjoyed coming to the quiet waters of the cove when her mother was willing to make the trip. Her pod usually moved further south for the short days of the year, but Phinney, her mother, and a few other newborns stayed behind, as it would be difficult for them to keep up with the big party.

In the early fall, Phinney and her mother headed to the cove for some easy hunting and lazing in the warm water of the lagoon. As she crossed the bar, she noticed activity at the dock. A launch was unloading humans, and when she lifted her head, she could see Boy directing people toward the buildings. She let out a stuttering series of clicks and immediately got his attention.

Boy ran down the dock, kicking off his sneakers and tee shirt before jumping in the water, almost landing on top of Phinney. He floated on his back, and she nuzzled him in the ribs, cackling and shaking with excitement, much like a puppy. If she had a longer tongue, she would have licked him. They circled each other, splashing and frolicking to the amazement of the arriving guests who had never seen such interaction with a water mammal. Many thought Phinney might be a shark because of her size.

Boy worked his way to the small stretch of sand next to the pier and sat in water about a foot deep with his legs out in front of him. Phinney thought this was an invitation to play, and she beached herself between his legs, rolling from side to side, scratching her belly in the warm sand. After a minute she lay there, enjoying just being with him. Some human on the dock shouted at Boy. He reached for the top of her head and stood up, starting to walk away. Then he turned and, stretching his skinny arms forward, spoke to her. She felt he was trying to plead with her, but about what she could not determine. Her mother signaled it was time to eat, so she joined her at the rocks at the far end of the cove.

Toby was surprised that Phinney would be so still. He reached out and rubbed her jaw, noting that it was rough, as though she had been scraping it on something. He imagined her bumping into coral trying to root out fish from a reef.

"Toby, quit playing around and get these bags up to the cottages, and help the guests get settled. You'll have time for your friend before dinner. Come on; get a move on."

Pop could really be grouchy sometimes, but Toby knew the dolphin experience had made a lasting impression on the new guests, and the fact that his grandfather had played it down as a normal occurrence only added to the effect. Word of mouth about the uniqueness of this place would spread when these mainlanders went home. Toby rubbed the top of Phinney's head in a playful gesture and walked the short stretch of beach to the dock to resume his chores. Over his shoulder he waved and shouted, "Wait, Phinney, please, please wait! I'll come back in a few minutes!"

The luggage was tagged with the cottage numbers. Toby loaded it on the big-wheeled cart and delivered it to each cabin while the guests gathered in the lounge overlooking the ocean and enjoyed island rum drinks. On the pristine ocean-side beach were chaise lounges, umbrella stands, and folding chairs. Also available were water toys, including two easily rigged and sailed sunfish, paddleboards, and a huge mesh box of skin-diving equipment with fins of all sizes, masks, and snorkels. There was a line of coral heads dotting the shoreline within easy swimming distance of the beach, and it provided the most popular form of recreation for the guests.

Tied along the pier on the lagoon side of the inn were the Albury skiff and a Chris Craft Cavalier, a small thirty-one-foot plywood cabin cruiser powered by two Chevrolet V8 gasoline engines. It was used primarily to make supply runs and pick up guests from Nassau. Pop occasionally took enthusiasts deep-sea fishing, but most guests preferred to get deep-sea charter fishing boats from the mainland in Nassau, run by professionals who knew the deep water and were equipped to bring in the big tuna when they were running. To round out the recreational equipment, a twenty-foot cuddy catboat and a sixteen-foot Comet sloop were moored just off the pier.

Toby was learning how to use all the equipment. He enjoyed sailing the most, but handling the twin screw Chris Craft made him feel cool. He had learned how to reverse the motors, one in forward, one in reverse, to spin the boat in its own length, and he was on his way to being one of the better boat handlers on the island.

"Slow is Pro!" Pop had taught him. "Don't be in a hurry to do anything. Unless you're in a strong current or wind, the boat isn't going anywhere unless you make it, so, if you hit anything, you did it. Take your time, position the boat, and move it where you want."

Toby liked showing off for the guests around the docks. It made him feel more important. But Toby's first love on the water was sailing. It played to his need for independence and being responsible for himself. He could harness the elements and make them help him achieve his goals. He got to go places without the aid of motors, and it was a lot less work than rowing, which he hated. Pop made him row or paddle everything before he got to use the mechanization. It was some kind of rite of passage to Vernon. "Anything you work for will mean more to you later on," he would say.

The Comet was the most fun, because it was a high-performance racing sloop. Although it usually required a crew of three for the helm and mainsheet, jib sheet, and spinnaker, Toby could handle it alone unless he wanted to set the "chute," but he saved trips on it to be with Pop or Irene, who were both good sailors. Not as exhilarating, but simpler, was the heavy catboat with the gaff rigged, single mainsail. Everything was heavy, including the boat itself, which weighed nearly twenty-five hundred pounds with its lead keel, compared to the twelve hundred pound Comet with its metal centerboard. Even the mainsail, with its heavy canvas and gaff, took all of Toby's hundred twenty pounds to hoist but, once up, was easy to manipulate with the three-pulley mainsheet purchase used to let the sail in and out.

Toby finished sorting the luggage. He could never figure out what all could fill the suitcases after suitcases brought by the guests. They never wore much other than tee shirts and swimming suits or shorts during the day. Evenings were casual too, with the women wearing sundresses and sandals, and men wearing the occasional guayabera, which often substituted for formal wear in the hot Caribbean climate when worn with a cummerbund and bow tie.

When he was done, he headed for the beach and set the lateen sail in one of the sunfish and dragged it the short way to the water.

When he was knee deep, he pushed down the dagger board and rudder and sat in the shallow well in the middle of the boat. Pulling the tiller toward him, he brought the mainsheet all the way in and sailed close-hauled east into a light southeast wind. He needed a short tack to round a shallow sand spit off the northeast corner of the island. Freed by the wind, he payed out the mainsheet and reached off south to the entrance of the cove, over the bar, and into the still water of the lagoon. With not much wind, he barely made way toward the beach where he had last seen Phinney. No sign. He stood up in the small boat and surveyed the far shore where he saw dorsals moving among the rocks. He placed his index fingers in the corners of his mouth on either side of his tongue and let out a shrill whistle.

Phinney was tired of hunting, and her jawbone hurt from bumping against rocks trying to tease out small fish. It was easier when her mother just stunned one and left it for her to take at her own pace. She heard a high-pitched sound, loud, coming from above the water across the cove. She looked and saw nothing; her mother had taught her to first be cautious, but after a minute, she moved in the direction of the sound. As she surfaced for air, she saw Boy standing above the surface of water.

"These humans are strange," she thought to herself, but as she closed the distance, she saw that Boy was standing on a long platform. She moved toward him, head above water to see better. As she approached, he sat down, knees above his waist. She heard mechanical sounds, and the long platform started to move toward the pier. Boy splashed a hand over the side and shouted something to her, and she knew she was meant to follow.

The platform picked up speed, rounded the pier, and headed over the bar. It moved surprisingly fast for Boy, not like when he was splashing around in the water trying to swim, and it was gliding effortlessly. She had to exert herself just a little to keep up. Boy continued to splash the water with his hand, but she knew this was mostly to get her attention. Above the water, she could see a cloud of white with a blue stripe across it that the wind seemed to be pushing.

Without a thought of her mother, Phinney followed Boy out of the cove and around the south side of the island where the water was flat in the lee. Boy picked up speed, and Phinney thought, "This is more like it!"

As they passed the southwestern point of the island, the platform made a loud mechanical sound. Phinney looked and saw the white cloud had moved to the other side of the platform as it slowed just a little. Boy was sitting on the other side. Rounding the west side of Piper Cay, the little platform really picked up speed, and a white dorsal-like fin stuck out the bottom, as it leaned over a little.

Phinney kicked hard to keep up, moving to the front of the platform as she jumped from wave to wave. As they turned in the direction where the sun rose, the boy slowed and began a zigzag path across the top of the island. Phinney heard lots of mechanical sounds, and Boy kept moving from side to side as the platform leaned first one way and then the other as the white cloud moved from one side of the platform to the other.

A half hour had passed when they found their way back to the bar at the entrance to the cove. Phinney's mother was not happy. She was waiting at the sandbar. When her calf approached, she charged her, giving her a shocking bump behind her pectorals. This was accompanied by a series of shrill cackles and shrieks. This was the first time she and her calf had ever been separated by more than a few kicks. It had frightened her, but it also signaled her that her calf was learning independence. But with a human! She pushed the calf toward the cove entrance and signaled for her to follow. The two moved off in unison toward Rose Island and the pod. Phinney looked back with each surfacing breath, only to see Boy standing again on the platform with its white cloud, waving in her direction from the distance.

After Phinney followed him out of the lagoon and around the island, Toby felt as if he had circumnavigated the world with his best friend. At first she just seemed to swim around the sunfish, and he was afraid she would become distracted, so he tried to keep her attention by splashing the water with his hand. It seemed to work. She roughly followed him as he ran downwind, jibing at the southern tip of the island, with the dagger board up. But as he rounded the west side and came more across the wind, he got busy trying to hike out as he let down the dagger board and brought in the mainsheet. The breeze was enough for some exhilaration as the reach got closer and closer, and his speed picked up considerably. He lost track of Phinney for a moment, but he didn't give a thought to splashing the water, as he had his hands quite full. Then he spotted her in front of the boat, swimming vigorously from wave to wave, and then alongside as she looked up when he leaned out. Bottlenose dolphins have a fixed jaw, but was that a smile he saw? Must be his imagination.

Around the north side, Toby had to make short port tack hitches to beat his way back to the bar, where he was greeted with an angry mother who, with great animation, rammed her calf theatrically and screeched at her. He wondered if this is what he could expect when he started going out with girls and got his date home late. The two headed off to the east, but Toby could see Phinney look back as he stood in the sunfish and waved goodbye, knowing he had a real connection with his friend and the pair would be back.

———— • ◆ • ————

When the fall term started, Toby's days became filled with school, chores, guest entertaining, and the occasional cavorting with

Phinney. He tried to take advantage of some of the after-school programs at Queen Victoria's Christian Academy, but the transportation situation made after-school programs problematic. If he tried to join the soccer team, he finished too late for the last shuttle to the island, and that required Pop or Major to make a special trip in the Chris Craft. That was not convenient as it conflicted with the busy time when guests were preparing for dinner. Pop and Irene had obligations to them for cocktails and evening chitchat, which made the social experience special on the island.

Major didn't like running the big boat anyway, and he always had an excuse why he couldn't be available. So, as usual, Toby was limited to short-term friendships with children who occasionally came to the inn. His encounters with Phinney were random at best, so he invariably had to drop what he was doing to spend time with her, which now often involved teasing crawfish out from under the barge in the corner of the cove. The nets had long since been removed, so they were no longer a threat.

Among Toby's friends at Queen Vic's was Randy Bethel, whose family owned the liquor distribution rights for the Bahamian Commonwealth. His father was also a family friend. Pop and Irene invited Sir William and his wife regularly to festive events planned at the inn. In their stiff British formal way, Pop thought they added a little class to the island experience. Randy spent weekends with Toby at the island on occasion, and the two had fun exploring and fishing the reefs and coral heads that dotted the barrier islands outside the harbor. It was not uncommon for them to run into Phinney on these excursions.

Randy was skinny and tall, with jet black hair, a slow gait, and a proper countenance that contrasted well with Toby's carefree manner and his long curly locks, which were somewhat defiant of what was expected of a Queen Victoria Academy student. Randy liked to spend time with Toby because the girls always seemed to be in his vicinity, apparently finding him rakishly attractive. Randy tried to capitalize on this, but Toby's social adjustment just did not make him comfortable around the proper English girls. After all, he was only fourteen, but he wished he could be different, because he certainly thought about them a lot.

Randy and Toby spent the Saturday before Christmas shopping in Nassau on Bay Street. Toby found a few trinkets for Irene and Pop in the shops around the British Colonial, but it was at Thompson's Chandlery that he came across something unusual, a shiny brass ship's bell salvaged from an old merchant vessel. Toby had the perfect idea for it. He had to beg Randy to prevail on his parents for an advance of twenty-five pounds to buy it. He talked the merchant into including four carriage bolts and nuts he would need to attach it to the steel beam on the end of the pier at the inn.

Back at Piper Cay, Toby and Herbert—Major and Ossie's son—made a project out of Toby's brilliant but cautious plan. Herbert was a few years older than Toby and was an occasional companion and source of local lore in Toby's adventures, particularly when it involved fishing. The two prevailed on Major with promises of future unspecified favors to weld a flat steel plate on the top of the short beam at the end of the pier. Opposite it was the tall beam that had the range light used by locals to find their way over the bar into the cove entrance at night. When Major was finished, Toby and Herbert borrowed Pop's electric drill and aligned four holes in the plate, after they cooled it with a few buckets of water. The carriage bolts were a little long, but that was all right. Toby secured the brass ship's bell to the plate and tightened it as hard as he could with a crescent wrench while Herbert held the bolts in place from the other end.

When they were done, Major came to inspect their handiwork.

"You know dat's gonna corrode, don't you, Mister Toby? You got two different metals together in da salt air, and dey gonna' corrode like a battry."

"That's okay, Major; I don't want them to come apart, ever."

"Thass good, cause dey won't, sir!" Major chuckled. "What you gonna do wid dat bell? Ring foh dinner?"

"No, sir, Major. You'll see the next time my dolphin comes to visit."

"You and dat fish; you som'tin, Mister Toby. You gonna marry her when she grow up? My. My."

Herbert chuckled to himself at his father's attempt at sarcasm.

———— • ◆ • ————

Christmas morning the guests and staff gathered around a potted palm tree on the veranda and had an impromptu Christmas service. They exchanged gifts of little consequence, as they were far from home, most of them. The local staff celebrated at home. That evening, Ossie served hard-to-come-by turkey and dressing that she somehow managed to get from the purveyor in Nassau. The turkey was accompanied by tenderloin fillets, and in good spirit, the dinner was officially designated as Chirp and Turf.

Phinney and her mother didn't show over the holidays, and it wasn't until the start of the last marking period in March that Toby had a chance to see Phinney again. They came in the cove on a weekday afternoon, crossing the bar at around four o'clock. They announced their arrival in the usual way with a couple of full out-of-the-water breeches and some clicking; even Phinney's mother gave the display some energy.

Vernon was sitting on the veranda, poring over his post binders again. Shouting over his shoulder to the kitchen he announced, "Toby, your friends are here again!"

Word passed mouth to mouth until it reached Toby, who was coming up the path from the trash dump after finishing his chores. All were grinning, because they all got a kick out of Toby's friends, never having seen man and dolphin relate to one another in such a manner. Toby pushed the cart over next to the wall and ran across the terrace through the veranda to the dock, where he shed his tennis shoes and tee shirt and leaped in the water. The cow kept her distance, observing, while Phinney moved in closer to feel Toby's presence as he put his arm around her, muttering how big she was getting.

"Phinney, I have something to show you. Just wait here. Wait, wait, wait!"

Phinney understood this to mean that Toby was coming back. She watched him climb the lower dock and jump to the main dock at the end.

Toby began pulling hard on the rope handle attached to the clapper on the ship's bell, and it clanged like a firehouse truck. The bell was solidly bolted to the steel beam, which was in turn secured to the end of the dock, under which it was planted through three feet of marl into bedrock. Noise travels three or four times faster through water than air, and with the solid foundation of the beam, the effect was quite unexpected.

Phinney dived with her mother and headed full speed for the bar and out the cove.

Toby stopped clanging the bell after a few healthy pulls when he figured out that it was the bell that had startled the dolphins and chased them away. He had anticipated the opposite effect, and he was a little disappointed, as he had hoped that he had found a way to let his friend know when he was available to spend time together, instead of relying on happenstance.

He waited a few minutes, and Phinney finally returned, her mother nowhere in sight. She swam nervously back and forth at the end of the dock. Toby jumped in the water with her and she stayed nearby, but she did not look happy.

Pop walked down the dock and looked at the pair, assessing the situation, "That your idea of an island telephone, Toby? You certainly got everybody's attention in the cottages."

Toby noticed guests gathering in the veranda, milling around. Some showed concern.

"What is this; some kind of fire drill?" came from the crowd.

Pop took control. "Everybody calm down. Toby was just testing his new bell on the end of the dock. He didn't mean to alarm anybody." Focusing his attention on Toby, he suggested, "You know, son, that bell is pure brass mounted on steel in several feet of bedrock. That sound is pretty intense, particularly underwater. You might want to consider some discretion in its use. Put your head underwater and take a listen yourself."

Toby dived in the shallow water while Pop gave the bell clapper a gentle pull. The soft tone on the dock was greatly amplified in Toby's ears, and Phinney darted away again, not knowing what was coming next.

Toby felt stupid and embarrassed. Climbing from the water, he asked Pop, "Do you think it was a bad idea? I thought I could use it to call Phinney."

"I think it's a brilliant idea; you just have to use it with discretion. You ring that thing hard, and your friends will hear you from beyond Porgy Rocks at the other end of Nassau Harbor."

The days shortened, and as the water cooled when Gulfstream currents moved south, Phinney and her mother moved south with them. Their pod followed the currents to the Exumas where feeding was easier for such a large group of dolphin.

Phinney missed her visits with Boy, but she didn't have a lot of choice in the matter. Although she was growing steadily, over three feet and weighing nearly forty pounds, barely more than a year old, she still needed her mother to keep her safe from predators. Her conical teeth were all in, and she could handle most small fish that made up the bottlenose diet; she just concentrated on smaller ones and immatures.

In the fall, the West African winds came early that year, and with a light storm season behind them, the Gulf Stream moved north early in 1957, bringing the trades prematurely north with it. The cow's pod had moved southeast to the Exumas when the days grew short and, before long, found their usual place at the northwest end of the Exuma chain. Winter cold fronts moved in and left as the days continued to shorten and then began to lengthen again, signaling it was time to return to the big island.

As a high pressure kept the winds and seas up, Phinney and her mother found themselves in familiar water around Nassau. They decided to take advantage of the stillness of the cove for some relaxation and easy hunting. They passed Rose Island on the sound side and moved inside Salt Cay for the short dash down to Piper Cay, crossing the bar as the sun was lowering in the sky.

Phinney made a beeline for the end of the pier, jumping and splashing to get somebody's attention. Even her mother made some halfhearted attempts to elevate her bulk out of the water. Moments later, Phinney saw Boy running down the dock, taking the color off of his torso, as he jumped into the water without even looking. Only her agility kept Boy from landing on her, and with great animation, they nudged and rubbed against each other. Boy put his long skinny arm around her belly and said something to her. Suddenly he pushed himself away and climbed out of the water, intoning her to stay near. He climbed out of sight on the tall dock and walked to the end.

He was not in sight when all her senses were shaken by the loudest sound she had ever heard. It began sharply and continued, repeating itself again and again. Phinney's eyes bulged, and her head felt as if it were going to explode. Her echolocation sense was dis-

oriented. In a flash, her mother swam beside her and nudged her away from the dock, the apparent source of the noise. In a panic, almost swimming into the pier pilings and the boat moored alongside, mother and calf beat a hasty retreat over the bar and to the edge of the cove.

The ringing stopped, but they didn't know for how long. Boy seemed to be associated with it. Phinney knew he would not harm her, so she ever so slowly ventured back into the lagoon and to the dock. Boy jumped in beside her. Boy and the other human spoke for a minute, and then Phinney saw the other human move on the dock to where Boy was when the concussion had started. The sound came again, but this time it was very soft, almost pleasant, but still she moved away, not prepared to be frightened again. That was the end of the noise. Phinney stayed in the cove a short while, then rejoined her mother to move out to the reef off Rose Island.

Easter signaled the end of the season for the inn at Piper's Landing, and Irene and Vernon made the most out of it. They planned a Saturday night celebration for the guests and invited friends from Nassau to join. The Bethels, state department officials from the governor's office, the adjutant Sir Henderson and his family, and others were in attendance.

Toby was required to put on a tie and make his presence known. He knew most of the families from town because he went to school with their kids. His Queen Vic friends, Randy and Neil, were there, as were a few of his girl classmates and their parents.

The dinner was a huge success, as Ossie made sure the food had the island flavor the locals found so exotic, and the guests were impressed that their vacation choice allowed them to mix it up with English aristocracy, at least judged by their proper English accents, anyway.

While Neil and Randy hung around with the girls, Toby spent most of the evening with the guests telling stories about his dolphin friend and their adventures. The stories would be quite unbelievable were it not for incidents they had all witnessed in the lagoon. Phinney was a natural showoff, and she seemed to know when she was performing for an audience.

Toby introduced the local dignitaries to the guests and did a good job of making them feel comfortable with one another. The Nassau businessmen did not have much opportunity to socialize with merchants from Kansas City or St. Louis. When Toby did gather with kids his own age, it was usually with Randy or Neil Henderson, his closer friends from Queen Vic's.

———— •◆• ————

After dinner, when the guests had retired to the veranda bar for "make-your-own-drinks, honor system," and the locals had caught the late ferry to town, Irene and Vernon had a few quiet moments to themselves on the veranda patio overlooking the sound. In the glow following a few drinks, they held hands as they sat next to each other, gazing at the amazing array of stars that made up the Milky Way. Compared to the States, the stars were much brighter in the Bahamas where the air was clear and ambient light didn't diminish the effect.

Irene looked radiant with her short gray hair, dimples, and piercing blue eyes, yet her face showed a look of concern. "Vernon, I'm worried about Toby," she ventured.

"How so?"

"I was watching him tonight very closely. Did you notice anything?"

Vernon knew she had something on her mind, so he thought seriously about her question before answering. "Nothing special. He seemed to enjoy himself. He is absolutely great with the guests, and his conduct with the local dignitaries was nothing short of ambassa-dorial, I thought. What's concerning you?"

"That's exactly what I'm referring to. I'm not sure we're doing the right thing by him. I mean for his development, you know. Liv-ing his formative years here on this island, years that are so very important for his growth emotionally."

Vernon felt defensive. "What do you mean? Someday he will look back and realize he has lived a life that can only be dreamed of, growing up carefree in these islands. How can you think this doesn't compare to Peoria!"

"That's not what I mean, Vern. Let's be objective. Did you notice how he spent his evening? We went out of our way to invite parents of his classmates and his classmates, so that he could feel part of the evening. So it could be a little about him."

"Yes, I thought that was a good idea. We should do it more often, or maybe we should spend more time on the big island with him."

"But don't you see? He didn't participate in it that way. Yes, he was great with the Nassau people, and Lord knows, the guests love him to death. Other than sharing a few words with the Bethel and Henderson boys, he spent no time with the kids of his own age. He doesn't identify with them, and clearly he isn't comfortable around them."

"So, what do you suggest?" Vernon replied. "We can't *make* him spend time with them. He certainly has the opportunity, particularly with the girls. Did you not notice the MacArthur girl didn't take her eyes off him all evening?"

"Exactly! And Toby couldn't make eye contact with her at all. Vernon, wake up! Look at this objectively. I love Toby as my own, and his presence here has added a wonderful dimension to our lives. But let's face it: Toby's best friend is a damn fish! He is great with people, but only grown-up people. He has no real friends his own age, and he's terrified of girls, even though they are clearly attracted to him. He is not developing well; he is going to pay for it the rest of his life, and it will be our fault. He is going to be fifteen next month."

"Again, my dear. What do you have in mind?"

"I sat next to the Hendersons at dinner. They have some of the same concerns about Neil. They want to broaden his teenage horizons. They have found a prep school in Palm Beach, on the island. It is a small boarding school, coed, about one hundred fifty students, grades seven through twelve. They call them 'Forms,' I think she said. It has a good reputation, and Phyllis tells me they adhere to a rather formal culture, like the fancy New England schools. Kids from the best families all over the country go there. Much of the faculty live on the campus; did I say it's on the island of Palm Beach itself, so they are well supervised? It would be a place where Toby can be Americanized again and develop the social skills he will need when he grows up. It's nearby, so he could be home on long weekends and breaks, and he would still have plenty of time to enjoy the benefits of the lifestyle we have chosen, so he will be prepared for that if it becomes the path he chooses. At least he will have a choice."

"And you just heard about this tonight?" Vernon hung out there. "You seem to have put a great deal of thought into it for it having just come up."

"Honestly, Vernon, I'd never heard about this school, it's called Flagler Preparatory School, by the way, until this very night," Irene assured him. "Phyllis told me she thought it was started by the Flagler family in the twenties to accommodate families like theirs who were spending more and more time in Florida and wanted their kids nearby. With the concerns I was recognizing, which have been over the recent few months, her suggestion just clicked. It seemed to fit our situation perfectly. Toby needs to be in a structured, supervised environment in a small student community where he will be forced to adjust socially."

Vernon sighed. "We can give it some thought. It's not like he's tearin' it up at Queen Vic's, and he will need some alternative for high school in a couple of years, anyway. I just don't know how he will take it. That *damn fish* is a mammal, by the way! And I kind of like the relationship those two have developed. Toby is much more aware of our beautiful, fragile environment since that calf came into his life."

CHAPTER FOUR

Phinney was indeed not far from Porgy Rocks near Rose Island on the eastern entrance to Nassau harbor when she heard a faint ringing. She felt it in her jawbone as much as heard it, but she knew immediately what it was. Boy was ringing that bell on the dock at Pipers. She signaled her mother, who was foraging nearby, and started the trek inside the reef past Salt Cay and down toward Nassau harbor to see her friend, Boy.

Her mother followed at a distance. She no longer felt the need to stay nearby. Her calf was getting bigger every day, now three and a half feet and weighing over fifty pounds. She was of a size that she was no longer a target for other ocean predators, except the largest of tiger sharks and great whites, but these were not common inside the reefs, as they preferred to hunt on the deep side of the ocean walls in the sound. The one bull shark that did try to take advantage of Phinney's diminutive size got a surprise blunt high-speed encounter from Phinney's mother followed by another from her birth mate. The shark left the area.

It took Phinney twenty-five minutes to clear the northeast point of Piper Cay, and a moment later, at increased speed as her excitement grew, she crossed the bar into the lagoon. Boy was already sitting in the big catboat with the white gaff sail raised, tacking slowly back and forth from the pier to the middle harbor. He was standing, holding the tiller in his left hand and working the mainsheet in his right, as Phinney broke the surface and tail walked, stutter screeching her arrival.

This was going to be fun, Phinney knew. When Boy took to the big sailboat, it meant they were going to swim in the ocean and maybe hunt together. Boy hauled in the sail and beat out of the cove over the bar and into deep water. Phinney followed him northeast toward Salt Cay where coral heads dotted the western side of the island in about fifty or more feet of water over mostly sand bottom.

As the sailboat turned off the wind, Phinney could see the sail move out as Boy payed out the mainsheet, and the little catboat really took off, making about seven knots across the wind. Phinney had learned, over the many trips she had taken with Boy in the sailboat, the relationship between the wind direction and the boat's ability to perform. She originally thought speed was relative to direction, because Boy always went more quickly moving away from the cove and toward the big island, but she became confused after a front had gone through and the prevailing southeast breeze switched from the west, and everything she thought she understood about Boy's sailboat performance changed.

Phinney was intensely curious about everything human, and Boy was her portal to that world. She now understood that the boat went fastest across the wind, slower downwind, and had to zigzag into the wind. Boy turned the boat into the wind, and she could hear the sail flap gently in the breeze. This meant they had arrived and the boy would put down the big metal thing to hold his position. Then he would get in the water, and they would play.

She was surprised this time though. No metal thing, and the

water was deep, deeper than she had seen Boy swim. There was a coral head nearby, but it only rose to twenty feet from the surface. Phinney knew Boy had to breathe much more often than she. All of a sudden, she heard a loud splash, when over the side came Boy wearing his flippers and mask, holding on to the big metal thing.

Down he went like a stone, all the way to the bottom, holding his nose with his fingers. Phinney was very concerned, because Boy was almost three surface pressures deep, further down than she had ever seen him able to go. Once on the bottom, he looked around for Phinney and waved. His hair floated about his head like sea silk on flower coral. Phinney started for him, coming face to face, as he kicked his way to the surface. About midway, he stopped and looked around him, swam toward her lingering for a moment, and recommenced his ascent.

She could hear him surface and gasp for air. He slapped the surface to get her attention, and she came up next to him, head out of the water, looking him in the eye. Boy was shouting with glee, as he climbed back in the boat, Phinney swimming alongside. She heard the familiar, "Just wait. Wait there, Phinney."

He disappeared inside the boat and returned over the side with a big white stone, and again, down, down, down to the bottom where he stood momentarily holding the stone in one hand, with his fingers inside his mask with the other. Phinney swam to him again, and this time, they took a long time swimming together to the surface, leaving the stone behind on the bottom. She was happy about his accomplishment and, at the same time, concerned for Boy's well-being. He had never been this deep or stayed down this long before.

They spent the rest of the afternoon checking out the coral heads in the vicinity. Boy was able to pull one crawfish out of its hole far enough for Phinney to crack its carapace with her teeth before swallowing it whole. It wasn't very big. She wasn't surprised, because when they teased larger crawfish out of the rocks, too big for Phinney to swallow comfortably, Boy would usually get a good grip on the carapace and tear off the tail, using his swimsuit to protect his hand from the sharp edges. Then he would do the strangest thing. He would break off an antenna and shove it up the tail butt hole, and pull its guts out, before putting the tail in his swimsuit. Phinney assumed he ate the tails at home. Sometimes he would collect five or six when they dived the shallow reefs together or teased them out from under the barge in the corner of the cove.

Boy raised the sails, pulled up his big metal thing, and headed for Piper Cay. Phinney was already halfway back to Rose Island, so she squeaked a goodbye and headed off east, Boy waving to her as she turned.

In late May near the end of term, Toby had an epiphany; he could never dive the deeper water with Phinney because he didn't have the lung capacity, but he had read about a Canadian free diver who had broken all the rules relative to a man's ability to stay underwater. Jacques Mayol was the subject of a class presentation made by Neil Henderson at school. Neil loved the water and loved free diving. His report talked about the new sport of apnea diving where free divers used weighted sleds to go deeper than they could unassisted because it took less time to get down there.

Toby figured he could do that too if he just had some weight he could afford to leave below, since he couldn't bring it back up with him. In the refuse corner of the cove, he found the perfect object. There was a chunk of concrete left over from a failed patio construction attempt that weighed about twenty pounds. *That ought to do the trick!* he thought. He had to share his idea with Phinney. It was Saturday, a free day for Toby, so he decided to give it a shot.

"Where you off to with that piece of garbage, son?" Pop called as Toby headed down the dock.

"Phinney and I are going to experiment with it!" Toby replied. "I'll tell you about it when I get back."

Pop gave Toby a puzzled look and returned to his reading.

Toby swam out to the catboat, paddled it to the dock, and loaded up his fins and mask, the concrete, and a small jug of water. He gave the bell clapper four or five hard yanks, much to the annoyance of Pop.

Vernon could be really sarcastic when he wanted, so as Toby headed back to his room to put on dry trunks, he asked, "Why don't you just buy your friend a watch? If she's as smart as you say she is, she can learn to tell time and you can prearrange your rendezvous."

Toby acknowledged the obviously insincere recommendation with a wry smile.

A few minutes later, he returned to the boat to wait for Phinney. He raised the sail in the lee of the dock, pushed off, and tacked back and forth until he saw Phinney come over the bar. He hardened up and beat his way out of the channel. When he rounded the point on the corner of the island, he payed out the mainsheet and took a starboard tack out to the deep sandy patch west of Salt Cay. The greenish-blue water turned darker blue. Toby headed into the wind and in irons moved to the front of the boat to get the anchor.

It then occurred to him, he only had one weight, but the anchor was heavy, and if this worked, he didn't want to have come all this way for one deep dive. After securing the anchor line to the heavy bow cleat behind the stem, he put on his mask and fins, hyperventilated a little by taking in several lungsful of fresh air, and looked over the side to make sure Phinney was clear. (He had had close calls landing on Phinney when she stayed close in her excitement.) Then he jumped in holding on to the anchor shank, making sure all the chain came with him. He hit the water with a crash, and before he knew it, he was passing twenty feet and he hadn't even started clearing the pressure in his ears, which was building rapidly.

The anchor was now going first, Toby behind holding on with one hand, reaching for his nose with the other. The pain in his sinuses was intense as the pressure continued to build up quickly. He blew as hard as he could and only got partial relief. The pain was sharpening, and he gave one last blow, as hard as he could, knowing that if he failed to clear his ears, he would have to abandon his experiment and let go of the anchor. *Relief!* His ears cleared.

Immediately the pressure started building again. He was going down so fast the current almost pulled his mask off his face. The water was noticeably darker as he saw the sand bottom coming up fast. He had only been in the water ten seconds and already he was standing on the bottom in eighty-five feet of feet of water, the anchor and chain barely reaching the bottom. His ears cleared more easily now, as he surveyed his surroundings. He felt no demand to breathe yet.

Phinney came from mid depth and looked right into his mask, which he had now cleared of water since he removed his fingers from his nose. He didn't know how much bottom time he had, so he started cautiously for the surface. Still feeling no lack of oxygen, he stopped at about twenty-five feet, circling with Phinney. At the first sign of a need for air, he continued his ascent, Phinney right by his side, to the surface, where he exhaled and took in a deep breath. He knew Phinney was concerned; she had never seen him go so deep before. Had she nudged him upward at mid dive? He couldn't be sure.

He realized his problem with the piece of concrete. If he held on with two hands, he could not clear his ears as he went down, so he needed to figure out a way to hold on with one hand. Back aboard, he took a short rope and attached it to an exposed piece of wire mesh on the slab of concrete and fashioned a grip out of it. This time he tried to pre-clear his ears at the surface to give him a head start. Over the side he went. Holding the piece of rope he fashioned, he was prepared this time as he literally went down like a stone, keeping his sinuses and ears equalized all the way. On the bottom, ten seconds later, he was already more settled.

Phinney was right with him, and he knew he had more than thirty or forty seconds to surface, even more if he needed it. He took more time to swim with Phinney. He felt like a superhero, like Aquaman, if there was such a superhero—he thought there was—as he and Phinney worked their way to the surface. Near the surface, Toby's vision narrowed a little, and he thought he would talk to Pop about that.

Considering his experiment a success, Toby and Phinney cruised around the coral head, where he teased an undersized crawfish out of the reef and held it out for her. The calf quickly dispatched it, and Toby found a nice one for himself, which he tailed and cleaned, putting it in his swimsuit to take home. Toby pulled himself over the gunnel of the boat and nodded to his friend. Phinney made it clear she was going east, so Toby raised the mainsail, pulled up the anchor, and headed for the inn.

It took about thirty minutes to reach across the southeast wind back to the island, cross the bar, and moor the catboat. As he approached the mooring near the pier, he noticed a nice-looking sport fishing boat tied up to the dock. The name on the transom was *Molly Blue.* He lowered the sail, put on the sail cover, and swam the few strokes to the dock. Once he pulled himself up, he turned the dock hose toward the boat and, with pressure from his thumb on the nozzle, got just enough distance from the spray to give the boat a gentle hosing and produced a mild rainbow through the spray against the late afternoon sun. He walked down the dock, crossed the veranda, and passed the dining room where he saw Pop and Irene seated at dinner with guests. Pop signaled for him to come over.

"If you can clean yourself up and put on a fresh shirt in the next few minutes, I'd like you to join Dr. and Mrs. Bridegroom, your grandmother, and me for dinner. We have some stuff to talk about that may interest you. We haven't ordered yet. I think they're serving lamb tonight," Pop said.

Irene added, "I think you might be interested in Dr. Bridegroom's hobby, Toby. He's a diver!"

"Sure, Pop," Toby acknowledged his grandfather to be polite, while at the same time he was totally distracted by his grandmother's comment about diving, especially considering his experience over the last couple of hours.

He turned and headed back to his room on the other side of the kitchen, jumped in the shower, and put on his shorts and a fresh alligator shirt and tennis shoes. He let his hair dry as it fell. Back in the dining room at the table, Vernon made introductions all around. They shook hands, and Toby took the empty seat at the table next to Dr. Bridegroom.

Once the introductions had been made, Vernon said, "Toby, Dr. Bridegroom owns the Rybovich tied up in the lagoon. He came over from Miami to do some SCUBA diving on the reefs around here, so I thought you two would have a lot to talk about." Turning to his guest he continued, "Hugh, my grandson here knows these waters as well as any native. He's been bringing us fresh fish for almost three years; so, I'm volunteering him as a guide if you would like. I know he's free tomorrow. Maybe you can show him some of that fancy SCUBA equipment of yours."

Toby assessed Dr. Bridegroom, deciding he looked outdoorsy and adventurous. His wife was a pretty brunette with an air of independence, looking as though she was capable of sticking up for herself when she wanted.

"I'm pleased to meet you, Toby. Your grandfather has been telling us all about your aquatic adventures. I'm particularly interested in the dolphin you are so fond of. It's a rare opportunity to be able to spend time with a wild animal in its environment."

"I like to think it's my environment, too," Toby replied, somewhat breathlessly. He was so excited at the prospect of being introduced to underwater breathing equipment that he could hardly contain himself. It presented boundless possibilities for him and Phinney. "Do you think I could try some diving while you are here? I can free dive to almost a hundred feet on my own," he exaggerated, thinking of his earlier experiment, "but I would love to stay down there longer."

"Sure you can, Toby. I would look forward to it. Frankly, it's unwise to SCUBA dive alone, and I assumed I would find someone around here to be my dive buddy, but Vernon tells me there isn't much demand for it here on the island, so I was going to have to go into Nassau to find somebody anyway. Your knowledge of the waters will be a great help to me, so I would be happy to show you the ropes. Mrs. Bridegroom isn't keen on swimming in the ocean, although she likes to come along and look after the boat while I'm down. She suns and reads to kill the time. Say, a hundred feet. That's a long way down! How do you manage that? You must hold your breath for well over a minute." Dr. Bridegroom sounded impressed.

"To tell the truth, sir, that's the deepest I've gone, and I did it only just today, out by Salt Cay. I took in a lot of deep breaths to get more air and rode the anchor down to get there faster, but took my time coming up. Phinney was with me. The second time I jumped in with a chunk of concrete." Toby was impressed with himself, but Dr. Bridegroom looked a little alarmed.

"Did you feel all right, Toby? Nothing unusual physiologically? I mean, did you get dizzy or anything? That can be very dangerous."

Vernon picked up on Dr. Bridegroom's concern, remembering the hunk of concrete Toby had carried down the dock that afternoon. He was never completely comfortable letting Toby wander the reefs for hours alone, but it was the one of the few things the boy truly enjoyed, and he didn't want to deprive him of it. "How so,

Hugh? Some of the natives dive that deep and even have bottom time to find a fish or two."

"It's not just about holding your breath, Vern. Just as SCUBA diving has its limitations, free diving has its own, as well. We are just learning about it medically, as apnea divers are challenging deep-diving records around the world with mixed results."

"What's apnea diving, Hugh?" asked Irene.

"Apnea diving is the sport of free diving to great depths without the aid of compressed air. The depths being challenged are really quite astounding, but the results are sometimes very surprising. Divers regularly go below fifty meters, about one hundred fifty feet, and reach the surface safely most of the time. But sometimes they do not for no apparent reason, even when the dives are considerably shallower than previous attempts by the same diver. They just black out. We are learning that deep breathing before a dive sometimes fools the body into thinking it has more oxygen that it has, and the divers don't feel the natural compulsive need for air when their oxygen runs out. They just pass out, sometimes quite near the surface. Then they drown."

"I did notice my vision getting narrower on the way back up on the second dive," Toby confessed.

"That was your body telling you that you were at your limit," explained the doctor. "I would be very careful, if I were you, young man. If you're up for it, tomorrow is Sunday. If you will show me some good reefs in about fifty feet of water, I would love to introduce you to SCUBA diving, if it's all right with your grandparents. We can talk about this other stuff in more detail then. What do you say?"

"Oh, dear!" said Irene. "Now methinks we will never see the boy again, Vern, with another water diversion."

"How can we deny him this opportunity? It might give him something to look into over the summer," said Vernon.

"Can we bring Phinney, Dr. Bridegroom? She would love it, and it would give you a chance to meet her."

"How on earth would we ever get such a big fish on the boat, Hugh?" asked Mrs. Bridegroom. Confusion crossed her face when everyone started laughing.

"Mrs. Bridegroom, she won't have to ride on the boat. She'll just follow us," Toby said shyly. He was concerned he had embarrassed her. "She's really very bright." Mrs. Bridegroom's smile eased his fears, somewhat.

Toby felt like he was on the moon, he was so happy. When dinner was served, he had trouble focusing on the meal; a new world of possibilities was opening up for him, as images of adventure with Phinney in her world flashed through his mind. "I'll be happy to clean up your boat for you when we get back," he volunteered. "The sun will be high enough by ten o'clock for us to see our way around the water, so we can pick our way easily through the reefs, and it will be behind us on the way back, which will be even better."

"Ten o'clock it is, then," Dr. Bridegroom agreed. "I'll see you on the dock about a quarter of. You have a mask and fins, I assume. Bring them. Vern, Irene, do you want to join us and make a day of it?"

"Much as we would like to," Irene began, "we have obligations here at the inn, but thanks, anyway. Toby, you be of help and not a pest, you hear? This is the Bridegrooms' vacation, you know."

Toby imagined he was going to be nothing but a pest; presented with this opportunity, he was going to get as much out of it as he could.

The group broke up as the steel drum band started up on the veranda, and the dining room cleared for some after-dinner Bahamian music in the lounge.

———— • ◆ • ————

When Toby got to the dock with his gear the next morning, the back of the Rybovich was already uncovered, and the Detroit Diesels were droning away as they warmed up. The Bridegrooms were already aboard, and Mrs. Bridegroom was slathering up with Skol suntan lotion in the cockpit. She brightened behind her sunglasses as Toby came down the dock. "Good morning, Toby. Did you get a good night's rest?"

"I was a little restless, because I'm really excited," he answered truthfully.

Dr. Bridegroom was on the bow taking off the spring line and coiling it in preparation for leaving the dock. "Hi, Toby. Jump aboard; I'll be ready to go in a few minutes."

"Can we wait a few minutes, Dr. Bridegroom? I need to call Phinney. She'll take about ten to fifteen minutes to get here after I call her." The Bridegrooms looked perplexed. "Not on the phone." Toby laughed. "I call her with the bell on the dock. She can hear it for fifteen miles, and she knows that I want to see her. Cover your ears; the bell is loud."

Toby grabbed the braided rope on the clapper and clanged about half a dozen times. Everybody in the inn knew to expect the dolphin in a few minutes.

It took about fifteen minutes for Phinney to make her way from the reefs east of the harbor. She crossed the bar and jumped several times off the end of the dock, one a complete summersault. With a few clicks and a quick stutter screech, she got everyone's attention for the aerial show.

Toby whistled to her from the lower dock platform and told her that he was going diving on the reef past Rose Island, that she should follow him in the big sport fishing boat. He felt rather silly when he noticed the Bridegrooms looking at him as if he were nuts, talking to an animal as though it were human. To be sure, Toby had no idea if Phinney made any sense of his gesticulations and verbal calls, but it made him feel better about his relationship with the dolphin to treat her as an equal. He made sure Phinney saw him board the boat, and he made waving gestures from the cockpit as she poked her head out of the water.

With the lines gathered in, Toby joined Dr. Bridegroom in the tower, a separate set of controls above the cabin where the captain could see all around the boat, particularly the fishing cockpit and the water around it. Dr. Bridegroom worked the stern out, levering the bow against the piling on the end of the dock, the way Toby had learned in the Chris Craft. Then he spun the boat around so it was facing out of the cove. He put both engines in gear and headed toward the bar.

"The *Molly Blue* draws about five and a half feet. I assume we can clear the bar?" he asked.

"Yes, sir! The bar carries almost six feet at low water. Just follow the inflatable buoys over the center. Stay between the red and green ones, just like a real channel." Toby grinned.

Dr. Bridegroom advanced the throttles to a fast idle after they cleared the bar, and the props began to sing as he synchronized the engine speeds.

"Where are we headed, young man?" Dr. Bridegroom asked.

Toby stopped waving at Phinney and turned around to survey the way out of the lagoon. "Turn northeast and go around the outside of Salt Cay, that's the next island you can just see on the horizon. Give the sand spit on the end about a hundred yards to clear some coral heads, then go east, leaving the island on your right. It's all good water on the sound side of the island. We're going to go all the way around Rose Island to the other end of Nassau harbor, and there are some big coral formations on the other side, just north of the Yellow Bank. They are easy to spot; we can just pick the one you want and anchor in the sand nearby. We will have several to choose from, all within easy swimming distance."

"Can I run it up here?" Dr. Bridegroom asked. He seemed worried about Phinney keeping pace and staying away from the propellers. She was right behind them.

"As soon as you clear the end of the island, your wake won't bother anyone," Toby replied.

Dr. Bridegroom gave the end of Piper Cay a respectful berth and ran the Detroit Diesels up to about eighteen hundred RPM. *Molly Blue* accelerated quickly to around twenty knots as her wake narrowed behind her. Her fine entry forward cut through the light chop out of the east, and an occasional light spray blew over the starboard bow.

Phinney struggled behind, but quickly tired from the strain, dropping well back. She was able to follow the song of the props with her superior hearing, so she knew which direction to go.

"Toby, are you comfortable running the boat? You have a better idea where we are going."

"Sure thing, Dr. Bridegroom. Pop lets me run the Chris Craft all the time, and this looks pretty much the same," Toby said with confidence.

The Rybovich was about ten feet longer with three times the displacement. He took the helm as Dr. Bridegroom moved to the seat on the other side of the bridge. It was a little wetter, but he didn't mind. Toby was amazed at the perspective he got from being so high above the water, having been used to the limited visibility he got from sea level. The additional ten or twelve feet elevation gave him a lot better awareness of the seascape he was negotiating. He could see the bottom clearly as he turned a little north to clear the shallow bar that stuck out from the end of Salt Cay. The water turned a deep indigo blue as he got into the deep stuff and headed east toward Rose Island.

Dr. Bridegroom went below and returned to the tower with a navigation chart sealed in plastic. He put it on the console between him and Toby and requested, "Show me our position on the chart, Toby." Toby pointed to the edge of the island in the sound. "Wow! The chart shows we're in over a thousand feet of water!" exclaimed the doctor.

"It's even deeper just a little farther out," said Toby. "We're in the far side of the tongue of the ocean that runs between New Providence and Andros. You crossed it getting here from Miami. It's many thousands of feet deep. The water can get pretty rough out here. It's really in the North Atlantic. The next stop out that way is Europe, after you get past the Bahamas." Toby pointed ahead to the east.

Meanwhile, Mrs. Bridegroom spread out some towels on cushions in the fishing cockpit and lay down to read and get some sun. She was reading Sloan Wilson's *Man in the Grey Flannel Suit*, a *New York Times* best seller. They rode in silence for about twenty minutes as the shorelines of Salt Cay and Rose Island passed by on the starboard side. As they rounded the end of Rose Island, Toby turned south a little, and they headed toward some light blue water.

"That's Yellow Bank up ahead." Toby pointed. "We're going to stop at the edge of the lighter-colored water. The sun is high enough; we will be able to see the coral heads as they come up in front of us." He throttled back to a fast idle to be cautious. As the water turned lighter, they could see patches of brown and yellow as they came upon the reef protecting the Great Bahama Bank.

"Over there is a continuous stretch of reef, Dr. Bridegroom. I think we should try to pick our way around these heads and anchor in the lee of them where the water will be smoother. It will be more comfortable for your wife. If you take the helm, I'll go forward and point you through and handle the anchor. We will find a nice sandy bottom there, too."

Before he left the tower, he searched all directions for a sign of Phinney, but saw none. With abandon, he stepped down from the bridge tower and walked around the side of the boat cabin to the foredeck. At the bow, he opened the anchor lazarette and pulled out the cumbersome yachtsman anchor and chain from the well. The boat had no bow rail, so he moved carefully to the stem where he could read the water and bottom. With hand signals, he guided Dr. Bridegroom around several coral heads on the back side of the main reef.

The water was a medium blue and crystal clear. The coral formations were three dimensional, rising vertically within fifteen feet of the surface, some higher. The inside of the reef was about thirty-feet deep over a sand bottom, while the ocean side was much darker blue, indicating deeper water.

"This looks perfect, Dr. Bridegroom. I think we should put the anchor down here."

"Okay, Toby. Let it straight down so it doesn't foul on the chain. There are over a hundred fifty feet of rode for you to let out. When it settles on the bottom, hold it for a minute so the anchor can orient itself, and then pay out what you need. Make the bitter end off to the recessed cleat on the bow. The wind will bring us away from the reef."

Toby tied off the line and held it in his hand so he could feel the anchor make a purchase in the sand. When he had a good bite, he signaled Dr. Bridegroom to cut the engines. The droning engines went still and the world became silent, with only little waves splashing against the white hull. Toby looked around anxiously for a sign of Phinney, but still saw none. He settled down when he realized it would take her more than twice as long as they did in the boat, so she wouldn't be due for another ten minutes. He knew she would be along when she could and would make her presence known.

The Bridegrooms and Toby gathered in the spacious cockpit. The fishing chair was still in the middle, but it now served as a pedestal for the cooler containing two jugs of water, assorted soda pop, and some beer. Mrs. Bridegroom moved back to her cushions and lay down to sun herself and resume her reading. Dr. Bridegroom motioned Toby over to the port side where he was putting the diving rigs together. "Why don't you watch me as I put on the regulators, and I'll explain how these tanks work."

Toby moved in closer to get a better look. The tanks were made of steel and were held in place by a simple metal rack, padded in a few places to avoid chafing. They had nylon straps for the shoulders and waist to attach them to the diver. Dr. Bridegroom held up a regulator with two accordion-like hoses coming out of it that came together at a mouthpiece. Toby had never seen one in person, but he had seen them in magazines.

"This is a two stage U.S. Diver regulator. It fits over the valve on the top of the tank like so." He showed Toby how the fitting on the bottom of the regulator slid over the valve. "Notice the little rubber ring in the valve stem, Toby. That's very important to make a good seal with the regulator; otherwise air will leak out. This regulator has two stages, which means the first stage takes the filled tank pressure, about twenty-five hundred pounds per square inch, which is a lot! . . . and reduces it to about one hundred fifty pounds, which is still too much pressure to breathe. That's where the second stage kicks in. It's the nifty one, because it takes the hundred fifty pounds and reduces it to the pressure of the water around you, which as you know changes as you go deeper. So you always have the right pressure to breathe. You try to take air in, and the little vacuum you create between your lungs and the second stage opens the valve to let air come to you. So you will always have air at the pressure you need, as long as there is sufficient air in the tank. Now, let's mount the regulator. I'll do mine and you watch, then you do yours."

Dr. Bridegroom turned the tank around to face the other way, loosened the thumbscrew on the base of the regulator, and slid out the protective piece of plastic. He slid the attachment over the valve stem on the tank, positioned the fitting carefully around the rubber ring and grooved fitting, and tightened the thumbscrew. The regulator was now firmly attached as a single unit with the hoses facing away from the tank to go over the diver's shoulders and into his mouth.

With a little guidance, Toby assembled his rig and looked up for his next instruction. They opened the tank valves located on the sides of the valve stems, and Dr. Bridegroom showed Toby how to open the valve all the way and back a half turn. He also showed Toby how to put a few lead weights on his tank straps. "This will help with your compensation as you use air from your tank and become more buoyant. You will have to work a little at first to stay up, and later in the dive, you will have more trouble staying down. When you get really light, it means your tank is probably near empty, and you should surface. That's the only way you know. Now, Toby, I'm not going to bore you with a lot of information about diving physiology, which can be complex, but there are a few things you need to know that are very important, so I need you to really pay attention. Don't worry about your dolphin friend right now. I need you to focus on me."

Toby's attention had been wandering toward the water from time to time, so he made a mental effort to listen very carefully.

"We will stay together all the time. I don't want you to ever be more than two or three kicks away from me at any time. This dive is just to familiarize you to the process. If you want to do more, you should probably get specific training. Rule One! Never move vertically very fast. You won't need to clear your ears as much as you do when you are snorkeling, because you are putting pressurized air in your body, which does some of that for you. A good rule of thumb, don't come up faster than your bubbles. Rule two: Never, never, ever hold your breath! Always be breathing in or out. If you hold your breath from a lower depth and ascend to a higher depth, your lungs can explode, or worse, you can force air into your bloodstream, either of which will kill you. You got it?"

"Yes, sir. You have my attention." Toby tried to imagine what it would feel like to have his lungs explode inside his chest. Whatever it would be like, it didn't sound like fun.

"So, while we are down there, probably about forty-five minutes, if we are close, we can help each other out if we have an equipment malfunction. It's uncommon, but it does happen. We can just share each other's air until we reach the surface. If you are on the bottom and you have a problem with your air supply, and for some reason can't get to me, you can shed your equipment and head for the surface, but remember, you have to expel the air from your lungs on the way up, or—"

"I know; my lungs will explode," Toby finished for him.

"Okay, let's get in our rigs, but first let's drink some water. Your body needs lots of water out here." Dr. Bridegroom pulled his fins and mask out of a military-looking bag and put it by the side of the cockpit. Then he pulled a ladder with big rounded ends on the top from the aft lazarette and set it over the side of the boat. The hoops hugged the gunnel, making the ladder secure for boarding.

"We don't want to forget the ladder, do we?" The doctor laughed. "That's why I like Mrs. Bridegroom along; in case I forget, someday."

Mrs. Bridegroom looked up from her book, smiling. "And you better hope I really love you, 'cause I might not put it in."

"That's the real trust in a strong marriage, Toby," said Dr. Bridegroom, laughing again. Toby chuckled; he got a kick out of sharing in the Bridegrooms' playfulness.

Toby and Dr. Bridegroom put on their masks and fins, and standing their tanks on the bait box at the transom, bent over and strapped on the dive rigs. Toby followed Dr. Bridegroom's lead and put in his mouthpiece, sucking in a few breaths to make sure everything was working. His excitement built as he anticipated getting in the water in SCUBA gear for the first time.

"I suggest you sit on the transom and roll backwards into the water holding your mouthpiece in your mouth firmly with one hand, and your mask over the faceplate with the other. We'll go one at a time being careful not to fall on each other. When you get oriented, swim to the anchor line at the front of the boat, and we'll meet there and go down the line together to the bottom. I will keep signaling you to see if you are okay, and you should respond with the same sign." He showed Toby a heads-up hand signal with a circle of index finger and thumb and three fingers extended. "Here I go."

In a flash Dr. Bridegroom went over backwards, making a big splash as he hit the water. He surfaced and shouted up to Toby, "The water's great, come on in!"

Toby followed suit, holding his mask and mouthpiece. He hit the cold water a little harder than he would have liked, but the surprise made him take in a big breath, and sure enough, everything worked fine. There were tiny bubbles everywhere, and at first Toby didn't know up from down. After a few seconds, the bubbles cleared away, and Toby could see the bottom. He was descending slowly, but he could control it by swimming. He worked his way to the bow. He was still wondering about the whereabouts of Phinney, but he needn't have. She was waiting for him by the anchor rode with a grinning Dr. Bridegroom, who was hanging on next to her.

Phinney was in her usual feeding territory toward the west end of Rose Island when she heard and felt the ringing of the bell on Piper Cay, and her heart jumped in her breast at the thought of spending some time with Boy. She signaled her mother and her friend that she was setting out for the cove, which they acknowledged before returning to their ritual entrapment of unwary fish straying too far from the safety of the rocks and coral.

The water was very calm, the visibility good, as she made her way inside the islands and across the short deep stretch to the cove at Piper Cay. Over the bar, she could already see and hear activity at the end of the dock. She couldn't resist announcing her arrival with a show of jumps. The last one was so high she actually fell over on her back almost making it a three-sixty!

Dancing on her tail, Phinney squeaked and clicked a few times until she saw Boy moving to the end of the dock. He put his spindly fingers in his mouth and whistled for her attention, then he waved his arms back and forth before pointing repeatedly to the large rumbling boat tied up to the pier. He talked to her in an excited voice. Although Phinney had no idea what Boy was saying, she clearly understood that he was going to do something on the boat, confirmed when she saw him board at the back as the boat moved away, engines droning. She had no choice but to follow.

Keeping up was easy until the boat cleared the lagoon. She could still see Boy waving from the back as she did her best to keep up, but soon, the boat picked up a lot of speed and she could not keep pace. The wake narrowed as the speed picked up. Phinney enjoyed jumping through the foam the boat left behind. It and the sound were easy to follow, which she did patiently, long after it was no longer visible to her. Soon the boat outdistanced her two miles to one, but she continued to follow the sound, soon realizing they were heading around the outside of Salt Cay in the deep water where she seldom went, even with her mother. There wasn't much to eat out there, but there were predators.

Across the length of Salt and Rose Islands toward the shallower water near the reefs at the east end of Nassau harbor, Phinney swam effortlessly, and finally in the distance, she heard the engines slow. She could tell the boat was maneuvering as the sound changed, and she continued. After a half hour of swimming, she knew she was close when the noise from the engines stopped.

She followed the churned-up water as it meandered among the coral heads, finally seeing the anchor line stretching from out of the water by the boat to the sandy bottom below. She could not see anyone on the boat, but she could hear voices, including Boy's. She expected to see him jump in the water momentarily, so she cruised the coral heads below, biding her time. The coral here was different from where she usually hunted. Huge red fans floated back and forth with the current and wave action, and there were a lot of skinny fingers of coral sticking out of the top of the reef. Although there were fish, they were not of interest to Phinney, as they were not the kind she ate. They did have a lot of strange, unfamiliar colors, but they were bigger than the small tropicals she saw around the pilings in the cove.

Suddenly there was a loud crash as something big fell into the water behind the boat. Amid thousands of bubbles, she saw a human wearing a lumpy piece of metal emerge from the foam and swim to the front of the boat, blowing bubbles from his head. Another crash from above, and there was Boy, in similar gear, crashing through the surface with his funny face mask and fins on him, thrashing about the way humans do.

Phinney moved to where the other human was waiting, holding the anchor line, and watched as Boy, now moving more efficiently in his fins, but also blowing bubbles out of his head, swam toward her. She greeted him with a few clicks as though she had been expecting him. He reached out for her, but just then his head let out a cloud of bubbles. She could see the long rubber hoses coming over his shoulder to his mouth, and she could also see that the bubbles were coming out behind the back of his head from that clunky metal thing. The other human and Boy made hand gestures to each other and slowly started sinking and swimming down the rope to the bottom, bubbles releasing every so often from each of them. She became concerned, because yesterday, when Boy had gone to the bottom, he had jumped in with the anchor and reached the sand in a hurry. She knew humans could not hold their breath for very long, and this was taking far too long.

Down they went anyway, to the bottom where they stood and looked at each other. Boy waved for Phinney to come closer, but she was afraid of the bubbles, which she had never seen before except from speeding boats and stormy seas washing across exposed coral. Boy was below the surface way too long, but he seemed calm. She came closer, moving away at the sight of more bubbles, and then closer still. Her mind was racing when she started to think of what she knew. She could hear breathing, just like hers, but more regular like a human, and she thought of the bubbles. Air! The bubbles were air! Boy and the other human were breathing air! It must come from those hoses in their mouths.

Boy and the other human seemed fine. She moved closer still. She could see in Boy's mask and look into his eyes. Boy and the human waved their hands around each other and left the anchor line, swimming toward the reef. They moved slowly as Phinney followed to see what they were up to. They swam among the rocks at the base of the reef, pointing to each other, sticking their heads in the coral, looking around the small caves, and moving on to the next group of rocks.

Phinney followed with interest, noting that they weren't doing anything much but looking. She saw Boy reach in among the rocks and pull out a spiny lobster by the carapace and tail it, putting the tail and one antenna in his swimsuit. Phinney made fast work of the carapace. She always did well following Boy around the reefs. He always found her some morsel, but she couldn't understand why he kept the hardest part of the lobster to eat and discarded the easiest part.

He was trying to show the other human how to do it, but all he came up with was an occasional piece of antenna. Once the new human nearly got the lobster out, but it wiggled free, cutting his hand in the process. As soon as the blood hit the water, dozens of small sergeant majors, with their yellow and black stripes, crowded around them, looking for the source of the wound, which usually meant disadvantaged prey. Boy and the human tried brushing them away, but they were persistent. After a period of sightseeing and blowing bubbles, they worked their way back to the anchor. Boy tried to engage Phinney by rubbing her belly, but she wanted no part of it. It was unnatural for Boy to be in the water so long without surfacing. She had been to the surface and back three times already.

A confused Phinney watched as Boy and the other human moved up the anchor line to the surface and swam to the back end of the boat where they removed their gear, handing it to a female human in the back of the boat, and climbed a ladder out of sight. Phinney could hear them talking and the sound of gear thumping as it tipped over inside the boat.

She jumped to get Boy's attention, which he acknowledged with a wave and some talking. She waited until she heard the motors start up with their annoying sound. She knew they were beginning to depart as the anchor started coming up. She wanted no part of a return voyage chasing a boat that was far faster than she was, and besides, if she wasn't going to be spending time with Boy, it wasn't worth the bother. She wasn't far from the pod and the rest of the party, so she headed northwest in their direction.

Toby swallowed some water, grinning from ear to ear; he struggled to hold on to the base of the ladder as he removed his tank straps, fins, and mask. Next to him Dr. Bridegroom was doing the same, the two of them bumping into each other as they held on to the lower rung.

"Toby, hook your waist straps from the tank around the ladder, and you can leave it be, while you hand your fins and mask up to Mrs. Bridegroom."

Mrs. Bridegroom was reaching over the transom to retrieve the equipment. Toby passed her his fins one at a time and then his mask. Her husband did the same, and she tossed the gear behind her on the cockpit teak deck.

"We'll climb in the boat and then bring up the tanks; they're not going anywhere strapped to the ladder."

Toby and Dr. Bridegroom climbed aboard and lugged the dive tanks over the sideboards and lay them by the transom.

"How was the dive, boys?" Mrs. Bridegroom inquired as they dried themselves with towels she provided. "Did you see anything interesting?"

Ignoring her question for the moment, Dr. Bridegroom asked, "Vera, darling, hand me that small towel by the sink, would you, please? Toby introduced me to catching a lobster by hand, but I'm afraid the little bugger got the best of me." Dr. Bridegroom held up his right arm so his wife could see the small cut on his palm, which was still bleeding. "I don't want to make a mess of the teak."

He wrapped the towel she handed him around his wrist, using his other hand to apply a tourniquet grip on his arm to slow the blood flow, which soon stopped.

"It's all in the wrist," joked Toby, pulling the six-inch tail out of his suit to show her.

"Toby made it look so easy. He just grabs them and tails them right there on the spot," Dr. Bridegroom said with some admiration. "My attempts just got me a few pieces of antenna, and the one I got a good grip on was unfortunately at the tail where the shell has sharp edges, how it got me. Say, Toby, show Vera how you clean 'em."

"That's the best part of lobster here in the islands, Mrs. Bridegroom. It's the easiest fish to clean there is, although it's not really a fish." He took the section of antenna he had saved and shoved the thick end up the tail's rectum until the spines caught hold, and then he pulled it out. Along with it came the entire intestinal tract, a gooey mess, which he threw overboard along with the antenna. "That's all there is to it. You can clean enough dinner for a family of four in about two minutes." He dropped the tail in the cooler for the trip home. He figured Ossie could cook it up as an appetizer for the Bridegrooms' dinner.

"Lovely," replied Mrs. Bridegroom, her voice laced with sarcasm.

"But the best part, Vera, was we were not alone. Toby's pet dolphin met us here as soon as we got in the water, and she stayed with us the whole time. Was it Phinney you named her? She was right with us until we got out of the water."

Just then Phinney leaped clear out of the water, as if to remind them she was still there. "Hey, girl!" shouted Toby as he went to look over the side. Phinney treaded water on her tail, bobbing her head as Mrs. Bridegroom came over to look. She stuck out her hand tentatively. "Go ahead and rub her forehead, Mrs. Bridegroom. She likes that."

The doctor's wife leaned over the side and gave Phinney a couple quick pats on her brow. Phinney responded with a few clicks and stutter squeaks.

"Amazing! Simply Amazing!" she mused to no one in particular. "Wait until I try to explain this to our Canasta Club at Jackson Memorial," referring to the Miami hospital where her husband was on staff.

Toby went forward and started pulling up the anchor, while Dr. Bridegroom started up the diesels. Toby rinsed the chain and anchor by dipping it repeatedly as it neared the surface and secured it in the anchor well. It was only about 1:30 in the afternoon, the sun was high, and the water was glassy. Everyone had a clear view of the bottom and the reef below as Dr. Bridegroom maneuvered out through the coral heads.

Mrs. Bridegroom handed out sandwiches given to her by Ossie

at the inn earlier that morning. She opened and gave Toby a root beer and, using the church key hanging on a string tied to the cooler, punched two triangular holes in a steel Heineken beer can for her husband.

Toby felt excited by his first SCUBA experience, considering it a success, but at the same time, he was a little confused by Phinney's reaction to being underwater with him; it really wasn't what he had expected.

"What else did you see, Hugh?" asked Mrs. Bridegroom, after they all squeezed onto the tower and idled back toward the northwest. "Was it up to your expectations?"

Toby threw a last wave to Phinney who was already ahead of them, working her way toward Rose Island.

"Very much so, dear. The water is much clearer here than in the keys. We could see every grain of sand on the bottom from the moment we put our faces in the water."

"You weren't down very long. I barely read a chapter of my book when I heard you surfacing. Did that cut on your hand do something to shorten your dive?"

"Yes!" Toby jumped in. "Dr. Bridegroom was attacked by fierce sergeant majors, so we had to come back up." Dr. Bridegroom gave him a look, and Toby knew he had overstepped a little. Backing off, he said more seriously, "The blood attracted some tropical fish, sergeant majors, and they wouldn't leave us alone. They try to nibble around any cut you have that is bleeding, and although not a real bite, it is not pleasant either. They are pretty little tropicals with yellow and black stripes, like on an army uniform, hence the name. Pretty or not, pound for pound, they are about the fiercest fish in the ocean, and they have no fear."

Dr. Bridegroom nodded toward Toby, acknowledging that the boy's explanation had made him sound less incompetent. "Should we go back the same way we came in?" he asked.

"Your choice, Doctor. We're outside the reef, so I guess so. We could have gone back inside Hog Island, and come out the harbor entrance by the lighthouse. But the water is flat, so this is the most direct way."

Dr. Bridegroom pushed the throttles up and headed off toward Piper Cay.

———— •◆• ————

The trade winds established themselves for the summer months, blowing a steady five to twelve knots out of the southeast, and the school days slowed in pace as Toby anticipated spending the summer on the water with Phinney. Final exams came and went, and Toby spent most of his time on cleanup detail and simple repairs at the inn. He went to the mainland on New Providence at every opportunity with Major and Herbert, shopping for supplies, or to drive the Chris Craft on trips with Pop when he went in for other business.

He saw Randy Bethel occasionally in town, and Randy spent occasional weekends on the island, where the two would dive and sail together, sometimes joined by Phinney when it was an adventure where she could participate. Toby knew she would not migrate with her pod until the winter months, so for the time being, she always came when he rang the bell. Neil Henderson summered back in England with his parents, finding the tropical heat a bit too much, so he could not join them on their diving adventures.

Dr. Bridegroom had left one dive tank and regulator with Toby at the inn, with the promise and understanding that he would never dive alone and that Phinney did not count as a dive buddy. This limited Toby to an occasional trip with someone from the commercial dive shop in downtown Nassau. This didn't happen often, but it was the only place he could find other divers and get his air tank filled.

As luck would have it, the only movie theater on the islands, on

Market Street, got movies years after they were released in the States. This did give Toby the chance to see the movie *Frogmen* starring Richard Widmark about U.S. Navy divers in World War II. The action scenes convinced him that he wanted diving to be in his future, and he imagined himself coming ashore during an invasion of some sort accompanied by Phinney where their actions would save Allied forces in some manner. He couldn't quite figure out how, but he and Phinney would receive medals for their valor.

———— •◆• ————

The smell of the refuse collecting in the harbor at Potter's Cay could be quite strong at low tide, conflicting with the fried fish for sale at the stands along the straw market, causing Toby to give it a wide berth coming in the channel and heading over to the public docks. After securing the Chris Craft at the city docks, Toby and his grandparents made their way to the British Colonial Hotel. Toby marveled at its beauty. It was so regal in pink with white trim, guards in uniform, and traffic police standing on their intersection boxes directing the local traffic flow. There was a lot of old-fashioned "stiff upper lip" and all that, but Toby knew they had to be melting in those heavy formal uniforms and pith helmets.

The air conditioning at the hotel was refreshing, but Toby had no idea what occasion had prompted his grandparents to want to treat him to a rather formal luncheon at the hotel. He had jumped at the invitation mostly because it was another chance to show off his skills in the thirty-one-foot cabin cruiser on the way over; otherwise, he would have preferred some of Ossie's conch fritters on the island. Pop had a manila envelope in his hand, and he seemed a little nervous. He had found nothing to criticize in Toby's boat handling, unusual to say the least, and Toby had seen him and Irene casting furtive glances at each other from time to time. Something was up!

They went through the lobby and past the interior courtyard to the terrace restaurant overlooking the water. A waiter seated them at a nice table where they could see the commercial traffic coming in and out of the harbor, going about business. Pop and Irene took their seats and Toby sat between them. He felt surrounded as they ordered iced teas.

After a couple of fits and starts interrupting each other, Irene began with, "Toby, your grandfather and I have a matter we want to discuss with you, and we thought making a day of it away from the inn might be a good way to go about it."

Now Toby was really concerned. This was strikingly similar to the conversation he had had with his grandparents when they had surprised him in Chicago in the fall of 1954 to inform him that his parents had died in the plane crash. His stomach did flip flops as he nervously tugged at his shirt collar and squirmed in his seat. Suddenly, the world became very still, and he leaned forward rigidly. Had he done something wrong? Were they shipping him back somewhere? His eyes pleaded with Pop's, but Pop turned away and looked at Irene.

Irene put her hand to her mouth. "Oh, dear. I believe I've gone about this wrongly." She had obviously sensed Toby's concern. "Toby, everything is fine. Your grandfather and I just want to talk to you about your future. Vern and I have been thinking about your life here in the islands and whether this is appropriate for your development."

If this is supposed to put me at ease, she is still going about it wrongly, Toby thought. "What's the matter with my life here? I go to school, get passable grades. I like it here with you. Where else would I go? What are you talking about?" Toby stuttered. He was flustered now . . . and scared, too.

Irene continued cautiously, "Your grandfather and I have been discussing your preparation for being an adult, and the appropriateness of these islands and your life here. Toby, let's be realistic; more likely than not, your future lies in the States. In three years, you will be out of high school and going off to college. You will need to focus on your education then, and you won't need the distraction of having to adjust to a new cultural background while you are doing that."

Toby looked pleadingly at his grandfather.

"Irene's right, Toby," he began haltingly, "although it pains me to say that, because I know how much you love these islands and your life here. But let's face it, you have only one close friend, and you don't spend a lot of time with him; two, if you count your dolphin friend. You spend more time with her! Have you been on a date? If you ever do, where would you take her? You don't have a social support system of friends the way most people have when they are growing up. You are very comfortable around adults, impressively so. We are so proud of you, your maturity and judgment. We just feel you need a more varied environment."

Toby frowned. "I don't know what you mean. Are you sending me away?"

Irene smiled reassuringly and placed her hand on Toby's. He did not find this comforting, as he knew this gesture was intended to make him accept a decision he would not be in agreement with.

"Your grandfather and I have been discussing the possibility of your going to prep school, at a boarding school, in the States." She paused to let this sink in and to gauge his reaction.

Toby felt conflicting emotions. At least they weren't sending him to another relative or abandoning him, but prep school? Oh shit, winters in New England. No water, no sand, no diving or spear fishing, no Phinney! He wouldn't know anybody! Emotions of dislocation flooded his brain and his heart pumped double time; yes, he was scared. He was looking for a life preserver. *Catcher in the Rye* had been required reading at Queen Vic's, and Toby worried that his grandparents saw him as the troubled teenager, Holden Caulfield, from that book.

"Your grandmother has come up with something interesting," Pop said with a smile. "Although I must admit, I will miss not having you around for cheap labor during the busy season, we were thinking of having you join Neil Henderson at Flagler Academy, a small co-ed prep school on the island of Palm Beach. Neil will be starting in the fall, too, so you would have at least one friend when you start out, and for what it's worth, there will be girls there."

Irene reached for the manila envelope and pulled out the school's brochure. It was in a classy, flat black-and-white format. Toby could see on the cover a Mediterranean mansion with a few students, girls in uniform dresses, boys in slacks and dress shirts under jackets; in bold print, it said: FLAGLER ACADEMY PREPARATORY SCHOOL. Sliding it across the table to him, she said, "This will give you an idea of the lovely campus where you would be staying. The campus is divided between the girls' side and the boys' side. They apparently have a lot of activities you would like, even a sailing team."

Toby took the brochure and started flipping through it, as the iced teas arrived. The waiter stood by attentively waiting to get their attention so he could take an order, which broke the tension for a moment. The distraction allowed Toby a minute to relax and catch his breath, as he scanned the menu before returning to the brochure. They ordered sandwiches, and Toby began absorbing the information presented to him, forming impressions of what he faced.

The campus looked like an old mansion on the ocean, apparently where the girls resided. Across North County Road, the main drag up the island of Palm Beach, was a more conservative-looking dormitory for the boys with lots of open space for tennis courts, ball fields, some cottages, and at the end by the Intracoastal Waterway, a large boathouse. The water on the west side by the Intracoastal was about a mile across. Moored off the docks were about eight or nine sailboats, most about twenty-feet long. He did recognize two Comets among the moored boats, which he found of interest.

The students all looked like what he saw at Queen Vic's. Boys and girls were dressed rather formally, except for the pictures of sporting activities. He was surprised to see the young men dressed in tuxedos at some of the evening affairs. The girls were in gowns. Toby had never worn a tuxedo before, but he had seen Pop wear one when he went to the governor's mansion in Nassau for big parties. Pop had complained about the attire when he had to wear it, and Toby didn't feel too excited about it either. "How often will I be able to come home?" he asked.

Irene answered with "It is a boarding school, Toby. You will spend most of the school year there, but you will be able to come home for special occasions and over Christmas and spring breaks. There are flights to Nassau from Miami, about seventy-five miles away, and right there in Palm Beach. You will have plenty of time to be on the water here in the islands. And, remember, we do run an inn; you will be able to bring friends with you if their parents approve. I'm sure that will be an attractive proposition for you to offer. Of course, you will have all summer, which is your favorite time here anyway."

Toby still felt very conflicted. In his head, he knew this was not a bad deal, but his heart told him otherwise. He knew he was nervous about learning to meet new friends and have to get along with them while he was living with them, but that wasn't the real issue for him. Suddenly it clicked. He would not see Phinney every week. Would she forget him? He became overwhelmed by sadness. He started to mutter, "But what about Phinney?"

Vernon noticed and caught on right away. In a gentle voice he said, "Son, that's kind of the point, don't you see. You have this rare experience with an animal, something very few people get to do, but Phinney has become disproportionate in your life. You two have become very dependent on each other for companionship, and as wonderful as that may feel right now, as a full diet it may not be what's right."

"For either of you," Irene chimed in. "Did you ever stop to think that this might not be the best for the dolphin, either? She is after all a wild animal, and her relationship with you might be affecting her development, too."

This became too much for Toby. His emotions got the better of him, and he burst into tears, burying his face in his arms, sobbing uncontrollably. "You think I'm bad for Phinney?" he choked out between sobs.

Irene slid her chair closer to Toby's and put her arms around him. Vernon squeezed his shoulder. Both were rather emotional themselves. "Of course not, Toby," they said in unison.

"We see the way the two of you are when you're together, and it fills us with joy," Irene said gently. "We can only imagine what you must feel, and we are so sorry to have to have this conversation with you. But because we see your pain doesn't mean we can ignore the bigger picture."

The waiter approached then, and Vernon nodded for him to begin placing the dishes on the table. "Here comes our lunch," he said. "Let's enjoy it and continue our discussion later."

Toby settled down, but he couldn't really enjoy his sandwich. They finished their meals pretty much in silence. Vernon paid the bill, and they walked down to the public docks to the Chris Craft. Toby got the lines while his grandfather started the engines.

"Don't you want to drive, Toby?"

"I don't think so, Pop. I'm not in the mood right now."

Irene knew this was serious, and she set about trying to find a way to deal with Toby's disappointment. Toby *always* wanted to drive the Chris Craft; now he was just sitting by the transom looking back at the small wake as Vernon eased out of the harbor for the short trip back to Piper Cay. She felt better when, as they crossed the bar into the cove, Toby stood up and asked his grandfather if he could dock the boat, which he did smoothly and efficiently. Tied up and secure, he made his way down the dock to his room where he stayed until dinner.

Only one guest cabin was occupied, so the dining room was quiet when Toby sat at the table with his grandparents that evening. He was thoughtful and introspective when he asked if the decision had been made.

"We feel it's best, Toby," Pop said cautiously.

"Then if you don't mind, I would like to take as much time off this summer to spend with Phinney as I can. I'd rather not make another trip to the States like we have in summers past, so I can be with her."

"That will be fine with us," agreed his grandmother. "Your grandfather and I may have to go stateside for a brief period, but you are comfortable here with Ossie and Major to look after you. The kitchen will be open for the summer, and there will be people about looking after repairs and such."

"You will still have your responsibilities, however," Pop added. "Your indentured servitude doesn't end until you report for duty at Flagler," he said, smiling nervously.

"And we have a lot of shopping to do to get all the proper clothing you will need for school in the fall. Remember, we need to get you a tuxedo. The brochure says every Saturday night is formal. There isn't much use for the clothing you have on this island, tee shirts, flip-flops, and swimming suits, and your Queen Vic outfits won't be totally right either."

Toby felt a release; no need to fret over a decision that had already been made. He had learned to make do with the hand he had been dealt, and he could not resist the warm, dimple-filled smile he got from his grandmother. Her blue eyes beamed love for him, contrasted with Pop's crusty smile that covered a cream-filled center.

The following morning, Toby was up at six to get his chores out of the way, and by nine, he was on the dock yanking on the clapper. He thought today would be a great day for a sail with Phinney, and he threw his dive gear and some of Ossie's conch fritters in the catboat, and rigged it while he waited for his girl.

They sailed all the way around Rose Island together. Upon completing the circumnavigation, Toby beached the catboat off the pristine sandy beach on the west end of the island and anchored it so the rising tide wouldn't let it drift away. With his cooler floating alongside in tow, he splashed ashore and then sat waist deep in the water, digging in his toes so the small waves washing ashore wouldn't tip him over.

Phinney wriggled alongside and beached herself between his knees, scratching her belly as she rolled in the sand. Toby put his hand on her brow, and they lay together basking in the Bahama sun as it reached its zenith almost directly overhead. Today was the solstice; the sun wouldn't get any higher than this. Phinney lifted her head, and Toby splashed some fresh water from his pitcher in the cooler in her mouth, which she promptly spat out. She sighed from her blowhole, and Toby felt a brief sting of sadness at the thought of not seeing her whenever he wanted, but that passed in the solitude of the moment. He slowly tried to explain to her what was happening, knowing she could not possibly understand.

———— • ◆ • ————

As the summer wore on, except for days when Toby was tied up with chores for Pop or someone needed a ride into Nassau in the Chris Craft, he spent his time on the water with Phinney. He took a week off with his grandmother to go to the States, where he acquired the necessary wardrobe for his fancy prep school. He was able to get almost everything in Palm Beach at the Prep Shop on Worth Avenue, the store that was identified as the school's official clothier. Mr. Newman, the proprietor, advised Toby on what was considered "in" from a fashion standpoint, which was a great relief for Toby who had no fashion awareness, having been dressed in a school uniform or tee shirts and shorts for the last several years.

Although the school was closed for the summer, Toby and his grandmother did have a chance to stop by and get a brief tour of the campus by an administrative aid. He had to admit, he was impressed. It was nicer than the governor's mansion in Nassau. The ocean side where the girls stayed was a classic Mediterranean villa, complete with loggias and breezeways, a small concert hall, and classrooms. The west side of the campus, reserved for the boys and athletic fields, was more spartan. A brief walk beyond the athletic fields passed a chapel on the way down a hill to the boathouse and docks on the Intracoastal side. The sailboats had all been stored for the summer. Toby could not imagine himself in this environment, because he had no reference, but he had to admit to himself that the possibilities were promising. Maybe Pop and Irene were right.

———— •◆• ————

The hot summer days passed languidly as Phinney and Toby sailed, fished, and just sat together. Pop had made good on his promise not to give him any difficulty about all the time spent with Phinney. Other than an occasional ribbing or sarcastic remark, he seemed sensitive to Toby's feelings. His grandmother tip-toed around the subject.

Finally, the week in September came when Toby knew he would be spending his last day with Phinney before leaving for school. His steamer trunk containing all the new clothes he'd gotten had been shipped to the school as instructed, and he was to report to the campus over the weekend. He had been assigned and received a nice letter from a "big brother" to mentor him through the acclimation process, some guy named E. Gerald Gale, IV, which conjured all kinds of thoughts about the society he was about to join. It was filled with welcoming enthusiasm one might expect from an obligated fellow student.

Toby did have a chance to visit with Neil Henderson when his friend returned to Nassau from his summer abroad, and they compared notes about what they had learned about the school. Neil's mentor was someone named Corrado Manuel Martinez y Lopez, quite a mouthful, from Venezuela. He had written a nice letter to Neil in the most beautiful handwriting Toby had ever seen, telling Neil what to expect when he got to school.

On the second Saturday in September, his last before heading off to his new school, Toby rang for Phinney early. The pair exhausted themselves by visiting all their old haunts, finishing late in the afternoon in the lagoon. Toby sat waist deep in the water by the small beach with Phinney cradled between his legs, as he stroked her brow. He was overcome with sadness while he talked softly to his friend, trying vainly to explain that he must leave, promising to return at Christmas, if not before.

He began sobbing, his shoulders shaking, as Phinney rubbed his thigh with her snout, sensing his grief. After a long time, he calmed and stood, giving Phinney his best smile and wave. He urged her out of the cove. With one last look over her dorsal as she took a breath, Phinney eased toward the bar at the entrance.

Phinney spent most of her time with the pod in the late spring. Boy called occasionally, and she came whenever she heard the bell. Sometimes they would just frolic in the lagoon or sit together on the beach in the corner on the far side of the pier. The sun was rising higher and higher as the days wore on, and Phinney began to realize there was a pattern to Boy's calls. They seemed to be several feeding days apart, but on a regular basis, and then followed by two days in a row.

She didn't measure time in weeks, rather in daylight or seasonal cycles, determined by her in how high the sun rose during the day, water temperature, which dropped when the sun stayed lower on the horizon, and stormy seasons. She had been through a couple of these now, and the seasonal differences were discernable. This lasted a while after she had that strange encounter with Boy when he stayed underwater too long and blew bubbles out of the back of his head. She really knew it wasn't the back of his head, but that he had some kind of breathing device. Either way, she was still uncomfortable with it.

However, recently he had been calling every day. Something must have changed, but she could not imagine what. Either way, she didn't care; Boy was fun, and she enjoyed being with him. She reflected on the first of the continuous days: Boy had led them for a long sail in the big sailboat, the heavy one, and they had stopped on the beach near the reef where she did most of her feeding. She had stranded herself a little between his skinny legs, and he had poured some of that funny water in her mouth. It had a peculiar quality to it, not like the water she lived in. Phinney thought it tasted bitter. She spit it back at him, and he made a funny grunting sound from his stomach. He did this when she did something unexpected. She didn't know about laughing, because it was foreign to her, but she knew it was associated with joy and affection in some way.

That day they had just stayed together for a long time. He made sounds to her. She heard them go on for a long time. She knew he was trying to get her to understand something, but it was just all noise to her. The only sound she could recognize was when he called her. It was a lot of air, and soft. So she knew her name to Boy was Phinney, which she could recognize by the sound.

She and others of the pod were very intuitive, capable of understanding other dolphins' needs by gestures or sounds, so she was good at reading Boy's moods. She knew he was sad, and she suspected it had something to do with her, but she could not imagine in what way. Boy finally stood up, and she started to work herself off of the sand by bending her belly and wriggling sideways, so she could get some purchase on the sand with her flukes to push off. Boy reached down and grabbed her by the flukes and pulled her into deeper water, then with his cooler floating alongside, waded to the waist-deep water where the boat was anchored. Boy climbed over the side and raised the sails. Into the wind, in irons, Boy leaned over the side and gave Phinney a brush on the brow and smiled. She moved to deeper water and gave him a good jump and a few screeches as a goodbye, as his sails filled and he reached off toward the cove and home.

This pattern continued as the days grew shorter instead of longer. Almost every day, Boy would ring for her and the two would sail or fish together among the reefs between Yellow Bank and Piper Cay. One time they went the other way toward the entrance to the harbor on the big island. A new jetty had been built of rocks and cement shapes jutting from the entrance to much deeper water. It had attracted a lot of fish.

The two of them made a pair as Boy caught and tailed spiny lobster and left the carapaces for Phinney. For her, it felt as when she hunted with her mother when she was just a baby calf. She was almost a quarter grown now, weighing over a hundred pounds. The daily sun height was almost halfway to its lowest point, and the pod was preparing for a journey southeast to more protected water.

Boy called her one morning, and they spent the entire day together going to all of their favorite places, ending their day in the lagoon at the small sandy beach adjacent the pier. They lay together in the shallow water for the longest time. Boy talked continuously, and he was making that movement from his belly, but it wasn't laughing. Boy was sad, and water was running out of his eyes, as his whole body shook. He stroked her brow anxiously as he talked to *her. His chest heaved, and Phinney felt a sorrow wash over her for the pain she felt in Boy's heart. At length, Boy stood and waved to her. She knew it was time to go, but she did not feel good about it, looking back at him as she kicked toward the sandbar at the entrance to the lagoon.*

After a summer of adventures in the water, Phinney didn't hear the bell anymore, so there was no more time with Boy. Phinney went to the cove several times, and she could see the bell still on the end of the dock, but no sign of Boy. The whole place seemed quiet. Many of the boats that had been moored in the cove were gone, and the nurse sharks that used to gather at the end of the dock were no longer there, having moved on to find a more reliable source of food.

She rejoined her pod for the seasonal move into the Exumas. Her life adapted to the ways of her party, feeding and resting, occasionally moving from one island to another. Phinney's new focus became the calf of her mother's companion, which she had given birth to recently. Phinney was given the responsibility of shadowing the newborn to help with his breathing and to make sure he didn't wander from the protection of the reefs.

CHAPTER FIVE

If it weren't for Neil Henderson, Toby would have felt isolated during his first few days at Flagler Academy. The other kids were nice to him, but most had been at the school for years. Associations had been made, relationships built, and he felt like he was on the outside looking in. It took him a while to learn the do's and don'ts.

The second floor of the boys' house, what they called the men's side of the campus, was devoted to six dorm rooms of twelve boys each. A common group shower and bathroom divided every other dorm room, so things got crowded in the mornings when twenty-four teenagers tried to pee, brush their teeth, and groom for the day in each common bathroom.

The supervisors were assembled from the faculty, most of whom lived on the school property in the dorm facilities or in cottages on the campus. The ground floor was given over to the common areas shared by everyone. The main great room was a comfortable space with leather chairs and sofas arranged in compatible settings, much like a hotel lobby. A grand piano occupied one corner and a twenty-inch, black-and-white television the other. A billiard table was the center of attention in the screened porch adjacent. The headmaster of the men's dorm had a large, comfortable apartment at one end, which included his office, a place the students avoided as much as possible. Rarely was someone called to that office to be complimented on what a wonderful job he was doing. It was also a place where students could receive a phone call from home and enjoy some privacy.

Sunday, Toby's first afternoon was spent unpacking his steamer trunk under the watchful eye of dorm prefects to insure his attire was appropriate for the school standards. A campus utility truck hauled all the emptied luggage down to the boat house where it was stored until it was time for the process to reverse at the end of the school year.

Toby was in the second dorm room on the north side, sharing a bunk bed with a new student from Washington, D.C. Across the room was a spacious five-drawer dresser and hanging closet, which held all his personal effects, clothing, etc. Gerry Gale, Toby's mentor, was in the Fifth Form, one grade advanced from his Fourth Form, which was the equivalent of a junior in high school to Toby's sophomore year.

He came by to introduce himself as Toby was unpacking, taking Toby's back by leaning on the prefect, who was really just another student in Toby's class with a few years of history at the school. The prefect was giving Toby a hard time on his wardrobe selection, which excepting the clothes he had bought at the Prep Shop with his grandmother, did not look like the other kids'.

Gerry otherwise seemed to be in a hurry to be with the older students. After shaking hands, he gave Toby a polite brush off with "Just go with the flow. If you have any questions about what you're supposed to do, just ask one of the old timers or see me at vespers." Whatever the hell that was, it would be Toby's first question of his prefect.

"It's the daily chapel ritual" was the prefect's reply. "At five o'clock the girls come over from their side and we all walk to chapel for a lecture of some sort."

The afternoon was free time, and the students organized themselves in groups to play tennis, softball, or shoot billiards. Toby followed Neil to the softball field where neither of them was picked early for a team, because nobody knew them. Besides, Toby looked a little different with his longish hair, and Neil was a little smaller than the others. The game was shortened by the threat of rain, although Toby did represent himself well with a double on his only time at bat. The billiard room became quite crowded as all the kids sought shelter from the drizzle. Many lit up cigarettes; Gerry Gale explained that if you had your parents' permission and you were at least sixteen, you were allowed to smoke.

Toby and Neil stayed together and tried to join conversations of some of their roommates, but the cliques were hard to break into. They finally started up a conversation with some of the kids they had played softball with, Toby receiving acknowledgment for the double he hit to right field. It was a good conversation starter, but slowly all the boys angled for the stairs to go to their rooms and get dressed for chapel and dinner.

Toby followed the lead of the others in his dorm room, who were putting on slacks and dress shirts with ties and school blazers. He found the required clothes and went to the commons, the large living room downstairs where his classmates gathered in small groups and gossiped about the day.

A lot of attention was paid to the driveway that ran the length of the boys' campus from County Road to the docks. At around five o'clock Toby figured out why, when the girls started walking by on their way to the chapel. Some of the boys paired with girls they had known from previous years; others just joined in where they were comfortable. Toby stuck close to Neil, and they slid in between two groups of girls, all dressed in shirtwaist dresses of pastel colors. The smell of perfume overpowered the Florida humidity as the two worked their way with the others toward the small chapel on the hill past the athletic fields where they had spent part of the afternoon.

The chapel was a classic, white, wood-frame building with a small spire at the peak in the front. Some of the windows were stained glass. Pews lined either side of the center aisle. They filled rapidly as all one hundred forty of the students took seats, almost by plan, girls on the right, boys on the left, as was the obvious tradition. Dr. Oestreich, the headmaster of Flagler Academy, took the podium and welcomed the students to the inauguration of the twenty-ninth year of the school's history.

After the expected boilerplate, the headmaster got into some of the rules and philosophies of the school. It was emphasized that boy-girl associations were discouraged, that the student body should be inclusive in the development of personal relationships. It didn't take a lot of imagination to figure out that about the only problem that could not be overcome would be an unexpected pregnancy of one of the girls entrusted to Flagler's care.

Dr. Oestreich was a tall man, and he spoke with eloquence. His countenance made a person want to pay attention, and Toby took in all he had to say regarding the responsibilities he had as a result of the privileges he enjoyed, enabling him to attend such a revered institution whose beginnings traced back to the Flagler family itself. In fact, the entire student body was instructed to write a 200-word essay to this effect to be turned in at the first English class attended.

After reciting the school prayer and singing the alma mater, introductions were made of the senior administrative staff. The new students were requested, row by row, to stand and introduce themselves. Toby heard a murmur run through the student body when he announced that he was born in Chicago, but now lived on a small island in the Bahamas outside of Nassau. This seemed to make him a curiosity of sorts, which Toby found peculiar in that Neil Henderson got no such acknowledgment when he announced that he was from the Bahamas. Toby also hadn't noticed the way the girls were looking at him.

After the conclusion of the proceedings, the students were dismissed to file orderly and solemnly out the front for the return walk to the girls' campus where the dining room in the old estate was located. The groups mingled, some mixed boys and girls, some just boys or girls, and made their way slowly along the half mile to the mansion. In the dining room, the sexes were separated again, one to each side of the large dining hall. The students identified by placard the tables set for them, which were matched to the dorm rooms. At the head and foot of each table were members of the faculty or administrative staff to oversee the dining process.

The meals were served rather formally by students selected by a posted rotation, complete with finger bowls to conclude the meals. On this first dinner, the servers were return students who already knew the drill. Coincidentally, Toby's table was served by his dorm prefect, a student who was returning for his fourth year, the one who had tried to give him a hard time about some of the clothes he had unpacked earlier in the day. He had the air of one in charge, the all-knowing oracle, and he made those around him feel uncomfortable.

The courses from salad and soup to entrée and dessert were served from the left, old courses removed from the right. Toby felt like he was on another planet when he compared this to the laid-back dining at the inn at Piper's Landing. What had Vern and Irene gotten him into?

Conversations were muted, mostly about young people getting to know one another, feeling out their boundaries. A lot of comparison was going on, how things this year compared to last, who was dating whom, who had targeted the outrageously good-looking girl from Brazil.

The food was really quite good, and there was plenty of it for those who wanted extra portions. Dessert was simple, a slice of apple pie; *How appropriate,* thought Toby. Most of the students tried to act the part of sophisticated city dwellers, drinking coffee they didn't seem to really like. This continued after dinner when the boys and girls retired to their respective campuses.

Back at the dorm the boys gathered in groups, discussing what they knew and speculating about what they didn't. Many smoked cigarettes that they knew they shouldn't, but felt more adult for it, with sport coats slung over their shoulders and ties loosely knotted at the collar. At ten thirty the prefects called for return to dorm rooms and lights out. Toby had made associations with about three members of his dorm room, but spent most of his time with Neil and Charlie, his upper bunk mate. After the lights went out, the boys in his room abed, conversation flowed more easily in the anonymity of the darkness until the room eventually fell silent.

———— •◆• ————

Toby's first morning at Flagler began with a call from the prefect, Barry Hutchinson, that it was time to rise and begin the day. Twelve boys from each side of the common bathroom facilities piled in queuing to use six urinals and six stalls. Some just stripped and headed to the showers where they relieved themselves while getting clean. An occasional lad tried to shield a morning erection from the shaming of others. Toby found this amusing, as he waited his turn, holding his Dopp kit in hand. He finished his morning ablutions and dressed for breakfast consistent with the others in khakis and an oxford shirt under the school uniform jacket. Slowly the dorm rooms emptied to the downstairs until the order was given to walk the quarter mile across County Road to the girls' side and the dining hall.

They entered from the boys' entrance and took places at the assigned tables where the process from the night before was replicated over scrambled eggs and bacon. Breakfast was followed by a series of informational talks by teachers and staff as to the routines that were to be followed, protocols, rules, etc. Dr. Oestreich spoke at length about what it meant to be a privileged member of the Flagler community, how to treat others with respect, and the usual philosophy one would expect at a prep school. With nothing in his background for comparison, Toby accepted what he was hearing and took Gerry Gale's advice to "go with the flow."

Each student was assigned an advisor and a time during the day when schedules would be given and classes assigned. Toby got his instructions from his foreign language teacher—he was taking Spanish—who explained his schedule in detail and gave him a map of the classroom locations, all of which had been halls or large bedrooms of the estate at one time or another.

And so began Toby's new life at Flagler Academy. In the weeks that followed, the routines flowed nicely. Getting dressed and prepared for the day was followed by the walk to the dining hall where learning socializing skills seemed to be the order of the moment. Toby was making friends quickly as his alternative background as an islander made him somewhat unique. Questions about island living came naturally from the other students, but Toby's shyness kept him from volunteering his relationship with Phinney. Otherwise, he had a never-ending litany of stories, which, although very normal to Toby, seemed magical to kids who came from Cuba and South America, New England, and the Midwest.

The school permitted Toby his longer curly hair, which, coupled with his long lashes and deep blue eyes, set him apart from the others in ways the girls found irresistible. More than once Toby caught them evaluating him in groups as they gossiped about who knew what. This made him uncomfortable, knowing he was the object of their conversations, but he did not know how to take advantage of their attraction, which made him all the more desirable to them.

A half hour following breakfast, classes started at eight forty-five lasting until noon with a juice break midmorning served on the loggias in the tropical Florida climate. Although the concept of couples was strongly discouraged, the opportunities for socializing certainly promoted the older boys and girls to pair off.

After lunch at twelve thirty, the afternoon was devoted to another hour of classes, followed by sports, which were assigned each semester just as were the classes. Toby elected sailing and tennis, which he did on alternate days, including Saturday, when abbreviated classes were scheduled. Following sport activities, the students returned to their dorms to clean up for vespers and the walk to chapel, where some nugget was delivered in a formal presentation and campus announcements were made. These comments usually contained some reference to what the staff now referred to as "twoing," the observation of faculty and Dr. Oestreich of a particular boy and girl spending too much time in each other's company.

On his first Saturday, Toby sailed in his first race in one of the school sloops, a lightning, where it became obvious to the skipper, an older student named Joe, that Toby really knew his way around a sailboat. That evening he had his first experience with a tuxedo. Gerry Gale took a few minutes on the way back from the docks to explain the Flagler ritual where the gentlemen were expected to be comfortable in formal attire, and so, each Saturday night dinner was to be served as a formal occasion.

Following dinner, there would be some mixed, boys and girls, event organized by the school. Typically, alternate weeks occasioned a dance with a student-featured recital on the others, usually involving a musical instrument. During the dances, the students were not allowed to dance with the same partner two dances in a row, which only meant to the couples who had already paired off that they skipped every other dance or swapped by prearrangement with another couple.

This first night was a dance held in the library, tables pushed aside to make room for a dance floor, music by Victrola. The faculty chaperones tried to play faster foxtrots, but students substituted slow dances to accommodate a little groping in the recesses of the library. The staff did their best to keep the students at least four inches apart, but to no avail. Youth has its ways.

Toby knew the basics from the dance school his parents required him to attend in sixth grade back in suburban Chicago, and he danced with a few of the girls who surrounded him. After a few dances—he was really the only one to follow the consecutive dance rule—he became more comfortable around the young women. They certainly smelled nice, but the talking was awkward. One of the girls put her head on his shoulder and moved in close during Pat Boone's "Love Letters." Toby was relieved when a proctor moved in and separated them. He could feel her breasts push into his chest, and the thought of that excited him somewhat.

The walk back to the dorms was filled with raucous laughter and bragging about who had done what and with whom. Bow ties were unclipped, top buttons unbuttoned, while the cooler, older Form Fivers and Sixers who could actually tie a bow tie, undid them and let them hang as Humphrey Bogart would have had he been in residence. The occasional cigarette hanging from the lips of a callow teenager completed the effect, but Toby found it just a little pathetic.

"Hey, Toby. It looked like Chrissy Mallen had more than a passable interest in you," said Charlie Briggs, his bunkmate. "Too bad you got busted by that nosey proctor."

"We were just dancing a little too close, is all. It wasn't anything." Toby felt a little bigger that anyone had even noticed. He could still smell her perfume, and he looked forward to chapel tomorrow. Perhaps he would have someone to walk with. After lights out, the chatter continued a little longer than normal. A couple of the older kids could be heard sneaking downstairs for a last smoke in the billiard room or maybe a rendezvous down by the docks. Toby's imagination was starting to get the better of him as he drifted off.

After breakfast, the boys waited at the dorm for the girls to pass by on the way to Sunday services. Toby leaned around the corner to try to spot Chrissy Mallen, the girl he had danced with the night before. He kept ducking back, not wanting to be too obvious. Finally he spotted her blond hair, as she walked with two other girls, which made joining in awkward. He didn't know them well; they were older. Chrissy shared English and biology classes with him, and after her actions on the dance floor with him, he felt comfortable that he would not be rejected if he asked her if he could join her for the walk to the chapel, but the other two girls complicated matters. What if she was having a private conversation with them, or if she felt it would look uncool to accept his invitation? As they neared, he was preparing to step back behind the corner of the building when she spotted him and gave him a beaming, dimpled smile.

Too late now, Toby said to himself as he ventured into the mass toward the trio.

"Toby, do you know Daphne and Laura?" Chrissy introduced him. They smiled and whispered to each other, as Chrissy punched Laura in the arm, turning over her shoulder and said, "Cut it out, you guys!"

"Hi, Toby," said Daphne. "We've seen you around this week. You're new this year aren't you?"

Laura actually stuck out her hand. "I sailed against you yesterday. You were with Joe Gardner on *Ole Blue.* I was on *Leprechaun,* the new lightning we got this year. We only beat you guys by a boat length at the windward mark. *Ole Blue* is kind of a dog. Heavy. Doesn't do well to weather, but you did all right yesterday."

"Yeah, Joe knew a few tricks, and we made good time on you on the wind shift, plus I think there is a little more current in the middle of the course when the tide's coming in. We stayed along the shore, and that helped a lot. You're right though, that boat feels heavy. It's old and been in the water a long time." Toby was a lot more comfortable talking about sailing than anything else, and he could see that it put Chrissy off a little. He turned his attention to her. "Do you sail, Chrissy?" Bad choice of topic, Toby sensed immediately, so he shifted gears. "That was fun last night, don't you think? It's a first for me; I've never worn a tux before."

Chrissy's smile softened a little. "My first formal, too, other than my cousin's wedding."

The four of them walked the short distance talking about nothing, and it was over before Toby had a chance to reflect on it. He didn't have an agenda, but he still felt as though he had missed the mark a little. Maybe he could do better on the way back to the dining hall, a longer distance to put a plan in place. "Hell, a plan to do what, exactly," he muttered to himself as he took a seat on the boys' side of the chapel.

The service was more formal than the evening vespers during the week. Hymns were sung and readings from the Bible were followed by a brief sermon from a minister visiting from Choate, a New England prep school affiliated somehow with Flagler. The format was easy in a nondenominational, protestant style not particularly offensive to the students of other faiths and not very filled with ceremony and dogma.

On the walk back to the dining hall for the midday meal, Toby walked alongside Chrissy, but the group had grown to five or six, eliminating any chance for a private conversation between the two. Chrissy sent signals that she preferred it this way, so Toby took the opportunity to get to know some of the other students better.

He liked the idea of having a connection to a girl on campus, as it seemed like the order of the day, particularly with the juniors and seniors. He would put more effort into the relationship in the free time he could find during the school week. About halfway back from the chapel, as they were passing the men's dorm, Daphne volunteered they all go sailing during the free time in the afternoon. There was always an informal race in Lake Worth Sunday afternoons organized by the Sailfish Club near the end of the island, and Flagler students' boats were always welcome to join.

"Joe and I have signed *Leprechaun* out. Toby, why don't you and Chrissy join us? We're pretty competitive in this fleet."

They all agreed that was a good idea and planned to meet at the docks at one thirty.

"I may just make it," said Toby. "I have to serve today. It's my first time, so I may be a little longer finishing up."

Toby would have his first rotation as a server for a full meal at his table. Breakfast had been easy for him. He just followed what he had been witnessing all week, but the main meal was a little more complicated with so many courses and finger bowls and such. He ate after the meal with the other servers, which ran a little later, but it had the advantage that he could have as much as he wanted, including desserts. He had a feeling he would be rushing today to take advantage of the opportunity to spend time with Chrissy on the water where he was so comfortable.

Things went smoothly, which meant he didn't spill anything on anybody. He rushed through his turkey tetrazzini, skipped dessert, and headed to the dorm to put on shorts and a tee shirt. On the docks, the fleet master, a crusty old gentleman nicknamed Cap, had already rowed everyone out to their moorings, so after Joe and the girls had rigged the boat, they sailed it by the end of the dock where Toby could step aboard as it passed by.

They headed to the middle of the lake, Joe clearly in command, and definitely enjoying a much closer relationship with Daphne than

Toby had realized. They nuzzled together near the rear of the cockpit. Joe had the tiller in one hand, Daphne in the other, and as soon as they were a comfortable distance from the eyes of the fleet master, they exchanged a few quick kisses.

"I didn't know you two were such good friends," Toby stated with some surprise.

"Then we're doing our jobs," Joe replied. "I'm sure you have noticed that couples are frowned upon around here. If you want to be with someone in particular, you have to be very careful, or they will separate you. We never walk to chapel together, and we try to avoid spending time with each other during free time when we are being watched. Daphne and I have been going together for two years, haven't we, sweetie?" Joe smirked as he gave Daphne a peck on the cheek.

"You know I'm your gal." Daphne smiled.

They set about working in among the lightnings, about a dozen or so, at the starting line. At the five-minute horn, Joe got down to business and started barking instructions to Toby and the girls, how much to trim the main and jib. Toby observed that he was skillful at positioning the boat toward the weather end of the line to try to get an advantage at the start. His face was tense in concentration as he shouted to the boat next to him to "bring it up" as he brought the lightning closer to weather trying to push the other boat over the starting line early.

"Fuck you, Gardiner!" came the reply from the classmate who was forced to tack away. Toby did not know a lot about the rules of racing, but he knew how to make a boat go fast. He soaked in everything he was seeing as Joe explained.

"The leeward boat has the right of way and can point straight into the wind if it wants to and the weather boat has to avoid contact. That's why he had to tack or risk a premature start, which would require him to sail all the way around the starting line and begin all over. Now he's out of position and we are at the preferred end of the line for the start."

The starting horn went off as Toby saw the small committee boat raise a blue flag, starting the race. It all made sense now as *Leprechaun* led the fleet in clear air toward the first weather mark down by the Colonnade Hotel, just this side of the bridge over the Intracoastal.

Joe pointed to the mark off in the distance explaining to the girls, mostly for Chrissy's benefit, as he had spent a lot of time on the water with Daphne, that they would tack against the wind until they rounded it, and then return downwind to the leeward mark by Peanut Island at the inlet, and finally to the finish midway on the course where they started.

"Move to the high side of the boat and keep your weight in the center. Daphne, keep the jib right about there in this wind. Bring it in a little if the wind picks up. Toby, same with the mainsheet."

They beat their way to the mark and rounded in first place just ahead of the lightning they had forced to tack at the start. Madison, the other skipper, and Joe's bunkmate in the Form Six room, only had a crew of three. His boat was lighter and performed a tad better off the wind. Coming from behind, he took some of *Leprechaun's* air and moved steadily past into first place. Taunts about manhood were exchanged until Toby pointed out, "Hey, we're the ones with the good-looking women aboard!" which earned him smiles from Daphne and Chrissy. "Joe, can I make a suggestion?" Toby asked tentatively, not wanting to exceed boundaries.

"I'm all ears, Nassau." Toby had a nickname, it seemed.

"Have you ever tacked downwind?" Toby asked.

"Never heard of it. What's the point?" Joe look confused.

Toby explained thoughtfully, remembering the days of light air when he tried to get the lumbering catboat to move at a reasonable pace and the trick Pop had taught him, "Well, you know we will go a lot faster on a reach. The boats I've sailed can reach at an angle downwind going enough faster than straight downwind like we're going now, wing on wing"—the main was on one side of the boat and the jib on the other, so as not to interfere with each other's wind—"that the increased speed more than makes up for the extra distance."

Joe eyed Madison steadily increasing his lead. "Here, you take the tiller and show me. We'll try it for a few jibes and see how it works out."

They all repositioned slowly so as not to upset the air that was filling their sails. Toby took the helm. "I'm going to head up slowly. Let the jib across when it wants to and trim it by letting it out until it luffs, and bring it back in just a little. Keep testing the trim to make sure we are maximizing the draw of the sail, as I maintain a course about forty-five degrees off of dead downwind. Joe or Daphne, trim the main the same way and stay on it, always letting it out a little and retrimming it to make sure it's doing the best it can. Everyone move to the back of the boat as far as you can to get the sail plan up higher and increase the waterline. Joe, put the centerboard down about halfway. Make all your movements slowly."

Toby had made all his commands quietly and confidently, completely in his element. They did as he requested while he slowly brought the boat up about forty-five degrees from their target. They picked up speed immediately, but moved away from the fleet, which was heading in a straight line toward Peanut Island and the next mark.

As they got further and further from the rest of the boats, Joe became a little anxious. "Are you sure about this, Nassau? We're getting pretty far from the fleet."

"Just wait. We'll see after we jibe and rejoin them whether we made up any ground. Then you can decide."

The day was spectacular as they moved quickly through the

water, occasional wavelets splashing cold water on them. Toby gave the tack about fifteen minutes and announced to prepare for a jibe, which they accomplished smoothly. With the sails on the other side, on a starboard jibe, the four of them had a great view of the fleet as they began to merge. It was clear after a few minutes that they had gained considerably. *Leprechaun* passed comfortably in front of most of the fleet and had a slight advantage on Madison's lightning.

"I'm pretty impressed, Toby. I've never seen that done before, but it sure works. Even though we will pass in front, let's take another hitch out to the middle of the lake, so we can preserve our starboard tack right-of-way advantage at the leeward mark if we need it. A little insurance."

Toby agreed, noting the tactical decision for use at a future time. He did not think in those terms, since he was not familiar with sailboat racing or its rules, but it made sense. They jibed again and back at the lay line to the mark. They rounded the mark about ten boat lengths ahead of Madison. Joe let Toby keep the helm for the weather leg back to the finish line, where they beat the rest of the fleet by three minutes.

Cheers went up, as Joe took the helm and headed for water more out of sight of Flagler's dock, so he could have a few semiprivate moments with Daphne. Back at the helm, Toby put his arm around Chrissy's shoulder as they sailed aimlessly, while Joe and Daphne slid down on the cockpit seat and made out. Toby didn't know what was expected of him, but Chrissy didn't seem to mind his arm around her.

"This is nice." She smiled up at him, moving a little closer.

The two soaked in the late-afternoon sun. When Joe and Daphne came up for air, they all laughed and headed back to the mooring. They put everything away, bagged the sails, and waited for the launch to take them to the dock, where they found they were the subject of conversation.

"You guys get lost out there?"

"We thought two of you might have fallen overboard. We could only see two heads above the deck."

Finally, Roy Madison ambled over. "That was some neat trick you pulled on the downwind leg, Gardiner. Where did you learn that? You really made up ground on us. I thought we had you beat."

"Not my trick, Roy. It seems Nassau here really knows how to make a boat perform."

They all turned their attention to Toby. He responded, "It works particularly well in light air, not so much when the wind is strong. The boat speed makes up for the extra distance, as you saw. I have a pig of a catboat at home, so I've had to learn a lot of tricks to get it to move. Don't know much about racing though. Joe knows the rules and how to use them."

Joe slapped Toby on the back. "We make a good team."

It was getting late, and the sailors made their way back to the dorms to get cleaned up for supper. Toby walked with Chrissy, as Joe and Daphne held hands as far as the men's dorm, where they quietly separated with an air kiss to say goodbye for the day. As they neared the dorm, no one would have thought they even knew each other, let alone were a couple, so practiced was their discretion.

———— •◆• ————

In the weeks that followed, Toby began to settle in to the routine of the school. Breakfast followed by classes filled the mornings. Toby was surprised at the rate he was making friends. At first he felt a little as though he was just a curiosity of sorts, but he finally accepted that he was likeable. His reserved manner served to draw people to him rather than push them away as it tended to at Queen Vic's' in Nassau. He had never mentioned to anyone about Phinney, although he thought about her all the time, wondering what she was up to, did she miss him or think he abandoned her?

It was only after Neil made reference to the dolphin that Toby began to get inquiries; however, when he mentioned an incident or two, he was met with disbelief. Even though Neil had seen Phinney on a visit to Piper Cay, he was given a good ribbing when he tried to corroborate Toby's stories. "Bullshit!" was the usual response, so Toby never brought the subject up, except with Chrissy, with whom he was spending more and more time. She was a little more sympathetic, although not truly convinced that Toby could have such a close relationship with a wild animal.

Toby spent two afternoons a week trying to learn tennis, but he seemed to have more enthusiasm for hitting the ball than precision. He was proud of hard, high overhand serves, which made it appear that he was better than he was. He rarely won a tennis match. On the water, it was another story. His sailing abilities were in demand as crew on all four of the lightnings in the school's fleet, and even though it was a junior or senior from the Fifth and Sixth Forms who was assigned the role of skipper, it was Toby who usually ended up making the sail trim and tactical speed decisions. He accepted this role graciously, as he was not yet fully schooled in the rules of sailboat racing, but he was learning fast. The week before the Thanksgiving break all the students were making plans to go home for the long holiday weekend; Cap approached Toby as he was walking up from the docks.

"Toby, you have accounted for yourself well for the last few weeks."

"Thank you, sir. I appreciate the opportunity."

Cap looked him in the eye. "Let's not kid ourselves, here. Our boats are not equal; we both know that. I can't help but notice that no matter which boat you sail on, or who you sail with, you either win the race or finish in the hunt. That's not an accident."

Toby nodded, feeling a little pride that he had been noticed.

"When you come back from Thanksgiving, I want you to take

over as skipper of *Ole Blue.* If you can make that pig of a boat go, it will be the best training for you to improve. Sailing one of the newer, lighter lightnings will not make you any better. You need the responsibility of authority to make the decisions, and you'll have to get a better understanding of the rules of racing."

He handed Toby a thin book that said LIGHTNING CLASS ASSOCIATION RULES OF RACING on the cover. "Brush up on these, and you will be ready when you get back."

Toby grinned from ear to ear, not just because of the compliment, but because of everything else. He was going home for a few days. He would get to see Pop and Irene, and more important, Phinney. He missed them. Although he had not felt homesick because he had been so busy with new experiences, the thought of returning filled him with joy. And did he have experiences.

After just ten weeks at Flagler, Toby had made the transition from island boy to sophisticate. He was comfortable in blazers and tuxedos, meeting people with the confidence that he would be accepted, and overall, he felt American. He knew kids from all over the globe, many of whom had backgrounds similar to his, coming from families that moved around at the will of the state department, or were from other cultures, such as the dozen or so wealthy Cubans who were sent to Flagler to get an American experience before going off to Ivy League colleges.

He had his first girlfriend and his first real kiss of many in the corner of the library at a Saturday night formal dance. He'd been nervous at first, but what he lacked in that regard was compensated by his eagerness, Chrissy's previous experience, and what he had gleaned from *Rebel Without a Cause,* which he and some upperclassmen had snuck off to see while they were supposed to be in supervised shopping on Worth Avenue. Mr. Newman had obliged their begging by driving them over to the theater in West Palm Beach and returning a couple of hours later to pick them up.

Toby was now regarded as the sailor to beat on the water and rewarded with a promotion to skipper. He received approving winks and nods from his classmates when they spied him going to or from some remote place on the campus, holding hands with Chrissy. Unfortunately, the newness of the experience lowered Toby's guard, and he was now under the watchful eye of the faculty and administration for violation of the school's antiexclusive fraternization policy. He and Chrissy had staged a visible, attention-getting breakup on the loggia during morning break the previous week, and they had avoided public contact with each other since. Only time would tell if the ruse had been effective. Daphne and Joe, on the other hand, continued their subterfuge with great success.

CHAPTER SIX

PALM BEACH AND BAHAMAS
⋅⋗⋅ LATE 1958–1959

On Wednesday afternoon of Thanksgiving week, Toby took the Greyhound Bus to Broward County International Airport where he boarded a Chalk's Flying Service Grumman seaplane for the hour and a half flight to Nassau, landing right in the harbor and pulling up on the city ramp by the city docks. The noise of the big radial engines reverberated in his head long after he stepped out of the airplane. Spying his grandmother waving at the gate, he waved back with the most excited of smiles. He walked through the informal process of customs and immigration without having to produce any identification, because Pop was standing right there.

They boarded the Chris Craft, and Pop, tossing Toby the keys, said, "You think you remember how to drive this thing?"

"It's like a bicycle, isn't it?" Toby snorted. He threw his soft bag below, started her up, and when Pop retrieved the dock lines, he spun the boat masterfully, levering off a piling, and headed out the harbor entrance for the fifteen-minute ride to Piper Cay.

His grandparents knew they were not the focus of his attention when he jumped off the boat before Pop had even tied it up, and yanked on the clapper of Phinney's bell as hard as he could. Then knowing he had a few minutes to get into shorts and a tee shirt, he ran off the dock toward his room.

"So much for the long-awaited homecoming!" said an exasperated Irene to Vernon.

With a perplexed look, Vernon replied, "I'm guessing the boy didn't suffer too much from being away from his family. We haven't seen him for two and a half months and all he's thinking about is that damn fish!"

"Dolphin," Irene corrected, "and she has a name, dear. Maybe she is his family now."

They ambled down the dock arm in arm, neither admitting to hurt feelings that they weren't the center of Toby's attention after being away so long. Well, they knew they would catch up at dinner.

Tomorrow, the Bethels were coming to share the American odyssey of a turkey dinner. Randy was coming along, too, so Toby would have someone to share his school experience with. Neil Henderson had gone directly to Washington, D.C., to join his family for the holidays. His parents had some state department function to attend.

Toby was back on the dock in minutes, shielding his eyes from the glare of the lowering sun as he anxiously searched the bar at the lagoon entrance for a sign of Phinney.

Phinney had given up listening for the bell over the last two months. She had returned a few times to the cove in hopes she would catch a glimpse of Boy, but to no avail. She returned to her pod, looking after the newborn, and preparing for the seasonal call to move southeast into the Exumas, where she liked playing in the clear shallow water with its white sandy bottom.

This particular day, noticeably shorter now as the cold water season moved in, Phinney was cruising the bank east of Rose Island around Porgy Rocks, keeping loose tabs on the calf, sort of babysitting, when she heard the clang of the bell on Piper Cay. Her heart leaped in her breast, as she shook from blowhole to tail flukes, so filled with joy was she. Excitedly she nudged her charge back toward the area where her mother was feeding among the coral heads on the Yellow Bank, and signaled that she was going on a mission. Her own mother, as well as her friend, knew the meaning of the bell, and they relieved Phinney of her obligations to the calf. In the blink of an eye, she was making a beeline around Hog Island on the deep side toward the cove at Piper Cay and her friend, Boy.

She picked up speed by clearing the water with a strong kick from her flukes about every ten thrusts. Phinney was stronger now than she had been in the early fall when Boy left, having gained another twenty-five pounds, and it was all muscle. She was going full speed now, over twenty miles an hour. Exhausted, she crossed over the bar twenty minutes after she heard the bell. Her heart was pounding from the adrenaline and exertion, and maybe a little excitement at seeing Boy, as she slowed toward the end of the pier.

Boy was jumping with excitement himself, tearing off his tee shirt and leaping in the water as always almost landing on Phinney, who stood on her tail and screeched, stuttered, and clicked, her emotions pouring out as Boy cannon balled into the water right next to her. Boy tried to put his arms around her in some sort of a hug, which was awkward for her, and she rolled on her back, pushing Boy beneath the surface. He took in a mouthful of water and started coughing. She could see him pumping his skinny legs rapidly as he tried to stay afloat.

"Phinney, Phinney!" he screamed.

She recognized her name, but not the words he said after, but there was no room to misinterpret how equally happy he was to see her. This made her feel even more joy, as she swam alongside Boy so he could grab her dorsal for stability, which he did. Then she moved gently to the beach where they renewed their ritual: Boy sitting on the sand waist deep in the water, while Phinney positioned herself comfortably between his legs. It felt good to rub her belly on the sand as she kneaded his thighs with her long nose. Boy kept babbling words Phinney could not understand, but she knew their meaning. She clicked in return to him, and they lay there for forty-five minutes, Phinney lolling between Boy's legs while Boy rubbed her brow, and fingered the edges of her mouth with a gentle motion. She knew he did this to show affection for her.

After the longest time, they moved into the deeper water in the middle of the lagoon and swam circles around each other, just enjoying each other's company. A while later the gray-haired lady human came out to the end of the dock, and she heard something "Phinney," as she waved to the two of them, but speaking briefly to Boy. His face saddened a little, and Phinney knew it was time for him to join the humans, but they had had a joyful late-afternoon reunion, and she had the comfort of knowing that Boy was back. She hoped she would see him the next day. Sadly, she kicked toward the bar and open water, hoping she would soon hear the call for her to return.

Toby was overjoyed to see Phinney's dorsal break the surface as she crossed the bar into the protected water. He pulled his tee shirt over his head and jumped cannonball fashion off the end of the dock without looking. At the last second, he saw Phinney below, and straightened out to try to miss her, but she stood on her tail and backed away as he careened into the water.

Without thinking he reached out for her to give her a hug, realizing too late that Phinney was not familiar with this behavior. As she rolled away, he took in a mouthful of seawater and began coughing. Out of breath, he struggled to stay at the surface. Phinney moved alongside him and offered her dorsal fin for support, which he gladly accepted. Then together, Phinney putting forth most of the effort, they angled toward the sandy beach in the corner of the cove where Toby sat in the shallows, his chest and shoulders above the water. Almost as if prearranged, Phinney slid between his legs and beached herself on the soft sand. She wriggled to scratch herself on the bottom, and he spoke to her softly, telling her how much he had missed her, speaking her name over and over. They lay together for a while, Phinney rubbing against his legs as he traced the outline of her mouth with his index finger and rubbed her nose.

"My, oh my, girl. Have you ever grown since I saw you last," Toby noted on Phinney's larger girth, the most noticeable, as well as her length. He guessed her to be about one hundred pounds now. A long time, they just basked in each other's company, until Toby started feeling antsy, and he stood up and waded into deeper water and began swimming. Phinney followed suit, as they circled each other.

Toby never stopped talking, but of course Phinney could not understand the words, but he sensed in his heart that she understood the meaning. After a while of just being together, Irene walked the length of the dock and said, "So nice to see you again, Phinney." She waved to the pair and informed Toby that dinner would be in an hour. In an ever so parental sense, Irene sent the message, "It's time for your friend to move along now. Say goodbye. You have the next four days to play together." Another wave and a pleasant smile, and she walked back down the dock to the veranda, where Vernon had mixed some tropical drinks for the weekend guests to enjoy as they watched the sun begin to kiss the horizon.

Phinney moved toward the open water as Toby climbed the ladder to the dock and used the garden hose to rinse off the salt.

"Toby, turn around and watch the sun go down," his grandmother encouraged. "See if you can see the green flash."

Toby turned as the sun was about midway down the horizon, moving visibly quickly into the ocean just off to the side of the big island. He had been told of the alleged "green flash," a retinal image of a reverse sun setting following its disappearance below the horizon, supposedly green in color, but he had never seen one, even after viewing hundreds of sunsets in the islands. He suspected it was something like snipe hunting, which he was introduced to in the fourth grade while he was away at camp. He never saw a snipe either, but he did see a lot of mosquitos, and he was reminded of this as the first of the no-see-ums began their kamikaze attacks timed for sunset.

Toby headed for the kitchen hallway to his room to dress for dinner. He started feeling bad that he had ignored Pop and Irene upon his arrival, and he was in fact more than a little excited to tell them of his time at Flagler. He hoped they would understand about his need to see Phinney. He chuckled to himself as he thought that he would have the next four days to fulfill their needs to learn about his adventures at school.

Dinner was a sort of pry-and-tell affair, wherein the parts of his Flagler experience Toby was eager to share did not coincide with what seemed to be of interest to his grandparents. At last he succumbed to divulging information about all of the classes he was taking, how he was adjusting to being away from home for long periods, and how he was making new friends. He also shared the news about his new position as skipper of one of the school's racing sloops.

Things were at something of an impasse until Toby mentioned the name of a girl, Chrissy, whom he liked to sail with. He moved on to the next subject when his grandmother looked inquiringly over her reading glasses at Vernon, who in turn interrupted with, "Let's back up there a minute son. Who is this Chrissy?"

"Oh, I didn't tell you? She's the girl I'm kind of going with."

All of a sudden the situation became brilliantly clear to his grandparents. All of their concerns for Toby's ability to adapt to his new surroundings evaporated. Toby had a girlfriend, a new center from which to measure everything else. Irene guessed that if he had a new girlfriend, then it follows that all of his social adjustments were falling into place. It explained why he had been so happy to see his dolphin again, before leaning on his grandparents for welcome support at his return for the holiday.

The new development rather closed out the rest of the evening discussion. Toby stayed through dessert, then asked permission to retire to his room. His relieved grandparents bid him a good evening and redirected their attention to their guests and the steel drum band that was warming up. The veranda was filling with vacationers who were enjoying the freshening breeze that blew in the tropical ocean smells. If the increasing surf was any indication, there would not be a lot of water activity the following day. Skirts were blowing in the wind, and the dockside candles were blowing out, but the holiday revelry continued unabated.

The next morning Toby was up early walking the beach on the ocean side of the island, cleaning up debris that was cluttering the sand from the strong wind. He found pieces of netting and glass bulbs and such, all of which were common booty unleashed during heavy winds from commercial fishing boats operating in the deep water. This was the only assignment he had been given since he had been home, and he enjoyed the solitude it brought, especially after spending the last two months at prep school where very little time was available in seclusion.

One hundred fifty students on a small campus did not allow such a diversion. This was probably the biggest cultural change for Toby to deal with, when contrasted with the majority of his time having only himself for company on the island. He had been so busy at Flagler that he hadn't had a chance to reflect on this in his time there, but it was front and center in his thoughts now. Perhaps it explained why he did everything so thoroughly, because paying attention to detail occupied so much of his free time.

His thoughts returned to Phinney as he finished his cleanup, and he racked his brain to try to figure out an activity they could enjoy in this twenty-knot wind. He was about to ring the bell for her when Major came out of the cabana area, shouting to him something about the dolphin, but Toby couldn't understand because his words were carried away by the wind.

As they came closer, Toby could hear from Major's grinning, ivory-filled mouth, "Dat girl of yours, she be waitin' for you, Mister Toby. Dat fish is in da cove. She don't even wait for ya ta ring dat bell; she just come by unannounced."

Toby crossed between the first two cottages and crossed the veranda to the dock where Phinney was patiently swimming back and forth, leaping out of the water occasionally to make sure her arrival had been noticed. Toby ran down the dock and, kicking off his flip-flops, sat on the edge of the lower dock and dangled his feet in the water.

"What do you want to do today, girl? It looks a little messy out there. I don't think we're going to get any diving in today."

Phinney acknowledged his words with some clicking of her own and a brief tail stand. To an observer, the two looked as if they were having a normal conversation about the weather. The dolphin acted antsy, as though she wanted to play, but Toby had no earthly idea what they could do together. The seas were running six to eight feet in the deep water, and there was little shelter from the east wind from the chain of islands running east and west outside the harbor entrance.

Toby felt an obligation to try something, so he returned to his room and put on a swimming suit. When he returned to the dock, he jumped in and swam over to the catboat, figuring it was the most stable of the watercraft in the lagoon. Since he was alone, he raised and put a double reef in the gaff-rigged main, disconnected from the mooring, and beat his way out of the cove across the bar and into the deeper water. In moments, he knew he had made a mistake, as the catboat with only a patch of sail up heeled over dramatically when he tried to reach off to the north. With Phinney close behind, he tacked and bore off to the south to find flatter water on the lee side of Piper Cay. He was already drenched, even taking one wave over the bow as he tacked, so he was trebly occupied with the mainsheet in one hand to control the sail, a plastic bucket in the other to try to bail out some of the water sloshing around in the bilge, and the tiller under his right armpit to pull against the considerable force caused by the catboat's natural weather helm, which always pushed the boat toward the wind in heavy air. He was really moving downwind now, dreading the thought that he would have to make his way back to windward to get home. Phinney, unaware of the difficulty Toby was having, followed with excitement, jumping in the wake behind the boat.

In what seemed like moments, Toby cleared the southwestern point of the island where the water was flat and shallow, causing the color to glow in the beautiful turquoise of the Out Islands, and it was time for Toby to jibe the catboat, bringing the sail across from the port side to the starboard side, a relatively violent maneuver in these wind conditions. His plan was to skirt the beautiful crescent sand beach on the west end of the island and bring the boat to weather for the beat across the north side to return to the cove. He considered tacking the boat, a safer maneuver to bring the wind across the front of the boat, coming about the long way 'round, but youth, self-confidence, and exuberance ruled the day.

With Phinney gallivanting around the boat, Toby slowly pulled the tiller toward him as he struggled to bring in the mainsheet to lessen the violence of the wind switching sides of the sail. Mid jibe, a strong puff of wind heeled the boat deeply to starboard just as the sail started to come across. The wind caught it on the other side and, combined with the rebound of the heeling moment from the other direction, forced the catboat on its port side in a violent catapulting motion. Toby knew he was in deep trouble when he became airborne and lost his grip on the tiller as he went over the side.

In the morning Phinney was so filled with excitement that she decided she would not bother to wait for the sound of the bell. She had no comprehension of why Boy had left or that he might some-day return, so the concept of separation was foreign to her. She awakened from her sleep in her usual surroundings near the west end of Rose Island, although for her this was not the same as Boy's sleep.

Half of Phinney's brain always stayed awake to direct the motor functions of her surfacing and breathing, so her mind never completely lost consciousness. The halves of her brain alternated the responsibility for her to maintain a source of air, which gave her an added benefit of the awareness of her surroundings for protection from predators, although with her increasing size, this became less and less of a threat.

She waited until the sun was well above the horizon, her clock of sorts, and made her way to the cove. Off the end of the dock, she jumped several times to get the attention of the humans, finally spotting the dark-skinned human hosing off the fish-cleaning stand on the end of the dock. He put his thumb on the end of the hose and squirted a stream of fresh water at Phinney, catching her in the mouth. She tasted the bitterness of the water, the same liquid as Boy drank when they were out together. The dark-skinned human ambled off down the dock, and after a short while, Boy appeared and sat on the end of the low dock with his feet in the water.

She could hear her name occasionally as Boy rambled on about something. Boy left and returned moments later, jumped in the water, and swam over to the heavy boat and began rigging the sails. Phinney knew it was windy; she had played in the big waves on her way over, and she was curious about what Boy had in mind. The heavy boat came free of the mooring, which Phinney could see was cabled to the bottom on a chunk of human-made rock, or some such thing, and started moving slowly toward the sandbar and out of the cove.

As soon as he was in the deeper water, Phinney knew that Boy was having a hard time of it. The boat tilted more than she had seen before, and she could see Boy struggling with whatever he was doing in the cockpit. The boat pointed into the wind and stood upright as the wind switched to the other side, and the boat now picked up speed, quickly heading toward the big island, and then toward where the sun went down along the shore of Piper Cay.

The boat accelerated and moved along at Phinney's cruising speed toward the far shore of the island, giving her the opportunity to jump in the flatter water all around the boat. She assumed boy was going to sail around the island, so she anticipated his turn to the northwest, but she was totally unprepared for what happened next.

The boat started to come upright, then tilted severely toward the island and immediately reversed itself to the other side as the big white sail came across the back of the boat. In an instant, Phinney saw Boy fly over the side of the boat into the water, holding on to one of the lines. In a cloud of bubbles, he rose slowly to the surface, coughing and sputtering. The boat wallowed for a few moments, rolling back and forth, heavily laden with water, which had shipped in over the gunnels during the severe broach, and slowly settled as it turned back into the wind. Boy swam the few yards to the boat, which was sitting low in the water and tried to hoist himself over the side, but each time he bore down on the side of the boat to lift himself in, the boat rolled toward him, and he was unable to complete reboarding. After several attempts and becoming visibly weary, Boy rested alongside the half-scuttled catboat.

Phinney knew she could help. As Boy pedaled his legs in the water, she rose up from beneath him and caught one of his pumping feet on her snout and pushed. His foot slipped off, so she tried again. After several attempts, he got a foothold on her nose; with a final big shove, Boy was able to lift himself over the side without putting a lot of weight in it. The boat stayed relatively upright as Boy moved to the middle of the cockpit. Phinney squeaked with delight as Boy started sorting out his circumstance and carefully brought the sail in just enough to work the boat toward the beach, but not so much that it would tip over.

She followed him until the water became very shallow and watched as Boy lowered the sail and secured it, then hopped over the side and started pulling the boat toward shore by the front end. Fearing she might strand herself, she maneuvered offshore a ways while Boy beached the bottom of the boat on the soft sand. It was clear he wasn't going to be sailing anymore this afternoon, at least for a while. When she was sure Boy was on top of things, she headed back out to deep water, making her way to the east.

Toby went in the water upside down, losing his bearings but holding on to the mainsheet for dear life. He payed out line as it grew taught, but kept his grip. Amid his bubbles, he resurfaced and tried to orient himself. The catboat was wallowing nearby after having shipped a lot of water, but apparently not in danger of sinking. The mainsail did what it was supposed to do, and the boat slowly rounded up into the wind where it sat until Toby could make his way to it. As he came alongside, he tried to lift himself up the side of the boat to climb in, but each time the water-filled craft rolled toward him as he put weight on the gunnel. After several attempts he became still, treading water while he tried to get his wits about him and think this situation through. His plan, if he could get aboard, was to beach the boat so he could deal with the problems on his terms and not be at risk of losing the craft. Facing Pop after such an occurrence was not an option as far as he was concerned.

As he treaded water, he felt something push against his right foot. At first he thought it might be something that had gone overboard in the melee, but then he felt it again two more times. Phinney, of course, it had to be Phinney. She was trying to help him get back in the boat. In another few attempts, he got a good purchase on her snout and felt her push him upward enough that he could clear the gunnel without having to press upon it. Success!

He tumbled over the side into the middle of the cockpit where the wallowing sailboat seemed more stable. He drew in the mainsail just enough that he could make way toward the beach, sensitive to the fact that if he pulled it in too far, the boat could capsize. He used his weight as ballast to help keep the boat upright. When the water was less than five feet, he carefully moved forward on his hands and knees so as not to upset the craft, freed the main and gaff halyards, and slowly lowered them into the middle of the boat. He furled the sail and tied it off with the length of the mainsheet, jumped over the side, and walked on the bottom, head just above water, to the bow where he pulled the waterlogged boat toward shore until it hit bottom.

He set the anchor high up on the beach, which made the boat secure for the time being, and Toby started bailing the water out of the bilge. There was over a foot of water in the boat, and the removable wooden slat seats were floating around in the cockpit as he began the laborious process of removing over fifteen hundred gallons of water with a two-quart bucket. He waved at Phinney as he saw her move into deeper water heading toward her pod, shouting his eternal gratefulness after her until she was out of sight.

Major and one of the staff came out of a stand of casuarinas further up the beach, beaming smiles from ear to ear.

"We thought you might be in a peck o' trouble, Mister Toby, when we saw you go 'roun' da island downwin'!" exclaimed Major. "I bet it dat fish, again. It goin' be da end of you, someday, or your grandfather, if'n he find out. Let's get dis mess cleaned up."

"Am I glad to see you guys, Major," Toby acknowledged. "Sidney, can you help me get the boat up higher on the sand where we can roll most of the water out of it? Then we can bail and sponge up the rest."

The three of them rolled the boat from side to side to spill out most of the water. When it was light enough, they were able to beach it higher and, using the mast as a lever, put it almost on its side to get the bulk of the water out. Once emptied and sponged dry, it required all their efforts to slide the lightened boat back to deeper water. Toby hooked the rudder back up to the transom, turned the boat around, and climbed it. Looking back at Major and Sidney, he invited them to join him for the sail back.

"No, sir, Mister Toby, sailin' be in you department," Major replied.

Major and Sidney waved after Toby as he turned into the wind and raised the still-reefed mainsail and reversed himself to follow the south shore back to the cove and safety, completing the return voyage without further incident. By the time he got back, the Bethels had already arrived in the marina and were having a cocktail on the veranda with Toby's grandparents. Randy was with them, now even taller than Toby remembered, with his dark hair slicked back; he looked like a young Errol Flynn just out of central casting.

Toby cleaned up for the Thanksgiving celebration and cornered himself with Randy while the others socialized before dinner. Randy wanted to know all about Flagler Academy, because, he explained, his parents had heard all about it from the Hendersons and Toby's grandparents and it seemed he might be headed there himself in the fall. Toby filled him in on the details, showing some enthusiasm for the ease with which he had slipped into a more sophisticated lifestyle. It was not lost on Randy that his life with his parents in Nassau was already rather formal contrasted to Toby's beach-combing environment. It looked as if the anomaly of a Bahamian in the Fourth Form might turn in to a populous segment at Flagler, three from the islands where none had been before.

Toby spent much of the rest of the holiday weekend cleaning the mess he had made of the catboat. He had to fashion a few new pieces that had floated away in the near capsize. Pop had noted the attention Toby was paying to the boat, but if Major or Sidney had said anything to him about the incident, he did not give it away. In fact, they *had* divulged their involvement in Toby's rescue, but it was Vernon's way of parenting that if the boy made a mistake, accepted the responsibility for it by ameliorating the results, and learned from it, then so be it. He saw his job as making the young man independent and responsible for himself, and it looked to him as if Toby was on track.

On Sunday, Toby rang for Phinney to say goodbye. The two babbled and clicked at each other for a while, ending the morning by sitting together in their usual position on the beach. Toby felt that Phinney had come to recognize this special encounter for what it was, so close was the emotional bond they had with each other.

Chalk's returned Toby to Fort Lauderdale later that day, where the plane took off in a cloud of mist and spray down the channel between Nassau and Hog Island, flying at a relatively low level over the light green and aqua Great Bahama Bank, passing Andros and the Berry Islands. Nearing the western edge of the bank, where the water returned to the deep blue of the Gulf Stream, Toby could see Bimini and Gun Cay to the left and the Great Isaac lighthouse to the right. Toby smiled as he recalled the stories he had heard from Major about the ghosts that haunted the lighthouse, which stood over one hundred feet above sea level and was made of iron, a peculiar choice for a landmark in the middle of a corrosive ocean.

———— • ◆ • ————

In no time at all, Toby readjusted to the routine of life at school. His romance with Chrissy was on autopilot, and although it gave Toby a sense of belonging and position at school, he no longer obsessed about her. He did, on the other hand, enjoy the private sessions he had with her in the time they were able to spirit themselves away on a sailboat or an occasional clandestine rendezvous after midnight at the boathouse. They had passionate sessions that always ended the same; he could only go so far, and although so far went a little further each time, the increments were tiny and the frustrations huge.

Before he knew it, the school had a free day, designated each year Toby learned, where the entire student body was let loose on Worth Avenue to do some Christmas shopping. Seventy-five young men in school blazers and uniform rep ties, mixed with a like number of young women in pastel shirtwaist dresses, played grownup in shops and restaurants on the famous Palm Beach shopping haven, with its Mediterranean architecture of white stucco and red barrel tile roofs, and quiet alcoves and loggias with wrought-iron fencing. Mr. Newman at the Prep Shop emptied his till to provide illicit cash for the kids he knew, covering the expense by adding the amount to the next bill sent home to unsuspecting parents.

Toby bought Chrissy a St. Christopher's medal, and she bought him a silver ID bracelet with his name engraved in script. Air Sunshine had added DC 3 air service from West Palm Beach to the new international airport serving Nassau, which enabled Toby and Chrissy to share a cab and a passionate goodbye at the airport where she caught a flight home to New York for the Christmas break. Toby had a couple hours to kill at the airport, which he spent with others from school who were awaiting later flights also. Everyone was eager to be off the campus as soon as possible to experience some grown-up freedom out from under the watchful eyes of Flagler guardians.

Toby didn't have to be back at school until January 4, so he had two and a half weeks to spend with his family in the Bahamas. His grandparents were happy to have him home, and this time he shared a little more of himself with them after he landed at the New Providence Airport with its tiny terminal and open air baggage claim. They stopped at the British Colonial in downtown Nassau for a snack and iced tea on the same patio where Toby had first learned of his grandparents' plans for his future at Flagler Academy.

It seemed as though years had passed since those emotional moments when he learned he would be going away to school. They chatted about small things; Toby avoided uncomfortable conversation about Chrissy, and they caught him up on goings on at the inn, which were not much. Irene told him Phinney had been spotted once or twice in the lagoon right after Thanksgiving, but had not been seen since. Toby assumed she had migrated south after the winter cold fronts started crossing the island chain. He guessed correctly that he would not be spending time with his water friend on this trip, so although disappointed, Toby was not surprised.

The inn was filled with holiday vacationers, and Christmas was properly set out with a lighted areca palm potted on the veranda. "Santa Clause" had found a place to land, absent a chimney to climb down. Sleigh tracks could be seen in the sand in front of the cottages, and somebody had eaten the cookies and milk left on the group coffee table in the lounge.

Toby got a full U.S. Divers SCUBA rig complete with wet suit and one of the new masks that had finger grips around the nose so that he could clear his ears without having the mask fill with water when he shoved his fingers inside. Vernon had gotten one for the inn as well so that he could accompany Toby as a dive buddy if he promised the old man he would be patient with him while showing Pop the ropes. Toby was excited as he anticipated sharing some diving with his grandfather in the beautiful waters and reefs in the area.

Grandfather and grandson got in a few dives around the coral heads on Yellow Bank where Toby had first experienced SCUBA diving with Dr. Bridegroom the previous summer. They were sitting in the cockpit of the Chris Craft one afternoon after a dive when Toby brought up a new subject.

"Pops, I've got a question for you."

"Shoot," Vernon answered, punching two triangular holes in a Heineken beer can with the church key tied to the cooler. He tipped the can to his lips and gulped a mouthful of the cold beer, while Toby toyed with a soda.

"I turn sixteen in a few months. What are we going to do about getting me a driver's license?" he asked, fearing the response. Until now, Toby's experience had been limited to driving around the island in the inn's rusty old jeep on the single road that serviced the cottages on one end to the dump on the other.

"What do you need a driver's license for, in God's name? You can't get one here until you are eighteen, and you have nothing to drive and nowhere to go when you're in Florida."

It was not the answer Toby was looking for, but not unexpected either. "I won't always be at Flagler when I'm in the States. All my friends are getting them. I don't want to be different."

Vernon thought about it for a minute, and he couldn't come up with a good response. He knew this was an important rite of passage for his grandson and what harm could it do, since he wouldn't be driving anywhere any time soon? It posed a problem, however, because he and Irene had deliberately divested themselves of all real estate in the United States, so that they could take full advantage of the tax-free status of the Bahamas. All of their investment assets were handled by the big bank in Nassau. Toby would need a residence to take the test in Florida, and Vernon agreed that if Toby were to have a driver's license, it should be from the U.S.

"Your grandmother and I will work something out, Toby. We have until March to figure it out, but I'm not against it."

They dropped the subject for now. On the way back, Toby noticed for the first time that his grandfather had aged somewhat. Where he used to jump around the boat like a monkey, he was now cautious, always holding on to something to secure himself. He noted to himself that he should keep an eye on Pop.

———— •◆• ————

Back at school, Toby finished his first complete semester, receiving respectable, if not stellar, grades. He finished the year as the designated captain of the sailing team for the coming year, having won or placed in all his races, save one. As captain, he would have his pick of the boats to skipper next year, and it was conceded by all that he would be impossible to beat in those circumstances.

For spring break, he had tried to convince Chrissy to join him in the Bahamas, but her parents would not permit it. They feared correctly that the two were getting too close, and encouraging an unsupervised relationship in the primitive islands of the Caribbean would be dangerous for their only daughter. Toby kissed her good-bye at the airport in West Palm and flew home on Air Sunshine to the islands.

Upon his return from spring break, he had a wealth of new stories to report on his adventures with Phinney, all of which were met with a little bit of disbelief and derision. It was not until one of the girls acknowledged that the parents of one of her friends from home had vacationed at Piper's Landing and had witnessed an appearance by Phinney that the possibility of the dolphin became credible. Toby had not been there at the time, but they were regaled with stories of the young lad who had rescued a dolphin and become fast friends with its baby. After this, some of Toby's stories gained traction, and he added a new element of eccentricity to his persona.

The school year ended with a whimper when Toby got the results of his first attempt at the practice SATs, the relatively new standard-measuring exam for college applicants. His scores were in the high nine hundreds, about average he was told, but not on track for an Ivy League education. His grades, although acceptable, were not stellar either. Much of his attention had been diverted by sailing and Chrissy.

He prepared for the summer with apprehension about how his grandparents would react to his academics, but he needn't have worried; Irene and Vernon were more than pleased by their decision to send Toby to boarding school. He was adjusting very well socially and even had a girlfriend, and that was sufficient for them right now. They surprised him by joining him in Palm Beach during his last few days at Flagler, arriving in their new 1958 Chevy Impala.

Toby was excited to show his grandparents the campus and introduce them to some of his closer friends. They really had only one friend in particular they were most interested in meeting, and Chrissy accommodated them by spending the afternoon walking the campus. At five thirty, they all attended chapel together, after which Vernon and Irene were invited to join Toby, sans Chrissy, at the headmaster's table for dinner. When Toby headed back to the dorm after dinner, his grandparents stayed behind and visited with Dr. Oestreich in his study for some time before returning to their hotel.

"What's that all about?" Neil asked Toby.

"I have absolutely no idea," he replied. "I don't think I'm in any kind of trouble."

Joe Gardiner overheard. "They're probably just checking up on how you're doing. Don't sweat it. It happens all the time when parents visit."

Two days later, with Toby packed and loaded up in the new car, he left the school, following a tearful moment with Chrissy where they promised to be faithful to each other during the summer. *Who would I possibly be unfaithful with?* Toby wondered. They couldn't agree to call each other, since telephone service on the island was spotty, unless he took a trip to Nassau to a public telephone, and then it was not very good. Most communications were made by marine band radio, and the States could be reached through the Miami marine operator when airwave propagation was good. They compromised on an agreement to write once a week.

Vernon surprised Toby by handing him the keys to the Chevy. "Son, you know your way around here a lot better than we do. Why don't you take us to one of those restaurants you go to when you're in town." It was a statement, not a question.

"You know I don't have a driver's license."

"We understand, but it's only a couple of miles. I'm sure it won't be a problem."

Toby headed off south on County Road, feeling on top of the world. There was diagonal parking in front of Hamburger Heaven, across from the fire station, but Vernon said he would rather they go to one of those fancy places on Worth Avenue, so Toby continued as directed, turned right on Worth Avenue, and stopped in front of deMillo's Italian restaurant. There was only parallel parking in front, something Toby had never done. He looked inquiringly at Pop, as if to say, "What do I do now?"

"You said you wanted to drive, so drive! Parking is part of driving."

Toby pulled alongside the car in front of the open space and maneuvered the Chevy into the spot. It took him two attempts, but he got it right. This was a lot better than driving the rusty old jeep on the island. After lunch, Vernon took them across the bridge to the West Palm police station, where they got a pamphlet on Florida's driving laws and instruction on what would be involved for Toby to take his driver's test in the morning. Toby spent the night in his room at the motel down the hall from his grandparents studying the pamphlet. In the morning, while his grandmother shopped, Toby and Pop drove all around West Palm Beach, following the rules of the handbook. They practiced parallel parking at every available space and changed lanes on the few four-lane streets they found, ending up back at the police station where in a very casual setting Toby took the written and driving tests for his Florida driver's license. The address shown was 690 North County Road, Palm Beach, Florida, prearranged by agreement with Dr. Oestreich the previous day during their private meeting.

"Your grandmother and I decided we would be spending more time in the States, particularly with you in school, so we have decided to make some sort of presence here. We are looking at a co-op in Fort Lauderdale, so that we will have a place to stay, just a two bedroom, and the new car is so we will have a way to get around. I just want to be clear; it's our car, not yours. Certainly you may use it on occasion with our specific prior approval, but do not even think about including it in your life while you are at Flagler."

Toby nodded, his imagination running away at the thought of all the opportunities this could open up. These and other thoughts preoccupied him as they boarded the Air Sunshine flight back to

Nassau. Things on the island were quiet, as one would expect during the hot summer days. Toby broke every diving rule in the book by making a number of dives without a dive buddy. He convinced himself that Phinney filled the important parts of the buddy responsibility, and for the most part, he never descended to depths from which he could not make a free ascent should an emergency arise.

The weekly letters from Chrissy arrived on schedule, the schedule meaning about ten days after they were posted. He looked forward to her ramblings about her summer on Long Island, the beach parties where she felt alone and out of place, and the part-time job her father had arranged for her at a law firm in Manhattan. She saw some of her Flagler friends who lived in New York on a regular basis, and they made it clear to everyone that she was spoken for, but that didn't stop the local boys from trying to break down the barriers.

Toby helped the staff make repairs and paint the cottages and main building during the summer months. The islands were spared any serious weather in 1959, unusual in this part of the Caribbean, for which the residents were thankful. Neil was back in England for the summer, but Randy was an occasional visitor. Toby had grown almost two inches from the start of the fall term at Flagler, and the work was filling out his body to one of a young man. He had broad shoulders and a flat stomach, under his intense blue eyes and long, wavy blond hair that gave him an independent air in a world of crew cuts.

Phinney had a fun-filled tropical season with Boy. They spent some time together at least two days a week. Phinney finally adjusted to the bubble machine that enabled Boy to spend more time under the surface of the water, and they ventured further from the cove on trips to good hunting areas. Occasionally, when they were close to each other, Boy would put the breathing hose under her snout and release a flood of bubbles. This surprised her, and Boy's body shook with laughter whenever he did this.

Boy was also able to spear larger fish with his bubble machine, because he could go to depths where the fish were much bigger. Occasionally he would attract predator sharks when he stayed in the water with bleeding catch in his fish bag, and Phinney would nudge him to make him aware of the danger. Mostly they were ordinary reef sharks, but that didn't mean they couldn't give a nasty bite; Boy would push them off with his spear pole if they came too close.

One time they attracted the attention of a larger tiger shark, which came up from the deep side of the reef on the sound and started stalking the pair as they hunted. Phinney noticed the shark and gave Boy a big nudge to get his attention. When Boy saw the tiger shark, he was much more concerned than he was with reef sharks, and he motioned Phinney to follow him back toward the boat. Usually the sharks returned to the reef when they left the area, but this tiger was different. He began circling them and got between Boy and the Albury runabout.

As the circles became tighter and tighter, Boy finally reached in the bag and took the fifteen-pound Nassau grouper out by the gills and shoved it toward the big shark. In an instant, the shark devoured the fish whole and, satisfied, left Toby and Phinney alone. Phinney's heart was pounding, and she knew Boy's was, too. After that, Boy returned each fish he caught to the boat before continuing with the dive.

After that incident, Boy didn't hunt with his bubble machine as much. Usually they just went swimming and free diving together, sometimes Boy using his weights to try for deeper descents. He could go to about three surface pressures in depth on occasion. This was how Phinney measured depth, by how much more pressure she felt in her body from the weight of the water above her. She could go much deeper, because she could hold her breath much longer than Boy, but there wasn't much for her to do or see. It got darker, and the coral lost all its beauty when the color faded. It was colder, too, especially at about two surface pressures where the change was sudden and dramatic. Besides, the fish down there were too big for her to swallow, and hard to kill as well. She did enjoy the freedom of going way down the wall, sometimes as much as ten surface pressures, but it was dark and eerie.

As the days shortened, Boy finally called for her and sat in the beach in the cove, and she knew that it was time for Boy to leave again. Although she was sad, and she could tell Boy was too, it was not as painful anymore. Phinney knew that Boy had to go away for periods of time, just as she did when the pod moved into the Exumas during the windy season when the warm water moved further west and south. He would be back in time, and they would be together again. She would listen for the ringing of the bell, and all would be as it was.

At Toby's return to Flagler in the fall, he felt like a veteran. He and Randy made the trip from Nassau together with Randy's parents, who joined to make sure their son was properly squared away. This proved something of an embarrassment for Randy, but Toby tried to run interference for him as he found his way around.

During the summer, Toby had received a letter from Dr. Oestreich advising him that he had been assigned the responsibility of being a mentor, just as Gerry Gale had been to him the year before.

Not surprisingly, his charge was none other than Randy Bethel. The note had said that they would be a natural pair, but cautioned Toby that he was to use his influence to see that Randy's introductions were across the Flagler community, that their past friendship was not to become a crutch for Randy and thereby stifle his social progress.

The headmaster needn't have worried. At the first Saturday night formal, Randy emerged from the dorm looking like he had just come from Rick's Café in Casablanca. He had his parents' permission to smoke, and he had that pose. Toby knew the pose, but he could never pull it off. Randy was tall and thin with slicked-back dark hair. Leaning on a column in the loggia with his left hand casually tucked in the side pocket of his white tuxedo jacket, cigarette held loosely in his right, he would have given Bogie himself a run for his money. The girls loved it. Randy's sense of humor and his British accent combined to place his status as one to be reckoned with. The girls swooned.

The year as a junior, or Form Five in Flagler terms, continued in routine fashion. Toby went about his days much the same as the previous year. He was not near a milestone he could think of, and as with most young men, he was just biding his time until the next rite of passage presented itself. Toby had one such rite in mind, but up to this moment, Chrissy had not been cooperative in her part of that collaboration. As it turned out, the next big factor in Toby's life had nothing to do with losing his virginity, finishing school, or the beautiful water of the Bahamas. It came from above.

CHAPTER SEVEN

Just before the Thanksgiving break Toby was summoned to the headmaster's office. Dr. Oestreich relayed a message from his grandfather that a guest of the inn and longtime friend was flying to the islands in his small private plane. Toby was welcome to accompany him if he wished. Arrangements were made for Clement Mills to pick him up at school Wednesday morning and fly him from West Palm Beach to Nassau. His grandparents would meet them at the airport in Nassau and transport them to Piper's Landing.

The idea of flying in a small plane touched something in Toby, and his excitement grew as Wednesday morning approached. At the appointed time, dressed in khakis and a polo shirt, he was standing in front of the boys' house with his soft duffle in hand. Clement Mills was a late middle-aged man, nice looking, dressed in a bush jacket and shorts. He seemed pleasant enough, suggesting Toby call him Clement.

At the airport, he turned in his rental car and accepted a ride from the agency to a small fueling operation on the south side of the airport, about midfield. The airplane was a high-winged Cessna

145

172 painted white with green stripes down the fuselage and accented in gold trim.

Mills walked around the airplane doing his preflight checks, draining fuel sumps and checking out the flap operation. After a five-minute inspection and a phone call to the Miami Flight Service Station to file a VFR flight plan, the two climbed in the airplane and threw their bags behind the rear seats. Mills, sitting in the left seat, started the engine, called ground control, and was cleared to taxi to runway nine right.

After taxiing the length of the runway, he pulled the aircraft over to the side of the taxiway and ran the engine up to seventeen hundred RPM, tested the magnetos, carburetor heat, and instrument vacuum. When everything checked out, he idled the engine, called the tower, and received a clearance to take off on runway nine right, next to the long commercial aircraft runway, on a runway heading.

The engine roared, and Toby saw the tachometer increase to the redline, clearly marked on the dial, as the plane swiftly accelerated. Before Toby realized what was happening, Mills eased back on the yoke, and the Cessna lifted ever so gently off the runway, climbing about six hundred feet a minute, past the airport, over the Intracoastal Waterway, above the Breakers Hotel and the homes on the island of Palm Beach, past the beach, and over the open water stretching endlessly ahead. Toby looked down, totally captivated by the view of the light blue water with gentle surf washing on the beach, the darker patches of reef about a hundred yards offshore, to the deep azure blue of the gulf stream.

They climbed for about ten or fifteen minutes while Toby absorbed everything he was seeing and feeling. The instruments, which had seemed confusing when he first got in the airplane, made logical sense now that they were in the air. He could see the attitude indicator in the middle, showing the airplane's flight characteristics; a compass beneath, which looked like a miniature of the ones on the boats he had driven; to the left, an airspeed indicator, which indicated they were going about one hundred fifteen knots; to the right, an altitude indicator showing they were at seventy-five hundred feet; and below that, a rate-of-climb indicator, which showed zero now that they had leveled off. . . . It all made perfect sense.

"Have you ever flown in a small plane before, Toby?" shouted Mills over the engine noise. It had quieted down after they leveled off, and Mills pulled the power back a little after the plane had accelerated to cruising speed.

"Never," Toby replied. "I think this is the most exciting thing I have ever done." Toby knew in his heart the minute they had cleared the shoreline that this was something he was meant to do, even more certain that he had done it before. It all felt so familiar and comfortable as if it had come from a previous lifetime.

"Let me show you a few things. Here, put your hands on the yoke and your feet on the rudder pedals."

Toby did as instructed.

"Now, no sudden movements. Slowly push the rudder pedals, first left then right. Notice how the airplane responds."

Toby pushed gingerly on the left rudder and the plane yawed a little to the left, and the left wing dropped a little. The aircraft responded similarly to the right with the right rudder.

"Now turn the yoke to the left and right."

Toby did as he asked, and the plane responded immediately and more smoothly, turning first to the left and then the right.

"Did you notice how much better that was than using the rudders?"

Toby nodded yes.

"Simply put, the rudders are used to align the airplane, and the yoke is used to turn it. To manipulate the plane correctly, you need a little of both. The yoke will bank the airplane so that as it lifts it does it at an angle moving it in the direction you want to go. A tiny bit of rudder will help align the fuselage with the new direction the airplane is going, although frankly, a lot of pilots don't use the rudders at all once they are airborne."

Toby didn't need an explanation. He felt and understood what was happening in his gut; it was as natural as breathing or diving. Mills let Toby play around with the controls for a while as they headed southeast, letting him climb and descend a little, but keeping it generally around seventy-five hundred feet. The Palm Beach tower had cleared them to the next frequency, but there was no one to talk to until they got to Nassau.

When Mills was confident that Toby could maintain a course and altitude, he pushed his seat back to the rear of the track and stretched out, letting Toby fly them toward their destination. A half hour out, Toby could see the island of Grand Bahama off the left side of the airplane. After another half hour, he could see the north end of the Berry Islands ahead and to the right. About then, Mills slid his seat back into position and turned to Toby.

"We should be able to pick up the Nassau VORTAC on the navigation radio about now, and that will give us a signal to track directly to the airport. It's relatively new; the old Windsor Field that has been refurbished."

Mills began fiddling with one of the radios in the radio stack in front of Toby. The top navigation compass rose needle came to life. Mills adjusted the compass until the needle centered, and it showed a heading of about 140 degrees to their destination. Mills told Toby to follow that heading. In a few minutes, the island of New Providence came into view, and Toby could see the airport on the west end of the island. He headed for it.

"Toby, just follow through with me on the controls, and you will get a feel for the approach and landing."

Toby kept his hands on the yoke and feet on the rudders and felt the energy of the airplane decrease as Mills cut the power a little and the RPMs dropped from 2,300 to about 1,700 as the little plane began a seven-hundred-foot-per-minute rate of descent. Mills showed Toby the round pitch trim wheel and showed him how to take pressure off of the yoke, so that it would continue to fly balanced and hands free, with little or no attention.

"When the speed of the plane changes, the nose will want to pitch up or down, depending on whether you are increasing or decreasing speed. The trim wheel adjusts a trim tab on the elevators to eliminate these forces to make the plane more manageable. You adjust it constantly to control these forces," Mills explained. "Roll it forward and back a little and feel what it does to the yoke."

Toby did that and understood.

Mills tuned in Nassau tower, calling in his position and intent to land and was told to continue and report a five-mile final. They slowly lost altitude as Mills instructed Toby to line up with the runway centerline a few miles offshore and then turn to the runway heading. As they intercepted the final-approach course, about five miles out, Mills called the tower again and announced he was on a five-mile final, and Cessna N52SC was cleared to land on runway one four.

As the plane slowed, Mills put in some flaps and adjusted the trim to compensate, and as the plane approached about sixty knots, he lowered the flaps all the way, adjusted the trim again, pulling off the power and adding carburetor heat to keep the carburetor from icing over and stalling the engine. They continued to slow to about fifty knots, gliding over the surf at the beach and touched down gently on the numbers.

Toby noticed how the controls needed much more input as the plane's speed decreased, when he followed through the landing sequence with his hands lightly on the controls. They rolled out about a half mile to the first taxiway and turned off. Mills changed frequencies and called ground control for a taxi clearance to customs. Ground advised him to proceed to the tiny green building adjacent the small terminal.

After some minimal paperwork, they were ushered through customs and immigration to the waiting area where Vernon had commandeered a taxi.

"Good to see you again, old buddy." Vernon stuck out his hand, which Mills brushed aside and gave his World War II amigo a big bear hug. "Welcome to paradise." Turning to Toby he said, "Clement and I go way back. Long before you were born, when I wore a suit and tie, I helped Mr. Mills finance a startup airline, which he later sold to Eddie Rickenbacker of Eastern Airlines, who bought it for the routes he had been awarded throughout the Midwest."

Toby's jaw dropped. His grandfather had never revealed much about his time in the real world before he took an early retirement and settled in the Bahamas. He could not imagine him wearing a three-piece suit and wingtips, though he knew he had been a city lawyer in Chicago. He noted to himself that he would have to dig further into this at some time in the future.

"How'd the flight go?" Vernon asked.

"Toby is a natural!" Mills replied. "He flew us all the way over, and followed through on the takeoff and landing. Want some advice, Vern? Invest in some flying lessons for the young man. It will pay dividends someday."

Toby grinned at the compliment and looked anxiously at his grandfather, who looked him straight in the eye. Toby couldn't read anything in his expression. They took a cab down to the city docks in Nassau.

During the long weekend while Toby was enjoying his visit with Phinney, his grandfather and Clement Mills were busy working out the logistics for Toby to take flying lessons when he got back to school. Vernon wrote a lengthy letter to Dr. Oestreich requesting the school accommodate Toby's desire to learn to fly by substituting three afternoons per week designated for his alternate sporting activity, which was tennis for this term, for an aviation training program to be developed by Clement Mills. Mills verified that the local fixed base operation at the airport in West Palm Beach had a flight school and instruction airplanes available for this purpose.

Toby made the return trip to West Palm Beach with Mills and presented the letter to the headmaster immediately upon his arrival at the campus. The request was met with some trepidation but ultimately indulged, provided Toby demonstrate evidence of progress toward the goal of becoming a licensed private pilot. Dr. Oestreich even allowed that Toby could receive some academic credit for the effort due to the mathematical and scientific skills he would master in the process. It took about a month for the details to be worked out and by then the Christmas holidays were upon them, but Toby was to begin his course in aviation in January upon his return.

Again, Toby pressured Chrissy to get permission to spend a few days with him in the islands, and again, her request was met with disapproval by her parents. The Christmas holidays were for family to be together, and that was that. In truth, the Mallens were becoming increasingly concerned about their daughter's involvement with just one man so early in her life. It didn't help that they could not conceive what kind of person lived in the wilderness, anyway. Certainly not someone who had a future in their daughter's life. The officials at Flagler were for the most part unaware of the closeness of the relationship of two of their students, or they, too, would have been concerned. Joe Gardner and Daphne had set the bar for "two-ing" under the radar, but Joe had graduated last year, and Daphne still had two years to go. She felt she was still in a relationship with Joe, but as pretty as she was, she remained a target for every available young man on the campus. Toby and Chrissy had learned a thing or two from them, and they enjoyed a healthy teenage romance that was hard to notice. As long as they didn't get caught in a midnight rendezvous at the boathouse, they would be able to maintain their relationship without interference.

Phinney had moved south into the Exumas by the time Toby got home, so he missed seeing her over the holidays. However, he was glad to have Neil Henderson around. His friend had taken up a keen interest in SCUBA diving, and he and Toby spent much of the vacation diving together on some of the wrecks on the reefs scattered around New Providence. Neil's parents had given him a full rig of gear, including a small dive compressor that could fill a tank in about an hour, so they didn't have to rely on the commercial dive shop in Nassau. They made a pact: Toby provided the boat, usually the Chris Craft, and Neil supplied the air fills.

Most of the dives were in shallow water around coral, which is why the wrecks were there, but a couple of commercial vessels had sunk in deep water during storms outside the harbor entrance, so Toby got to experience some deeper dives over a hundred feet. He and Neil followed the decompression tables religiously, stopping occasionally on the way back up from any deep dive that lasted longer than fifteen minutes.

On his return from Christmas break, Toby focused all his attention on his new flying pursuit. In ground school, he learned the principles of navigation and dead reckoning and the theory of flight, which he absorbed like a sponge from the classic book *Stick and Rudder* by Wolfgang Langewiesche, which was considered the bible for those studying the forces of lift and drag affecting aircraft performance. If he had devoted the same energy to his academic studies, Toby would have been a straight A student. As it was, his performance at school did pick up considerably just because he was learning better study habits. What he lived for, however, was the hour or two per week of dual instruction where he actually got to fly an airplane.

One day in late February, after weeks of flying square patterns, turns about a point, landings and touch-and-go's, Toby's instructor had him pull over to the side of the taxiway adjacent the short runway, nine right, at midfield on his taxi back to the approach end of the runway. Without warning, the instructor, a young man not much older than Toby himself, told the tower that his student pilot was ready to solo and, with that introduction, got out of the airplane. Standing in the prop wash, holding the door open and shouting so that Toby could hear him, he gave Toby his final instructions for his first solo flight.

"You are to make three takeoffs and landings as the sole manipulator of the controls and radios to a complete stop and taxi back. When you have completed all three, you are to taxi back here and pick me up. I will be watching from right here by the side of the runway. I only want to give you one last piece of information. You have all the skills to do this now; you've demonstrated that to me for weeks. The only difference you may notice is that the plane will feel much lighter, and the performance will seem enhanced. I only weigh one hundred seventy pounds, but in effect, your payload has been decreased by more than half. So fly the numbers you know; don't add any extra for a cushion; you don't need them."

Toby was flabbergasted, frightened, and excited all at the same time. He was going to solo for the first time. His instructor closed the door, and Toby secured it. Focusing on the centerline of the taxiway, he called ground control and received permission to taxi to the approach end of the runway. At the hold line, he called the tower and received his takeoff clearance from the tower. He lined the Cessna 150 on the centerline of the runway, glanced quickly at this pre-takeoff checklist, lowered the flaps to twenty degrees, pushed up the power to full throttle, and released the brakes. The little trainer jumped forward, and before Toby even got to the place where his instructor was standing, he was in the air.

"Cessna 45245, Palm Beach tower. Make closed right traffic, cleared to land nine right."

Toby climbed to eight hundred feet, pattern altitude, and turned crosswind, his heart leaping in his chest. *Please, please, please don't let me screw up,* he thought.

In fifteen minutes, he had completed three landings to a complete stop. On the way back to the fixed base terminal, Toby picked up his instructor, who congratulated him with heavy slaps on the back. The only thing that stopped Toby's grin was his ears.

The customer service representatives and staff in the building all greeted him with congratulations, one of them producing a pair of scissors; they cut the back out of his polo shirt, recorded the achievement with a felt tip pen, and tacked it to the wall of the pilot lounge amongst many others as his first time solo badge of honor. His logbook was signed off, and his student medical certificate was endorsed. It would serve as his license until he passed the full private exam, which would take him another forty or so hours of flying, most of which he could do by himself.

Back at school, he was somewhat of a sensation. Everyone wanted to go for a ride, but Toby had to tell them they must wait; he was only allowed to operate a plane by himself or with an instructor.

Chrissy pouted at all the attention he was getting. "Toby, I can see where I fit in your life now . . . Flying, sailing, your dolphin, and then me . . . a distant fourth!"

"Babe, it's all so I can do these things with you," Toby responded.

"Then, how does the dolphin fit in?"

"For that you have to come to the Bahamas to find out."

—— • ◆ • ——

Toby continued flying before and after the spring break, and in May, he met with a designated FAA examiner and passed his check ride for his private pilot certificate. Clement Mills learned of the accomplishment and gave him a call at the boys' house on campus.

"Young man, you are welcome to borrow my one seventy-two any time you like; just check with me to make sure it's available, and pay me for the gas you use. If you want, at the end of term, I will be happy to check you out in it, and do a test flight to Nassau, so you can see how the paperwork part of the deal fits in. It's more difficult than the flying, I'll tell you."

"I really appreciate that, Mr. Mills. I am done in two weeks, and I can leave anytime on Friday afternoon."

"Then you have a date, my boy. And by the way, it's Clement or Clem to you."

"Yes, sir; I mean, yes, Clement. I appreciate that, too."

Flagler gave Toby the same academic credit as a math or science class for his accomplishment, and he took Mills's offer of the check ride and trip back to Nassau. Vernon thanked him for the effort by comping Clement to a few days fishing and board at the inn, which was greatly appreciated.

Meanwhile, Chrissy returned to Manhattan, still unable to make any headway with her parents regarding a visit to Piper Cay.

She was thinking perhaps a formal invitation from Toby's grandparents might help, showing they were not savages in the Out Islands. She would bring it up the next opportunity, probably after the start of her senior year at Flagler.

Toby spent a few days reuniting with Phinney for the usual adventures. After the initial excitement of their reunion, their routine became so natural it was though they had never been separated. One evening, after Toby returned from hunting with Phinney, Pop approached him to see if he was interested in spending a couple of weeks on a cruise to Florida. He suggested they take the Chris Craft across the bank to Bimini and across the Gulf Stream to Fort Lauderdale, where he had finally made good on his promise to buy a small cooperative on the water at NE 32nd Street and the Intracoastal.

They fueled up in Nassau and made their way across the deep water to the Berry Islands and entered the Great Bahama Bank just east of Chubb Cay. The water was flat on the bank, their wake narrow behind them, as they made good time on the light azure blue and green shallows to the western edge, rounded Gun Cay, and turned north to the entrance to the Big Game Club on North Bimini, where they tied up for the night. They enjoyed a beer together at the Red Lion and dined on freshly caught grouper. Toby felt very grown up having a beer with Pop.

"Don't get used to it, young man," his grandfather cautioned parentally, deflating Toby's sails a bit. "You have had a big year, and I just want you to know how proud I am of your accomplishments."

In the morning they completed the last leg of the journey across the Gulf Stream to Port Everglades and ran north in the Intracoastal past Oakland Park Boulevard to the canal where the two-bedroom co-op was located. After they tied up and settled in, Vernon tossed

Toby the keys to the Impala, and they headed out to buy some groceries.

The next morning Toby asked if they could go up to the Pompano Air Center at the small airfield in Pompano Beach to check things out. At the air center, they met some local hanger rats, who gave them the lay of the land and introduced Toby to the head of the local flying club. With his grandfather's permission, Toby purchased a membership that entitled him to rent a variety of small aircraft at very reasonable rates, including a Cessna 150 and 172, with which Toby was already familiar. Following a club indoctrination and checkout, Toby was able to take Vern for a ride around the area. The confidence with which Toby handled the airplane and the communications impressed the older man.

Back on the ground, the owner of the air center talked to Toby about his flying interests. "Toby, I would imagine with your enthusiasm you would like to build some flying time. After you get a couple hundred hours, you might want to consider getting your commercial certificate, and you could get some free flying time towing banners. There isn't much work this time of year, but it picks up in the winter season when the tourists come into town."

"Thank you, sir. I don't think I will have much time for that when I'm back in school, but it's good to know," Toby replied. For the time being the club rentals would have to do, and he couldn't imagine getting two hundred hours. He only had about sixty so far.

Toby and Vernon spent the next two weeks shopping for supplies for improvements to be made at the inn, which included two washers, dryers, and refrigerators, items that were very expensive in the islands with the value-added taxes. Toby took advantage of the time in the States to fly each day for an hour or two, sometimes with Pop and sometimes alone.

They made one trip to Orlando to visit Rollins College. Toby had expressed an interest in going there because it was on Chrissy's short list. His grandfather had advised against it for the obvious reasons that he would be making a major life decision based on what were not the best of reasons. Still, Vern felt the experience would be worthwhile, so he went along with it, and it gave purpose for Toby's flying. The thrill of just going up in the air was wearing thin, as Toby began to realize that his new world was basically a form of transportation. If he had nowhere to go or a reason to go there, his desire to fly would wane over time. He set about finding a practical use for his ability.

As their time away from the island wound down, Toby and Vern treated themselves to a final celebration dinner at the Mai Kai, a touristy Polynesian restaurant on Federal Highway near the apartment. Vernon ordered the famous mystery drink served by a hula dancer, who placed a lei around his neck and gave him a sultry peck on the cheek as was the custom. The waiter, sensing the importance of the moment, gave the two an extra straw and looked the other way as Toby shared the potent tropical rum drink with his grandfather.

In the morning, the appliances were delivered, secured in the cockpit of the Chris Craft, taking up most of the space. Pop covered them with a heavy canvas tarp. They locked up the apartment and headed off for Bimini, first stop on the return trip.

The seas were not as smooth as on the way over, so they took turns securing and repositioning the cargo as it shifted during the voyage. After a night's stopover in North Bimini, the winds softened, and Vernon and Toby had a quiet crossing on the Great Bahama Bank to Russell Beacon, passed Chub Cay, and crossed the tongue of the ocean between Andros and New Providence. The deep, dark blue water was not as smooth as the sheltered bank, and again, the two took turns steering and repositioning the appliances.

Approaching Nassau harbor, Vernon veered wide on the north east side of the jetty and made way directly to Piper Cay, customs and immigration being a formality pretty much ignored by the locals. Besides, there would be all that paperwork and duty to pay on the household goods being brought back. Vernon was concerned that he was not setting a good example for Toby, but the boy took it good naturedly, feeling somewhat like an adventurous pirate, which was really consistent with the history of New Providence before it finally succumbed to the authority of the Crown.

Major met them as they tied up and summoned staff from the inn to help unload the appliances. Irene ventured by the dock and inquired of Vernon if he remembered to get the linens she requested. He nodded affirmatively, which brought a dimpled smile to her face.

"Toby, can you hose the boat down while Major and I wrestle this stuff up to the main house?"

"Sure, Pop," came the fast reply. "Would you and Grandma like to go for a sail in the Comet tomorrow? I haven't been for ages, and with three of us, we could set the spinnaker and run inside the reef past Cable Beach and back."

"You know, Toby, I'll bet your grandma would love that, at least the spinnaker part. Probably not so much the beat upwind back home, but it will do her some good to get out in the sun and fresh air. She needs to get some color back, been inside too much the last few months, I guess. I'll confirm with her, and we'll pick a time at dinner. It's just us; no guests this time of year."

The three of them had a quiet evening on the veranda, dining on a meal of fresh grouper and baked potatoes. Toby's grandmother was a little quiet, but otherwise in good spirits, looking forward to tomorrow's sail down the beach.

In the morning Toby took the Albury lapstrake to the mooring and readied the Comet for the sail. He raised the main and tacked over to the dock, pulling alongside the T-head into the wind, mainsail luffing, while Vernon and Irene climbed aboard with a cooler of refreshments.

"Okay, hotshot; show us what you do," said Vernon as he moved forward to undo the jib sail ties, and Irene pulled on the jib halyard, raising the small sail. Toby pumped the tiller to push the bow off the wind until the sails filled, and he tacked smoothly out of the cove, across the bar, bearing off around the south side of the island.

As they reached along the shoreline of Nassau, Irene steered a steady course while Vernon and Toby rigged the lines to set the spinnaker. It was a bright blue orbital spinnaker of old design, but it performed well off the wind, and they made good speed past the jetty and turned dead downwind to parallel the shore and its clean white beaches. Downwind was hot, as the sun rose toward noon, and they were sailing away from the wind. At a point midway down the island where the reef closed on Cable Beach, they dropped the spinnaker, each grabbing handfuls of light sailcloth and stuffing it below the foredeck.

Toby jibed and turned on the wind back toward Piper Cay. Close hauled with the jib and mainsails pulled in tightly, they could almost make way to the jetty, but as they neared, they knew they would have to make several tacks to clear the harbor and slide under the island to the entrance of the lagoon. The turn back into the wind brought welcome relief from the summer sun and heat.

On the way down and back, they talked about all sorts of things. Toby related again how he had gotten the attention of Cap, Flagler's sailing master, by demonstrating tacking downwind the way his grandfather had shown him. He talked a little about Chrissy, but not too much detail, knowing they were becoming concerned about his exclusivity with her. Unknown to him, Irene and Vernon had talked about it privately and had come to the conclusion that it was just puppy love and that Toby would move past it in time.

Irene positioned herself for maximum sun exposure to make Vernon happy, and Vernon amused himself with three Heinekens and a Cuban cigar he had picked up the last time he was in Nassau. As they sailed across the bar, much to their surprise, Phinney greeted them with a giant summersault in the middle of the lagoon. She seemed very animated. More jumps were followed by screeches and repeated stutter clicking. Toby suddenly became aware how much he had missed her while he was gone.

Major had moved the Albury from the mooring while they were away. Toby luffed the Comet expertly nose first to the mooring, which Vernon snagged over the side and made off to the bow cleat.

As the hot summer sun beat down on them, Irene slid over to the side of the cockpit well. "I can't remember when I have felt so hot. I'm not going to wait for a ride to the dock; I'll just swim in from here and cool off." With that, she slid on her butt to the edge and into the water.

Phinney jumped out of the way of her fall and came back to face Irene as she surfaced, her short hair plastered to the sides of her head. Phinney gave her a tender "Phinney" kiss on her mouth and moved off to give her some room to maneuver.

Irene treaded water for a moment and announced, "This is marvelous. We have to do this more often. Oh, Phinney, get away from my legs or I'm going to kick you accidentally."

Phinney moved back a little, and Irene made her way toward the beach until she could stand in about four feet of water.

Toby watched. "She must have seen that the Chris Craft was back and decided to hang out."

"She been here 'bout and hour, Mister Toby!" shouted Major from the dock. "She waitin' foh ya, been comin' by most days to check on ya. Ya'll don't worry about packin' up dat boat, boss. I be takin' care a dat foh ya. Sorry I took your ride off da moorin', but I be needin' it to run into Nassau for some parts in da kitchen. I'm sure sorry Mrs. Irene had to swim ashore."

"It's fine, Major," Vernon chimed. "She wanted to get wet and cool off."

"Phinney, what are you doing?" Irene shouted, as she backed up to Phinney's advances. Phinney was probing her belly with her nose, nodding her head in circles. Vernon jumped in and swam over to the beach to join them, Toby right behind. He put his hand affectionately on Phinney's brow and rubbed. "Most peculiar."

Phinney gave Vernon a little attention and returned to Irene and began probing her belly again, backing off and nodding her head in circles. She backed up and stood on her tail, screeching quietly, mixed in with some clicks. Again she returned to Irene's stomach and made soft whines. Backing off, she nodded her head in circles.

"I think she's just playing, Pop. But I've never seen her do that before. Sometimes she'll just sit with me in shallow water for a long time making all sorts of strange noises."

"This is different, Toby. Her whole demeanor has changed, and she's repeating the same process over and over."

Irene laughed. "I think she's telling me I need to lose weight, although for the life of me I don't know why. My clothes are just hanging on me now."

"I'll bet she is just warning you that you are going to have a nasty sunburn tomorrow," joked Toby. Indeed, Irene was looking very red about now.

"You know, that's a good thought, Toby," said Irene. "I think I might go in and break off a few aloe plant leaves and rub some salve on my shoulders. You happy now, Vern!" She directed a stern face to her husband, who was looking bewildered, trying to ascertain Phinney's intentions.

As they waded ashore and walked the beach to the veranda steps, Phinney followed with more noises and jumps. Toby stayed behind in the water for a while and sat with Phinney, who became very quiet, resting between his legs in the sand. Finally, they said their goodbyes, and Toby went off in search of some of the aloe his grandmother kept around for burns. He thought he would need some, too.

Phinney was happy that Boy had returned for the high sun season. She dived with him in their usual places for a few days, comforted that he had again returned after being away so long. She was getting used to the fact that he left for moons at a time, but now realized that he would always come back.

She associated the changes in seasons with his comings and goings, which took a lot of the stress off of his departures. So she was a little more than concerned when, after a few days of the high sun season, she did not hear the bell. She let a few more days pass and then she began swinging around the cove on her foraging routine. She did notice that the bigger, growling boat was gone, but she could not connect those dots, so she paid a visit each day. The dark-skinned human was often about the dock when she came by. She would acknowledge him with a jump and some screeching. She could hear him speak human sounds to her, but of course, they made no sense.

Finally, after days of visits without success, Phinney was rewarded with a change; the growling big boat was back, but one of the sailboats was gone. She hung out in the area for a couple of hours and saw the sailboat passing over the bar at the entrance to the cove, and she followed it to see if it would produce anything new. As it maneuvered to the buoy and secured, sails lowering, she could see Boy and the older humans aboard. She had spent enough time with them to understand they were family, as was she with her mother and others in her pod with their kin.

The female human slid off the side of the boat rather ungainly and splashed into the water. Phinney approached her and looked her in the face as she thrashed in the water to stay afloat. As Phinney came nearer, she shouted at her, making gestures with her arms to stay back. Phinney swam below her and tried to swim between her legs, but they were kicking up and down so erratically that she was afraid she would be hit, so she backed off.

Phinney could hear Boy talking to her, so she just swam around and waited for them to get off the boat. To her surprise, they all jumped in the water and made their way to the beach. She joined the group and shared the excitement of the reunion.

But something was amiss. Phinney used her echolocation as a supplemental sense continually. As she "sounded" them, she could not help but notice that the female was growing something foreign inside her middle. She knew from "sounding" pregnant cows in her pod that she could sense the mass of a baby calf growing in her mother, much the same as she could sense the mass growing in the belly of the older female human, but she knew it was not a fetus. It didn't belong with the other organs she could "see" in her body.

Phinney poked the human's belly softly to get a better idea. Backing off, she rolled her head in circles to settle her bearings, and probed again. Still she could sense the mass. She repeated it several times, but she felt Boy and his family were unconcerned or unaware of it.

After a while, the older humans went ashore and up the stone steps to the dock; Boy stayed behind and they sat in the sand at the water's edge for a while. Phinney was happy that Boy was home. They enjoyed each other's company for a while, exchanged good-byes, and Phinney headed out over the bar to join her pod around Rose Island. She was troubled by what she had observed, but the others seemed unconcerned, so she put it out of her mind as she swam east. She hoped Boy would ring for her tomorrow or the next day.

The high sun time moved on. Most days Boy rang for her, and they hunted together or sailed. Occasionally Boy brought his bubble machine, and they dived in the deeper waters. The high sun time was shortening a little when alarm spread through the pod, and as a group, they moved to deeper water, as they did when a storm was brewing. This time the leaders of the group appeared more agitated, as they prepared for some serious weather. Phinney could feel the pressure dropping as the winds built and the surface swells grew to steep, breaking waves.

Breathing became more difficult as Phinney and the others had to take short breaths, lest they take in water in their blowholes. The winds continued to build, wave heights mounting and crashing as they rolled over in cascades of white foam. The noise below was deafening. The reef fish scattered, making feeding difficult. Swimming near the reefs was dangerous to say the least, as the waves crashed above and through them. In the deeper water, things were more settled, and some in her pod actually played in the big waves, jumping clear of the water. Phinney had never experienced a weather phenomenon like this, so she stayed with her mother and a few companions.

Bright streaks of intense light shot from the skies, flashing the surface of the water, followed by booming roars of thunder. The closer the lightning strikes were, the brighter the flashes, and *the sooner and more forceful were the thunderous crashes of noise. As she surfaced to take a breath, Phinney noticed that the wind was so strong it picked up water and blew it through the air. Although the skies lightened a little during the day, there was no sun, and the powerful storm lingered.*

She found it a little frightening and thought of Boy on the island, wondering how the humans were enduring the ravaging winds and rain. She could not risk leaving the safety of deep water to find out. She imagined the surf and surge would make entry to the cove impassable, and she would have been right. Finally, after hours, the storm passed more quickly than it had arrived. The sun shone and the waters stilled, and Phinney's home returned to normal. The pod worked its way back to the reefs around Rose Island to find the corals damaged, particularly the staghorn and fans. In time, the reef fish returned and order was reestablished.

After a few days, Phinney heard the familiar ring of the bell on the dock at Piper Cay, and she rushed westward to the cove, over the bar. Boy was standing on the dock waiting for her. He sat on the lower level with his legs dangling in the water. He rubbed his feet over her back as she rose up to the surface to greet him. Boy talked to her gently, pointing with his skinny arms at the devastation around him. Part of the dock was loose, separating from the steel rails that held it. The sailboat that Boy liked to sail with his family was in the corner of the cove washed up by the shed where Boy had saved Phinney's mother and first met Phinney. Debris was all over the little beach. The other boats seemed to be secure, one sailboat, the fat one Boy seemed to like best, was firmly attached to its mooring, and the growling big boat was still tied to the dock.

Phinney sensed Boy would be busy for a while, so she didn't expect him to be spending much time with her. The days were shorter now, and she knew that this signaled imminent departure for the Exumas for the low sun season. The last several times she went exploring the beaches and reefs with Boy, he seemed distant and worried. Phinney could sense something troubling was going on in his life, but she was unable to turn his attention away from whatever it was.

Phinney had other concerns facing her. Her mother was going to have another baby and would not be a likely candidate for the annual migration to the Exumas. Finding a reliable companion was difficult in the best of circumstances, so most likely Phinney would also be staying behind to help with the situation. She had only done this once before, and that was right after she was born and too young to travel such a great distance.

In late August, the marine weather radio bands began talking about a tropical depression forming off the Cape Verde Islands. It moved swiftly across the Atlantic to the Caribbean, strengthening to a 140-mile-an-hour hurricane. With so much advance notice, Vernon, Major, and the staff at the inn had ample time to prepare. The big stuff they did early, waiting for the inevitable turn off the coast of Cuba to decide how seriously to take this one.

When it went north of the Cuba coast nailing Grand Turk Island, they knew they were in the path of a big one, now named Donna. She made landfall in South Florida with devastating results and turned northeast up the Straits of Florida toward the central Bahamas. The warm water didn't help as it crossed near New Providence and moved north for an eventual landfall in the Carolinas.

Piper's Landing was well prepared. Everything loose was brought inside, wood panels covered the exposed jalousie windows, and all the canvass had been taken down. The boats were double tied; the small ones were brought ashore. Toby, his grandfather, and all the staff were exhausted from the effort. Irene was not feeling well, so she spent most of her time inside with those details.

When the storm hit with its full force, Vernon, Irene, and Toby huddled in the common room, unable to see out for the wood covering on the windows. They could only imagine the damage going on outside from the noise of wind roar and rain pelting the building. Water began to seep under the doors, but it did not taste salty, so they were comforted that it was not storm surge, which would have been devastating. They were fortunate that the worst of Donna hit at a low tide. The roof had been built by experienced Bahamians, who knew how to secure and angle trusses so that they would support each other, reducing the risk of loss.

The air in the common room was still, humid, and uncomfortable. The rain came in bands, pelting the building; a small leak began weeping at the roof seam between the dining area and the common room, leaving an accumulation of water on the bar. Vernon put a bucket under it so the water would not work its way into the cabinetry below. The eye of the storm passed to the west of them, so they had no mid-storm relief to go outside and check things out. Slowly the winds clocked from north to west to south as the storm moved north.

As it abated, Major, Toby, and his grandfather ventured out through the kitchen to survey the damage. The sea grape on the ocean side was destroyed, but there was no other visible damage. On the lagoon side, the Comet had broken free of its mooring and washed up in the corner of the lagoon where it beached next to the work shed. The dock had lost some planking, but the Chris Craft was still securely tied to the iron I-beam posts. Remnants of rain pelted their skin in the waning breeze. They all felt lucky that the damage was not more severe.

Toby wondered how Phinney was doing, and he decided he

would wait until the next day to ring for her. He still had three weeks until he had to be back at school, and he was excited about the prospect of seeing Chrissy and beginning his last year of high school.

Major got the generator up and running again, so they had electricity for the inn. Everybody worked late into the evening to restore some order to the place. Irene spent most of the time in her cottage resting. In the morning she looked drained of all her usual energy, and she and Vernon spent some time alone on the veranda talking quietly. At noon Vernon called Clement through the Miami marine operator and asked him if he could fly over to Nassau and pick up Irene and him for a quick trip to the States. Clement was more than happy to do so, and arrangements were made for the following day.

"What's going on, Pop?" Toby inquired when he learned of his grandparents' plans.

"Nothing really important, son," Pop replied. "Your grand-mother has not been feeling well recently, so we are going to go to the apartment in Fort Lauderdale and have her checked out by American doctors, just to cover all our bases. We'll only be gone a few days. You're welcome to come along if you like, but I think it will only worry her if you do. Why don't you enjoy the last weeks you have before school, and we'll give you a full report when we get back."

They were gone most of the week, and when they came back, courtesy of Clement again, Toby noticed his grandmother looked awful. Her eyes were not as bright, and she had lost even more weight, but her smile was the same. Pop looked like he was dis-tracted as Toby maneuvered the Chris Craft to the dock at Piper's Landing.

Toby followed them inside; they all sat at a table in the dining room. Clement, who had accompanied them in from the airport, took a walk on the beach so they could have some privacy. Toby knew something serious was up.

"Things did not go as well in Florida as we hoped," Vern told him. "Our regular doctor referred us to a specialist at Holy Cross Hospital, a new hospital near the apartment. They have done all kinds of tests on your grandmother, and they have not found anything conclusive, but they fear she has something going on inside of her, possibly a tumor or something." Vernon let this sink in, and Toby's stomach started doing flip flops.

His grandmother took his hand, looking him in the eye. "Darling, they think I may have some kind of cancer. They are going to do a minor exploratory surgery to see if it can be removed. You know I have been losing weight recently, but we had no idea how much until I got on the scales and compared my weight now with my previous medical records. Now I know why my clothes have been getting so loose on me. I don't want you to worry about anything; I am in the hands of the best doctors in Florida. They have made great strides in cancer treatment in the last several years. We hope that if they do find anything, they will simply remove it, and that will be the end of it. They said I shouldn't wait, in case it is progressing, so I'm going to go back, probably before you go back to school, and have the surgery."

Toby's stomach felt as though he had swallowed a bowling ball. His eyes welled up with tears, as he was reminded of when he learned his parents had been killed in the plane crash. At least that had been final and over with at once. He knew he had to worry about this for a while before he could know what would happen. He felt that he had to do something to help, but he had no idea what or how. He also knew that grownups seldom tell the truth in situations like these to spare the pain of bad news.

Vernon ached for the look he saw in Toby's eyes. He bore not only his own pain, but Toby's as well. Irene was the core of his life, his True North, his compass. "There is something you can do to help, Toby," he volunteered. "Clement is taking Chalk's Flying Service back to Florida, and he is leaving the Cessna here for you. When we are ready, we would ask you to fly us back for the surgery, and then you can be there with us when your grandmother comes out of the recovery room. Then you can come back here and get ready for school. Would you do that for us?" Vernon correctly figured that Toby would feel better if he could contribute in some way, be part of the experience.

"You know I'd like that very much," Toby replied, his voice heavy with fear.

"It's all set, then," Irene said matter-of-factly. "We won't speak of this nonsense again until it's all over with. I don't want to waste these last few days of Toby's summer brooding over something that is unlikely. We will just hope and pray for the best. One good thing, Toby, is that while I am recovering from the surgery, I will be in Fort Lauderdale, not so far away from you. Maybe they'll let you out for a visit. They couldn't deny a request from an ailing grandmother, could they?" Irene smiled, her dimples as deep as ever.

Toby felt a little better, but he was still filled with dread. He spent much of the next several days gunkholing with Phinney around the reefs and beaches in the area, but his thoughts kept returning to his grandmother.

CHAPTER EIGHT

Chrissy sat on the edge of the dock on Lake Worth with Toby, looking across the Intracoastal to West Palm Beach. "Is there anything I can do to help? I know this is a really bad time for you, and I feel helpless to do anything about it. I feel lacking in some way, and that's selfish of me to say, because I really understand it's not about me right now."

The pair had been sitting quietly on a Sunday afternoon shortly after returning to school. Toby had declined skippering a race so he could be alone. Chrissy risked getting in trouble to be with him unsupervised.

The last month was a blur to Toby. He had taken his grand-parents to Fort Lauderdale in Clement's Cessna, as requested, and he had felt better about being of some assistance to his grand-mother. The trip on a commercial carrier would have been a burden if she had to make it. The Cessna took a little longer, but was much easier in the long run by avoiding all the rigmarole of the big termi-nal in Fort Lauderdale with its formal immigration procedures, as well as the proximity to the little executive airport they flew into, not far from the apartment on 32nd Street.

That was on a Tuesday; his grandmother went in to surgery on Thursday, expecting to be under for at least two and a half hours. Toby was surprised and hopeful when Dr. Morrell came into the waiting room an hour later with a poker-faced expression, asking to speak with Pop privately. Pop waived the privilege, squeezing Toby's hand as the doctor explained that the cancer was very advanced, much worse than first thought, and nothing could be done surgically. They had closed Irene back up and made her as comfortable as possible. Vernon and Toby could see her in a couple of hours when she came out of the recovery room. Toby was positive his grandmother knew as soon as she opened her eyes and saw their faces.

"That bad, huh?" she whispered through her foggy perspective.

She was five days in the hospital, then released to rest in the apartment with Vernon to look after her. Toby visited with her every day, but mostly, they just held hands and spent the time together. Irene's attempts to cheer anyone fell short, as the depth of the inevitable pressed upon them. Finally, she snapped at the two men to stop depressing her so much. "Everybody knows what is happening; let's just accept it and move on with the last few months in some kind of harmony," she pleaded.

When Toby asked if he could return to school late, his grandmother wouldn't even consider it. "What do you mean, late, Toby?" she asked. "You mean after I'm dead! I won't hear of it. You will move on with your life now just as you will after I leave this world. Now, go home and get ready for school." So Toby returned to the inn and packed up his things for his last year at Flagler.

Pretty much everyone at school knew about Toby's family situation from Neal and Randy. They were respectful of Toby's mood swings. Chrissy really got him, and he felt tremendous support and comfort from her.

The school was cooperative also, as Irene had prophesized, so Toby was free on weekends to go to Fort Lauderdale to be with his family, which he did several times. Then, one mid-October evening, high season for the presidential election, debates, politicking on grounds of principle—*Can we let Quemoy and Matsu Islands fall to the communists, or should we go to war over them?*—Toby got the dreaded message to report to the Dean's office of the men's house to receive a phone call from his grandfather.

"Toby, I'm going to come pick you up in an hour. Your grandmother wants to see you to say goodbye. She is not doing well, and she's back at Holy Cross Hospital. They doctors say it won't be long, now."

That night was the last time Toby saw his grandmother alive. Midmorning the next day, his grandfather called him again to tell him it was over. Toby reflected on his last visit with Irene. The compassionate nurses had taken time to help Irene fix her hair and apply a little makeup. Her eyes were as electric as ever, her dimples as deep as he remembered, but all of her expression lines led to craters in her face. She just looked spent. She spoke softly to him, telling him how proud she was of the fine young man he had grown into. She asked him to be strong for Vernon, that he would need a lot of nurturing and that she was relying on Toby to help him through the coming years, but not to sacrifice his life for her loss.

Toby went through the next two weeks on autopilot. Pop made the arrangements for Irene to be cremated, and when the formalities were complete, they flew in Clement's Cessna to Nassau with his grandmother's ashes in a beautiful brass urn. Friends and a few family members gathered for a service at Christ Church on George

Street next to Government House in Nassau, which was followed by a reception at the inn.

Irene's last wishes were to have her ashes scattered on the waters between Nassau and Piper Cay where the currents would spread her remains around the islands she loved. There was a lot of crying and grieving as Toby and Vernon said final goodbyes. Even Phinney attended, following the Chris Craft into the clear blue waters next to Piper Cay. She sensed Toby's sadness, circling the ashes as they drifted toward the bottom, the light diffusing in beams downward through the cloudy ash as it disbursed in the clear water. The Bethels and Hendersons joined others in a collection of small boats after the ceremony, and they headed back to the veranda at the inn to remember the vibrant life of a wonderful woman.

By the end of the month, Toby was back at school. The regimented daily grind diverted the young man's attention away from his grief. Chrissy was always by his side during the hours permitted, and no one on the staff interfered with the obvious affection the two shared for each other. She had asked her parents for permission to attend the services, but again she was denied, almost breaking her heart that she could not be with Toby during this difficult time.

Christmas was a sad time at the inn, as repeat guests were met with surprise that Irene was not there to share the holiday spirit with them. Toby spent a lot of time with his grandfather. They tried to engage in at least one activity each day, either sailing, fishing, or diving. Toby could not help but notice the vacant look in his grandfather's eyes when they went about activities they had previously shared with Irene. In rare moments, he would come back to life when they spoke of times they had shared together, and Toby resolved to try to be a constant reminder of the good memories to help his grandfather along.

Phinney, who strangely did not move south with her pod this winter season, was much more attentive to Vernon when they occasionally swam together. Vernon tried to hug her and lift her from the water on one occasion, soon realizing Phinney was no longer a calf, now five feet long and weighing in at over two hundred fifty pounds.

"Wow, Toby! This girl is getting big. I was thinking, you remember the day we went sailing and Phinney acted strangely with your grandmother, poking her stomach and shaking her head when we swam into the beach?"

Toby remembered with sadness how Phinney had prodded his grandmother's stomach and wound her head in circles. "Like yesterday, Pop."

"Do you suppose that she could sense something was wrong?"

"Maybe. You know, Dolphins have a kind of sonar they use for navigation. Maybe she could see something inside of her."

"I wish we had paid more attention, but I don't suppose it would have made any difference at that point. Strange though, nevertheless. I was thinking, we don't have any kind of marker for your grandmother other than the Atlantic Ocean. I wonder if we should do something. Maybe a plaque on a wall at the inn."

"Pop, that's a great idea. I have another. What if we had a headstone made that we could place in the water somewhere. You know those coral heads off the west end of the island. The middle one has a hole in the center where the light shines through onto a bed of pink-white sand. We could put it there, and it would have sun shining on it on clear days."

"That's better still, Toby. I'll have something made up, and we can place it when you come back for spring break."

———— •◆• ————

Following Christmas break, Toby returned to school to finish up his semester. Then, during the short break between semesters in early February, he headed back to Piper Cay to spend a few days with his grandfather and see how he was doing. Pop was spending less time with inn operations, although he visited regularly to welcome guests, but he had given up the day-to-day involvement.

Major and Herbert handled the routine operations. Herbert had just completed his two years at Miami Dade Junior College where he had been studying hotel administration and accounting. He had always been a great help around the inn, but when he received his associate degree, Vernon put him on the payroll as one of the office staff. He worked well with everyone, and the guests warmed to his big toothy smile and easy-going Out Island manner. He stayed on top of things, knowing what detail needed to be attended to and when. Toby was comforted knowing that his friend was available to keep everything under control while Vernon was preoccupied with the grieving process.

When Toby returned in April, he and Vernon went to the site Toby had identified, and using SCUBA gear and ropes, they lowered a deep red, polished granite headstone marked:

IN LOVING MEMORY
IRENE FARIS MATTHIAS
1892–1960

———— • ◆ • ————

It sat in white sand inside a glorious reef, highlighted by the sun filtering down through a large hole in the top of the rock formation. Toby and his grandfather sat on the bottom in the sand and watched as the changing light altered their perception of the monument's features. They stayed until nearly out of air, almost an hour thanks to the lack of activity, and wept quietly into their regulators. Phinney was in attendance but kept her distance, seeming to understand that this was a powerful emotional moment for Toby and Vernon.

———— • ◆ • ————

In the early spring, Toby got his SAT results, and while they were respectable, he knew he was not going to an Ivy League school. Chrissy had been accepted and planned on attending Rollins College in Winter Park, Florida, where her mother had matriculated.

Toby set his sights on the University of Florida in Gainesville, where he would only be a hundred miles away from Chrissy. Her parents were not thrilled about this, Chrissy had told him. They had only met Toby once when they had visited Flagler the previous year, and it was only for a couple of minutes. Although they had determined he seemed polite enough, Toby's long, unruly hair and questionable background made them wary. Toby felt the coolness from them.

They were particularly unhappy when Chrissy told them unequivocally that she would be spending two weeks following graduation with Toby at his grandfather's island in the Bahamas. She had to put her foot down when they tried to argue against it. Her decision had been made. She and Toby had not prearranged this discussion, so Chrissy was relieved when Toby accepted her self-invitation with enthusiasm.

"What do I need to bring?" she asked him.

"Nothing but tee shirts and swimming suits. Maybe some flip-flops, too!"

Toby called Clement and pleaded with him to permit the use of the Cessna for transport. He so wanted to impress Chrissy with his skills as an aviator, and he was not disappointed at her reaction when she saw all the instruments, switches, and gauges in the cockpit. She was not at all surprised by the calm authority he displayed as he preflighted the airplane at the FBO at the West Palm Beach airport; she had become used to it from watching him sail on Lake Worth.

He explained everything he was doing and why, trying to engage her in his passion. They flew at seventy-five hundred feet over the Gulf Stream until they approached the north side of the Berry Islands, where Toby began a decent to one thousand feet, so Chrissy could experience the beautiful colors of the Great Bahama Bank with its alternating white, turquoise, and deep blue waters. She was in awe of the splendor as Toby made his final approach across the Tongue of the Ocean to the airport on the west side of New Providence.

"The water down there is over fifteen thousand feet deep," he explained, pointing out the very dark blue stretch of ocean between Andros and New Providence.

"Wow!" she responded.

As they neared the island, Toby changed his mind and turned north, skirting the island to overfly the town of Nassau. Passing the downtown, he dropped lower still until they were only a hundred feet over the water as they covered the short distance between the main island and Piper Cay. He banked to the right to give Chrissy a good view of the inn.

Buzzing the inn, he could see Major waving from the dock where he was hosing off the fish stand. He waggled his wings in reply. They could easily see his smile from this altitude.

Herbert met them in the Chris Craft at the government dock for the short trip to the island. Smiling ear to ear, as ever, Herbert gave Toby a bear hug. Then, standing back to survey Chrissy he said,

"So this is the mystery girl we hear so much about!" Turning back to Toby, he said, "Good job, my man! But you know, you way outta' your league."

Chrissy blushed at the compliment, her dimples deepening as she smiled. Her shoulder-length blond hair looked natural in the island sun, her flawless skin lightly tanned. They shook hands, and after, Herbert pushed her arms aside and gave her a hug, too. "Phinney is not going to be happy about this, I suspect."

He was not wrong, as Toby would learn.

Pop was waiting on the veranda, all smiles to see Toby bring his beautiful young woman to the island. "So nice to see you again, Chrissy. Welcome to our little bit of paradise. I am so sorry that Irene could not be here today so that you could report back to your parents that we really are not savages out here in the wilderness."

Vernon was well aware of Chrissy's parents' contentious attitude when Irene's written formal invitation to their daughter to visit the inn had been rebuffed.

Toby was directed to his room in the main house, while Chrissy was ushered to the first cottage on the beach where it was not so subtlety made clear it was off limits to Toby except during daylight hours. Chrissy marveled at the attention to detail, from the king-size bed with the highest-quality Egyptian cotton and the quaint jalousie windows overlooking the ocean, to the brilliant watercolor paintings of island scenes on the walls. The walls were painted a subdued peach, the wood trim glossy white. A woven straw rug covered the middle of the room over tongue-in-groove walnut-stained flooring. There was a full bath with modern American conveniences.

"This is just wonderful, Mr. Matthias!" she exclaimed.

"Please call me Pop." Vernon smiled. "Why don't you get settled and come down to the veranda where we will get a light bite to eat. I'm sure Toby will have plans for you on the water, so we don't want you too full."

Later, as she finished a small conch salad with the others, Chrissy reflected on how totally at home she felt among these people. When she and Toby headed out for the dock in their swimming suits to ring the bell to summon Phinney, Toby could barely contain himself, so full of excitement was he to introduce his "girls" to each other.

While they waited for Phinney to make an appearance, Toby pointed out the corner of the lagoon where he had saved Phinney's mother four years earlier. It seemed like forever before Phinney made her way over the bar into the cove. She jumped, stood on her tail, and stutter screeched a tail walk off the end of the dock.

"My goodness, she's so big. I thought she was only a baby!" exclaimed Chrissy, watching the performance.

"Well, she was, but that was four years ago, Kiki," he said, using the nickname he had for her.

Toby decided to introduce them cautiously at first, so he led Chrissy down the dock steps to the beach, where they entered the water up to their waists, holding hands.

Phinney was at the far end of Rose Island when she heard the bell. Her heart leaped in her breast as she made powerful kicks to the island and the cove. She had not seen Boy since the lower sun, shorter days, and that was usually with his family, the older male human. She knew in her heart that the older female was gone, sensing that the ceremony some time earlier had something to do with that. She hardly noticed the other human standing next to Boy as she went through her greeting ritual, jumping and tail walking to get his attention.

Instead of jumping in the water, Boy and the other human

walked back down the dock to the stairs and beach, their skinny arms around each other as they walked into the shallow water. Boy seemed very happy. Motioning to Phinney, he pushed the other human in front of him to greet her.

Phinney could tell the human was a female. She was filled with caution as she watched Boy hold her hand out to Phinney to try to touch her brow. Cautiously she inched closer and felt her tentative touch on her nose becoming more assertive as she patted and rubbed her brow. Boy moved in front of Phinney with his arms out, and she let him circle his arms around her breast to hug her just above her dorsal, touching his mouth to hers in the affectionate greeting he always did. She let him hold her a moment and backed away, swimming between his legs, her bigger girth barely fitting; he lost his balance and fell on his behind, water covering his head and going up his nose. He sputtered and coughed up saltwater as he regained his balance. Placing his skinny arm around the female, he motioned for Phinney to join them at the water's edge.

Boy splashed the water around him and spread his legs to let Phinney snuggle between them, the female next to him touching. The two talked to each other, laughing as Boy moved his face to the female's and placed his mouth on hers. They turned their attention away from Phinney as their mouths lingered, and Phinney knew immediately that Boy and the female had bonded.

Phinney felt sorrow that another human was coming between her and Boy. Boy made gestures to have Phinney engage the two, but she no longer felt the special connection and wanted only to distance herself from them. She turned and moved out to deeper water. Boy shouted after her, but she ignored his pleas and swam back and forth across the lagoon. Boy and the female swam to the fat boat and climbed aboard. After a moment, Phinney saw the white sail rise in the air, and she knew she was to follow.

The female disconnected the mooring line, and Boy pumped the rudder to fill the sail; the fat boat gathered speed slowly and made its way across the bar, as Phinney followed reluctantly. She could hear the two of them talking and laughing as they made their way around the south side of the island. By the shallow sand spit, the boat turned into the wind and lost way. When it stopped, the white sail softly shaking in the breeze, Boy and the female slipped over the side.

Standing chest deep in the water, they called to her and she came forward slowly. Phinney loved coming to this part of the beach with Boy, but it was special to her, and she didn't like sharing with the other female. They dipped their heads below the surface and motioned to her again. Slowly her sense of loss was replaced with the joy of seeing Boy again, and she joined them, swimming about around the two. Boy let go his hold on the fat boat and let it drift, facing into the wind. He and the female waded to the beach and sat again, as they had in the cove. This time Phinney moved between Boy's legs and beached herself comfortably there. The female stroked her back around her dorsal, where it was sensitive, and Phinney understood that she was trying to be a friend. Phinney accepted her advances and rolled back and forth on the sand, scratching her belly, clicking softly to show her contentment. She felt them ladle cool water over her back as they lay there.

After a bit they waded back to the drifting fat boat. As they got into deeper water, skinny arms entwined, Phinney made a last effort to show her place. She moved swiftly toward them and pushed her way between the two, knocking the female aside. Boy and the female laughed, and Boy spoke excitedly to her. They climbed aboard the boat and made their way around the north end of the island, Phinney circling and jumping as they tacked into the southeast wind, around the end of the island and into the cove.

As Phinney watched, Boy and Girl (Phinney had decided to give her a name to distinguish her from the other female humans on the island) walked the crescent beach to the corner where Boy had saved Phinney's mother years before and where there were always small baitfish and spiny lobster around the rocks. Phinney grabbed herself a snack as Boy snatched three lobsters from the rocks. Kneeling, he could just reach deep enough in the rocks to get them. He tailed them on the spot and threw the carapaces to Phinney, who swallowed them whole. Girl made a few attempts, but her arms were not long enough to reach any. She did pull a few antennas from the rocks, but that was all.

The three frolicked a while longer until the dark-skinned human shouted across the lagoon to Boy. Boy shouted back and signaled to Phinney that he had to leave. Girl made a last effort to hug Phinney, but she dodged her and left for Rose Island, jumping over the bar on the way out.

Over the next many sunrises, Phinney saw Boy often, but always in the company of Girl. They were obviously close companions, and although she was a little hurt by the separation she felt from Boy when Girl was with them, she knew she was not going to be abandoned, just as her mother did not abandon her, although they were seldom together anymore since the birth of Phinney's sibling when she had played a role as assistant companion to her mother.

After the long period of sharing where Phinney came to enjoy the company of the girl with the big toothy smile, Boy rang for her often, and just the two of them returned to normal, hunting, diving, and exploring the waters of the area. There were no big storms this year, and Phinney and Boy played almost every day until the days grew shorter, and she suspected that he would be going away for a long period, as he had before, just as she and her group moved south into the Exumas during the cold season.

Phinney did not approach quickly or with the enthusiasm Toby was expecting. He held his hand out and gave her a quick kiss on the mouth, but when he tried to push Chrissy forward, Phinney would not engage. She let Chrissy touch the top of her head, but that was all. He moved in and gave Phinney a bear hug and she backed away, swimming around and between his legs, roughly knocking him off his feet. Unprepared, he got water up his nose and came up sputtering. He couldn't help notice how much bigger she had gotten, unable to swim so easily between his legs.

"Kiki, watch this." Toby put his arm around Chrissy and walked back to the water's edge and sat with his legs out in front of him, motioning for her to do the same. She came down in a crash, Toby wrapping his arms around her to cushion the fall. They laughed at how uncoordinated this must have looked to an outsider. As Toby turned to face her, he leaned in and kissed her quickly on the mouth. Her hands came up behind his head and held him to her, and their kiss lingered a while longer. Toby was eager to show how close Phinney and he were, and he splashed and called to her, but she would not come forward.

"I know what she will like. Follow me and we'll go for a quick sail around the island."

They swam to the catboat and climbed over the gunnel, falling inside. The boat was always rigged, so Toby raised the mainsail and told Chrissy to unhook the mooring line. He pumped on the tiller to give the sail an angle on the wind, and they moved slowly out the cove entrance. Phinney kept her distance, but she did follow as they made their way around the island to the shallow bar on the west end.

"I don't know what's the matter with her. She's acting strangely like I've never seen before."

Chrissy smiled. "I think she's jealous," she said. "Remember, she's never had to share you before."

"I guess that's right. What should I do? I don't want her to feel bad. She is following us, which is a good sign. I'm going to try again at another of our favorite places."

Toby headed to wind and let the momentum of the heavy sailboat carry them forward until he felt the keel gently brush the sandy bottom. "Hop out. We'll go sit in the shallow water again and see if she will come to us."

Once they sat, Phinney slowly moved in between Toby's legs and beached herself, rolling back and forth.

"Rub or scratch gently around her dorsal; she likes that," Toby instructed.

Chrissy did and noticed Phinney respond with some strange, soft noises, which she interpreted as contentment.

The three lay together for a while, as Toby and Chrissy cupped water and poured it over Phinney's back to keep her hydrated. Toby had never seen Chrissy with so little on, and he marveled at how perfect her skin was for someone with such a good tan, very few freckles and no blemishes. He noticed the contrast of the white skin around the edges of her bikini, and he imagined what lay underneath. The thought of that excited him, and he stood with his arms around Chrissy to keep her turned away from him to avoid his embarrassment. As they made their way back to the catboat, out of nowhere, Phinney charged between the two of them, pushing them apart. They laughed at her obvious intention.

"I guess she showed us her position on things," Chrissy chortled. "Now I know where I stand."

"Phinney always responds to a free meal, and I know just where to get her one."

They climbed aboard, Toby pushing the bow off the wind and pulled in the mainsheet. Close hauled, they made their way around the north side of the island to the cove and back to the mooring, as Phinney cavorted around them, displaying her inventory of antics. After they attached the mooring and Toby secured the sail cover, they made their way to the beach where Toby led Chrissy to the corner of the lagoon by the shed. Kneeling at the rocks by the old rotten dock, he reached in and produced a nice-sized lobster. Chrissy gave him an "Eeww!" and she jumped back, as Toby tailed it and pushed a piece of antenna up its rectum to clean it.

"How do you do that?"

Toby explained how to grab a lobster around the carapace, avoiding the tail so as not to get cut up, and pull it out after you have a firm grip. He removed two more, tailing them as well. "There's one more good sized one in there. Why don't you try?"

Chrissy's head went underwater as she extended her reach to get at the lobster, identifiable only by the antenna waiving around outside the rocks. She could not get a hand on it, so she tried to grab the antenna, but it broke off in her hands when she pulled, and the lobster drew back.

"I'm impressed. That's good for a first timer." Toby grinned. He turned and tossed the carapaces to Phinney, who dispatched them midair. "See, she does circus acts, too. Good girl, Phinney!" he shouted after her.

Major shouted from the dock. "Mister Toby, you grandpa be callin' foh ya! Time you an' Miss Chrissy be comin' in foh dinnah!"

Toby looked at his dive watch. It was only five thirty, but he knew Pop just wanted some company for the evening. "Tell him we'll be right in, Major!"

Toby whistled and waved to Phinney, hoping she was pleased with the peace offering. Chrissy and Toby walked hand in hand around the beach to the steps at the foot of the dock, hosing off at the spigot. They padded across the veranda to their respective rooms to clean up for dinner.

Toby was seated in the dining room early talking with his grandfather when he spotted Chrissy walking at the edge of the sand on her way from the cottage. She was barefoot and wearing a white linen sundress, carrying her sandals by the straps in one hand. The wind blew her blond hair from the side, and Toby could see she was wearing a thin pearl necklace. Her long tan legs, silhouetted through her dress by the setting sun, highlighted her frame, as she was lit from behind. Her eyes were lightly made up, but the effect was of a goddess from the pen of Shakespeare as she moved slowly toward the dining room patio. The evening breeze carried a light scent of her perfume, reminding Toby of late-night rendezvous at Flagler. Toby felt like a slob in his shorts and tee shirt.

Vernon was mesmerized by her, too. As she approached the table, he gasped. Then, speaking only loudly enough for Toby to hear, he let out, "Toby, you are in way over your head, young man."

Toby didn't have a chance to respond before Chrissy took her seat next to him.

They had a quiet meal together, Pop learning as much as he could about Chrissy's family and doing his best to embarrass Toby with stories from his earlier years. Before the meal, they had said a short prayer acknowledging Irene's presence from above, Vernon tearing ever so slightly.

Later, they sat on the veranda finishing the bottle of wine Vernon opened at dinner, and Chrissy mused again how at home she felt. Around ten o'clock, Vernon apparently felt his presence was no longer relevant, and he shuttered up the veranda and headed off to his cottage, shuffling slowly with drooping shoulders. Chrissy was aglow with fresh sun on her face, kneading her fingers as she nervously anticipated Toby's next move. Toby was as knotted up as a fishing reel trying to figure out how he was going to maneuver his way into Chrissy's cottage. Just as he was about to make his move, Chrissy cut him short.

"Toby," she said earnestly, leaning forward and placing her hands over his, "we have two weeks together. Let's not try to cram everything into the first day—and quite a first day it's been. Let's just go to our own rooms and dream about each other tonight. You know I love you, and I am yours in every way. Let's not disgrace your grandfather's trust the first day. We would both regret it."

Toby was so relieved. He did not know how to make the next move, but as always, Chrissy knew how to make it for him. Her message was clear; she was offering herself to him, so he had no need of fear of rejection. If he did things right, she would give herself to him willingly.

He smiled. "Okay." He knew better than to say anything else, and he also knew that this beautiful girl was a keeper, worthy of great respect and trust. He couldn't imagine being with anyone else. They headed separately to their rooms to dream.

Toby cherished the two weeks he spent with Chrissy. Her own affection for the blond boy from the islands deepened every day, learning about his way of life, his love and respect of the environment and the creatures that lived there, and the bountiful waters around them. Her love for him grew, and she did give herself to him willingly, as promised. Eager young lovers, they learned to enjoy each other, using limited resources to prevent an unwanted pregnancy. Most of the time they were successful, but not always, and the risk added an element of excitement to the process of exchanging their puppy love for a bond much stronger and permanent than as high school sweethearts.

Even Phinney came to accept that Toby came with some baggage, and she made her peace with Chrissy, even frolicking with her in the shallow waters they frequented. She even helped Chrissy tease lobster out from holes in the rocks when they dived, so that she could finally get a firm grip on one and get it in the boat. Chrissy left the tailing and cleaning to Toby, however.

Toby took his girlfriend to his favorite snorkeling places, and she marveled at the beauty beneath the turquoise waters. He even tried to introduce her to SCUBA diving, but this experience was a little extreme for a New Yorker whose idea of going to the beach was to sit on the sand and soak up rays. Once she got over the newness of breathing underwater, she did relax and open herself to the new world below the surface. When she saw her first reef shark, she nearly bit through her mouthpiece, clinging to Toby with a viselike grip. As she observed the big fish cruising the area not paying any particular attention to the divers, she slowly relaxed, but she never let the shark get out of her field of vision.

Toby sneaked up behind her and slipped her mask off several times to get her used to the idea of not seeing well underwater, until she was so adept at replacing and clearing the water from her mask, it became second nature. They sailed the catboat by moonlight, lying in each other's arms, abandoning an attempt at making love after suffering bruises and splinters from the rough woodwork inside the cockpit.

"Don't you think we would be better off in the nice soft bed in my cottage?" Chrissy suggested.

Toby readily agreed, as he came about and let out the mainsheet to reach back to the inn.

With tears and great sadness, amid promises of eternal love and fidelity, the two parted at the Chalk's Flying Service ramp in the heart of Nassau. They were next scheduled to see each other in the fall, when Toby would make his way down to Rollins College from Gainesville. Each hoped that an earlier opportunity would present itself before summer's end, but they both knew it was doubtful that Chrissy's parents would permit it. She was destined for the summer home in the Hamptons on Long Island, and she correctly figured that she had stood up to her parents about as much as she was going to get away with. She and Toby would just have to write; they couldn't even call except by prearrangement, since there was no phone service yet on the island. By arrangement, Toby could call her through the Miami marine operator, but that was cumbersome and expensive at best.

The summer did pass swiftly for Toby. He renewed his routine with Phinney. He had added chores around the inn, still making small repairs from the damage caused by hurricane Donna the previous year. In the quiet evenings, he would enjoy a beer with Pop, as they succumbed to the fragrant summer breezes bringing the sweet smell of gardenias off the bushes at the edge of the veranda, reminding them of Irene.

Pop was not much for conversation these days, but just having Toby sit nearby gave him comfort. The loss of his partner of the last forty-six years was taking its toll. Pop spent more time "finding supplies" in the States than he used to, and the last time Toby was there, he noticed a lot of mileage added to the odometer of the Chevy.

On this particular evening, Pop volunteered, "Toby, you know I was thinking how much I like your friend Chrissy. I know Irene would have felt the same if she had had a chance to get to know her." Toby's eyes welled up. "Forgive me if I belittled your relationship in any way over the last few years. I was just looking out for you. It's rare when you meet a soul mate right off, and you may have just done that. So now, I'll just shut my mouth." And he did.

Toby was overwhelmed by his grandfather's sentiments. It made him somewhat anxious about the future, but the fatalist in him calmed him. He couldn't control the future; on the other hand, he was in full agreement. Chrissy was special. He felt if he could keep some maturity about himself, he and Chrissy could make a long-distance relationship work with a lot of effort. He thought of making a trip to New York before the end of the summer, but money was a consideration, and the inn had not had a good year following the big hurricane, so Toby decided it would be best to allocate his resources more efficiently.

CHAPTER NINE

In the fall, Toby packed up his recommended clothing and accessories suggested by the freshman orientation list for his first semester at the University of Florida. He took advantage of a visit by Clement Mills to fly the Cessna back to West Palm, and boarded a Greyhound Bus going north. When he got off in Gainesville, he thought he had disembarked somewhere in Georgia by mistake, so foreign were the accents he heard.

He arrived early morning and made his way to Simpson Hall, a new housing dormitory geared to freshman where he met his room-mate, Chuck Ford, from St. Petersburg. They hit it off immediately, as they began unpacking before the mandatory dorm residents meeting later that afternoon.

Toby started a week of freshman orientation where he toured the campus in his alphabetically assigned group with Mansons, Matthias, and Mc-something or others, alphabetically forged. Most of what he learned each day was contradicted at the end of the day by the few upperclassmen residing in his dorm. He remembered something his grandfather had told him before he left for school:

"Son, I'll give you but one piece of advice for your next adventure in college. Please remember it." Placing his hand on Toby's shoulder and looking him squarely in the eye, he continued, "College is easy if you just remember one thing. Do the *minimum each day*." He emphasized MINIMUM EACH DAY. "The material you need to learn to make straight A's is not hard, but you cannot let a day go by that you don't do what is asked of you. Sometimes it's not much, sometimes it is. That's all I have to say about that."

For four years that lesson served Toby well.

Campus life became routine very quickly. Toby made friends easily, and although he was rushed enthusiastically by the ΣAEs and several other fraternities, he kept his distance, knowing it was a party atmosphere geared toward meeting women, and he did not want that kind of temptation.

One advantage he had was the telephone. It didn't take him long to find a reliable dorm number for him to call Chrissy at Rollins. They spoke once or twice a week, each quickly becoming the butt of jokes in their respective dorms. At all hours Toby would hear a sarcastically sweet shout down the hallway, "Tobeeeee. Chrissy's calling." Toby always rushed for the payphone at the middle of the hall; sometimes she was on the line, sometimes she wasn't.

Rollins had very strict regulations regarding female students leaving campus. In late October, Chrissy had to manufacture a parental permission for her to join friends on a weekend field trip to Jacksonville to hear some distinguished conductor lead the local symphony orchestra. Toby hitchhiked all Friday night to get there so he could surprise Chrissy with student tickets to the Florida-Duke football game being played in the Gator Bowl.

Toby wasn't all that impressed with Florida's 1961 football team, led by a one hundred thirty-eight pound quarterback, but he was excited when they went in for halftime up over Duke twenty-eight to three. As usually was the case, his excitement proved premature when the game ended favoring Duke over Florida thirty-five to twenty-eight. The loss was quickly forgotten when Toby and Chrissy had dinner and shared a motel room together for the night. They hopped a bus back to school the following morning, letting Toby off in Gainesville before continuing on to Orlando for Chrissy.

"Well, was it worth the wait?" Chrissy asked smiling as Toby stood to get off the bus.

"Always, babe." He grinned as he held his duffle in front of him to hide his excitement left over from the two-hour make-out session.

Chrissy and Toby got together at the start of the Christmas break, as well. Chrissy had delayed her departure a day so Toby could join her in Winter Park, where they stayed at the Langford Motel. They exchanged Christmas presents before separating for their respective homes. Toby had a busy vacation, as Piper's Landing was full, no vacancy, over the holidays.

Although Toby was disappointed that he would not see Phinney, because she had moved south for the season, he was delighted when Clement showed up with a brand-new toy, a state-of-the-art twin-engine Beechcraft called a Travel Air. He was more than happy to offer use of it to Toby, who found a Nassau resident qualified as an instrument-rated flight instructor. It took Toby about ten hours of instruction to prepare for a multi-engine rating, which he was awarded by a designated FAA examiner in Fort Lauderdale the day before he headed back to school.

Clement came to visit during the short semester break, which did not coincide with Chrissy's, so the two of them flew down to Orlando for a surprise visit. Chrissy had some good news; her parents were going to Europe over the spring break, and they asked her if she would like to spend the time with her friends, which of course she did, having just the friend in mind. Clement cooperated with the use of his Travel Air, which he insisted needed more use than the hundred or so hours that comprised an average flying year for him. Toby was more than happy to accommodate him.

Toby and Chrissy had a wonderful vacation on the island, spending a lot of time with Vernon, who was continuing to slow down, and Phinney, who continued to warm up to Chrissy as they spent more time together. The two of them put a smile on Vernon's face and a hop in his step when he was included in their activities. They made love every night, trying to be careful, although on occasion, Toby's excitement got the better of him, but the apparent success they were having carried the day, and they did not explore more sophisticated birth control options. Vernon could see the deep love blossoming right before his eyes, and he was happy for them. It made him remember being young again, while at the same time reminding him of how young he wasn't now.

Toby and Chrissy finished their freshman years. They got together as often as they could, but Chrissy was ordered to the Long Island home for the summer by parents who were angry that advantage had been taken of them when they learned about spring break. Since they controlled the purse strings, Chrissy had no choice but to oblige. In 1962, Commonwealth Telephone, Ltd. laid cable to Piper Cay, and the first telephone service to the island was established.

Toby, at some expense, could now reach out to Chrissy and hear her voice. They agreed to talk every Sunday night around seven o'clock. Toby was busy with the inn and flying at every opportunity, working toward his instrument rating. In the back of his head was an idea that if he could qualify with commercial and instrument ratings, perhaps his grandfather would consider getting a used twin-engine plane for island business, maybe even bringing guests to and from the States.

Phinney made up the majority of Toby's social life, and a welcome companion she was. Without her, Toby would likely have had only Randy, who spent most of his time in the family business, so he valued their time together. Herbert was usually busy with responsibilities at the Inn, where he was increasingly invaluable.

One afternoon in early July, Chrissy called midweek, which was highly unusual. Toby took the call in the main house office where most telephone business was conducted. Chrissy was very emotional, which concerned Toby, his antenna on high alert.

"Toby, I think we really messed up." She cried softly into the telephone.

"What's up, Chrissy. There's nothing we can't deal with. Are your parents upset again?"

"No, I think it's much worse than that. I don't know for sure, but I haven't been feeling well since I got home. You know, like I feel like I do when I've partied too much the night before, only I haven't been out since I've been home, and certainly not drinking."

"I'm sure it's nothing, Kiki. Why don't you go see a doctor?"

"There's more. I haven't had a period since the end of school, and I don't even remember when before that. Toby, I think maybe I'm pregnant." She paused.

Toby gathered himself as the significance sank in. He knew that his next words would be among the more important of his young life. "As you once told me: I love you; I am yours in every way. I now repeat that to you. I love you; I am totally committed to you in every way. At the very worst, this is news of great happiness for us. We will deal with this together. I will be on my way up there tomorrow morning; it will take me all day to get there. Can you see a doctor?"

She sobbed. "My doctor is my parents' doctor. He will tell them either way why I came to see him."

"I'm not sure he can do that, but if you're more comfortable, get a name out of the phonebook."

"It's not like that here, Toby. This island is not much bigger than your island. Everybody knows everybody, and they gossip! Are you really coming, coming for me?"

"Yes indeed," Toby replied without a thought or hesitation.

"Then, I would like to meet you in the city. My parents will give me a car for the day, if I ask them. We can see a doctor together. Could we do that?"

"That's a great idea. Will you meet me at the airport if I give you my flight information? Can you stay by the phone in the morning so I can call you with it; otherwise, we'll have to meet somewhere in the city, and as you know, I'm just an Out Island boy; don't know my way around too well," Toby said, belittling himself, but justifiably so. "I have an idea for a doctor that might work. Let me call you in an hour with some information."

"Okay," Chrissy agreed. "I feel much better. My parents will be at the club all day, and they're out tonight. I'll sit right here by the phone."

Toby filtered through the office desk drawers until he found the airline schedules for the summer. Eastern Airlines had a late-morning nonstop from Miami to Idlewild. He didn't bother to book it because he knew the plane would most likely be empty. Then he looked back through the guest logs until he found Dr. Bridegroom's phone number in Miami.

After explaining his situation, Dr. Bridegroom reminded Toby to call him Hugh. He gave Toby the phone and address of his roommate from medical school who was practicing obstetrics in Manhattan. He even agreed to arrange an introduction to make sure that Toby and Chrissy could get in to see him on short notice.

"Toby, I'm sure I don't need to tell you that Dr. Wargo cannot help you terminate this pregnancy, if indeed there is one."

"I would never, ever do that, Hugh," Toby replied emphatically.

"Does Vernon know about this?"

"No. He's in Florida for a few days. Why don't you call him and say hello? But, please, let me tell him in my own way. I don't want him to hear about it from someone else." Toby gave Hugh Vernon's Fort Lauderdale number. "Thank you ever so much for your help and understanding."

Toby rang off and called Chrissy with the new information. She was greatly relieved. "I'm just so happy you are going to be here soon. I'll be at the curb upstairs, since you won't have any luggage, at the departures terminal. It will be less crowded. I'll be driving a white Oldsmobile convertible with the top up."

———— • ◆ • ————

In the morning Toby raided the cash stash, what Pop called it, of two thousand dollars, leaving a note explaining he needed to leave for a few days for an emergency, all to be explained upon his return. He persuaded Herbert to take him into the harbor in Nassau to catch the early morning Chalk's seaplane to Watson Island in Miami, where he grabbed a taxi to Miami International Airport. A one-way ticket cost him $250.

As promised, he was met at the curb in the afternoon by Chrissy driving a white convertible. They embraced and laughed after Toby presented her with a complementary pack of four Winston cigarettes he had been given on the plane. They headed off for the city where Dr. Wargo, Hugh Bridegroom's college roommate, confirmed that Chrissy was carrying a healthy baby, approximately three months along.

They drove back to the Hamptons where Toby checked into a Howard Johnsons. Chrissy called her parents and explained she was going to spend the night with her friends after a beach party, that she wouldn't be home until the next afternoon.

Sitting on the bed, holding hands to comfort each other, Toby and Chrissy discussed their options. Toby only had one option, they were going to get married, with or without her parents blessing. Chrissy agonized over this, recognizing the pressure it would put on the two of them to bring their situation out in the open. Toby had always made his own decisions and suffered the consequences. It was a carryover from losing his parents so young, an event over which he had absolutely no control. It pained him to see the fear in Chrissy's face that she was not going to lead the life she or her parents had envisioned for her if she had this baby. To sound his thought process out, Toby turned where he always turned. With Chrissy's acquiescence, he called his grandfather in Fort Lauderdale; Vernon listened patiently until Toby finished with all of the details and his game plan.

"Well, you're thorough; I'll say that, young man." Positioning the phone between them so both he and Chrissy could hear, the two listened as Vernon continued, "Chrissy, if you and Toby feel you have thought through all the consequences that result from starting a family so young, and recognize the loss of a part of your lives that cannot be recreated, I will support you in every way I can. I am proud of both of you, but one more thing, Toby."

"What's that?"

"You must be a man and enter the lion's den. You must go and make your peace with the Mallens face to face. It is most likely not going to be pleasant. After all, in their minds, you have soiled their daughter, and most likely ruined her life—at least as they envisioned it. You understand?"

"Yes, sir."

The following morning, an unenthusiastic Toby and Chrissy drove the short stretch to Ocean Drive and pulled into the drive-way at the Mallens's house at about nine o'clock. Toby and Chrissy walked slowly up the back steps to the kitchen entrance of the New England wood-frame home. Chrissy's parents were attired in golf clothes and having a light breakfast in the breakfast nook. Chrissy's mother smiled momentarily, as her father looked up from his morning paper, directing an intense glare at Toby, the probabilities of this unscheduled circumstance formulating in his head.

CHAPTER TEN

Chrissy and Toby were married in a quiet ceremony at the inn on August 15, a month before Toby was due back at school. The Hendersons and Bethels were in attendance along with very few others outside of the immediate families. Richard and Dorothy Mallen, Chrissy's parents, reluctantly agreed to a wedding ceremony on Matthias turf mostly because they wanted to avoid the embarrassment of exposing their daughter's condition to their friends in New York.

Toby's approach to the lion's den had gone about as well as could be expected. Chrissy's parents tried to physically separate them in the kitchen in an effort to establish dominance over the situation, but the young couple stood firmly together, hand in hand. Their circumstances were easily forecast, but the decision to marry caught the Mallens off guard. Richard Mallen argued as persuasively as he could the case for giving up the child, so the two kids could have a chance at normal young lives.

Dorothy Mallen was mostly an emotional mess of tears. Richard argued passionately from the heart, urging strongly for Toby and

Chrissy to reconsider; however, he eventually recognized that he was not in control of this situation, having totally misjudged the closeness of the relationship flourishing under his nose these last four years. His sentiment was heartfelt, but in the end, his daughter's strength of mind and Toby's courageous calmness wore him down. He was moved to tears when he at last hugged his daughter; the best he could do for Toby was a handshake.

The rest of the short morning was reduced to the discussion of logistics. Chrissy planned to transfer from Rollins College to the University of Florida where she would be able to finish her first semester of her sophomore year, the university having adopted a trimester system where the first semester would end at Christmas break. The baby was due in January. The couple would decide on the furthering of her education after they had a chance to evaluate circumstances after the baby was born. Richard, although quite wealthy, made it clear that if Toby and his daughter could make such adult decisions, they could be responsible for the hard parts, too. He did volunteer to continue funding his daughter's education as though she was continuing, but nothing extra.

Toby was actually relieved to hear this, as he believed that his grandfather's resources were limited to some degree. The contribution of an education stipend for Chrissy would make things easier, so Toby wouldn't have to get a job, scarce in a college town, to make ends meet. He thanked Chrissy's dad and assured him he was not in the relationship for money. He also thanked him for his cooperation, acknowledging his feeling about the matter, insisting that he was going to devote his life to assuring Chrissy's happiness and the security of his family.

Reverend St. Claire officiated the subdued nuptials on the veranda at the inn. A steady trade wind kept the heat of the summer sun at bay. The reception was held there also, where the dozen or so in attendance could enjoy an aerial show in the lagoon put on by

Phinney. The Mallens did not know what to make of all this, but they were relieved to see that the living conditions were not as pagan as they had imagined from New England. To make them more comfortable, Vernon had suggested a rather formal setting. The English accents and the appearance by the governor added a touch of class totally unexpected, leaving the Mallens thinking there was more to this family than they had previously surmised.

Clement loaned his Travel Air and a North American Flight Services credit card as a wedding present, which made planning a honeymoon an adventure. In the end, Toby and Chrissy opted for travel between the islands and the States with a cruise through the Exumas on the Chris Craft for a celebration. Phinney followed them as far as Norman's Cay before turning back to join her pod.

Phinney was happy to have Boy back in her life as the sun began its cycle higher and longer. She did not see him every day, but he rang for her often. If he missed a few days, she would swing by and check things out, looking for missing boats in the lagoon to explain his absence. Just past the longest days, Boy disappeared for some time. She came by the marina often; all the boats were there, but no humans she was interested in were in evidence, so she was surprised and a little disappointed one day to cross the bar and see Boy on the dock with Girl.

She screeched her disapproval standing on her tail. Boy waved to her, but seemed a little distracted. For the next while he did not ring for Phinney, and when she came by the inn, she could see a lot of activity around the big house, the dark-skinned humans and others busying themselves with something or other. Something was up; Phinney could feel it.

Boy and Girl did call for her once, and they swam together in the shallow water by the beach. When Phinney first got close to Girl in the water, her echolocation revealed what was going on. Girl was going to have a baby, most likely Boy's baby. Phinney did not understand the concept of family beyond mother and calf, because dolphins are not monogamous. Her mother had many male relationships, and Phinney had helped with a sister calf, but they were not closer as a family than Phinney was with the rest of the pod. A part of her understood the significance of the connection between these humans, and she began to comprehend the idea of family. She had always felt the connection between Boy and the older human, and now it made sense.

Boy was talking animatedly to her, skinny arms waving, his voice rising and lowering as he spoke. He rubbed his chest and Girl's chest and clasped his hands together, then he rubbed Girl's belly where the baby was. Phinney understood this was something important to Boy, but she only vaguely understood that it had to do with their connection as a family unit. She would think about that later; right now, she just wanted to have Boy's company. They mingled in the shallow water a few moments longer before Boy signaled goodbye, and turning slowly to the beach, he walked hand in hand with Girl back to the inn.

Several sunsets later, Phinney heard the bell in the late afternoon, and she headed back to the cove. Crossing over the bar, she could hear music, odd mixtures of continuous sounds moving against one another, but not at all unpleasant. On the raised part of the building patio, Phinney could see a crowd of humans covered in heavy clothing. She could not see their skin except for their hands and faces. The females wore bright colors; the males wore dark. Boy and Girl were together and the other humans were paying attention to them.

A little annoyed, Phinney made as big a ruckus as she could, jumping clear of the water, summersaulting, tail walking, all the while screeching as loudly as she could. In no time, all the humans were gathered at the water's edge by the dock looking only at Phin-

ney. They shouted and pounded their skinny arms together in thunderous smacking. Boy and Girl called out to her, and Phinney realized she had been acknowledged, which made her feel a little better. She gave a repeat performance with the same result, quitting only when she became so tired she could only swim and watch.

After a while her novelty wore off and she returned to the east and her group, smaller now that they had split into two groups having grown so large over the years that the reefs around the big island could no longer sustain their concentration in number as one. Many had moved north to the islands and reefs of Eleuthera, but they still commingled once a year as the days grew short and the pods moved south into the Exumas.

For the next week Boy and Girl spent a lot of time with Phinney. They even went on an excursion deep into the Exumas, further even than Phinney traveled in the short day season with her pod, following the growling boat at a distance. The three of them dived new unfamiliar reefs and explored new and majestically beautiful turquoise waters. Just as Phinney began to feel removed from her pod, Boy and the Girl reversed their direction and returned to the big island and the home she knew.

Toby and Chrissy found half of a duplex a block off of University Avenue, close to the main part of the campus, and set up shop. Their days were filled with the spirit of young love in full bloom as they went about making the eleven hundred square feet a home. There was a small sunroom off the bedroom that they turned into a nursery. They left the final touches until after the baby was born, because neither had any idea what color to paint it.

By the end of September, Chrissy was showing, and her body was making changes in preparation for motherhood. The couple's social structure adjusted as many of their friends seemed young and immature. They made new acquaintances with some of the married students whose lifestyles were more suited to theirs. Chrissy took a normal course load of fifteen hours, mostly the same compulsory comprehensive courses, known as "C" courses, as Toby. With the added structure of a wife and home, Toby found it easier to follow Pop's words of advice about doing the minimum each day, and he found himself well prepared for the big multiple-choice exams, not surprised when he finished the trimester with three A's and a B. Chrissy mugged for him when she showed her grade slip with her 4.0 grade point average. With Toby's encouragement, she called her parents each week to keep the channels open for further healing. They were happy about her grades, but the "what could have been" image still filled their hearts.

By Christmas, Chrissy was uncomfortably huge and did not feel up to travel. Vernon's presence was required at the inn for the returning guests, and so, for the first time since he had moved to the island, Toby did not plan to spend the holiday with his grandfather. As a surprise, Chrissy reached out for Clement to ask a favor. On December 26, the day after their first Christmas as a married couple, Clement Mills flew to Gainesville and gave the use of his Travel Air to Toby, so he could visit his grandfather for a day or two.

"Clem, I don't know how to thank you," said Toby, overwhelmed by his friend's generosity. "What are you going to do while I'm gone?"

"I'm renting a car and heading down to Orlando to look at some property. Several friends, including your grandfather, have put together a land trust, and we are buying up farmland near Orlando, have been for years actually, because it's cheap, and we think it will be a good investment over the long haul. Central Florida is growing that way."

Toby thanked him enthusiastically, hugged Chrissy carefully, and made his way to Nassau to spend the night and most of Thursday with Pop.

Vernon was delighted to see Toby. The two made an afternoon of it to visit Irene's memorial; Toby rang for Phinney, but she did not come, having already moved with her group further south for the winter. The late-afternoon sun shined curtains of light, shimmering back and forth from the wave action over the hole in the cave. The confines of the cave were quiet, with the shifting sun highlighting the moss-covered rock, creating the illusion of deep red velvet. It changed its rich color because they were in forty feet of water, and red, which is the first color in the spectrum to fade in deeper water, had darkened to a ruby-like quality as ribbons of light fell upon it, giving the space a cathedral-like aura.

Toby departed Nassau that Friday afternoon. He left a note of appreciation to Clement on the clip over the control yoke, before returning home to Chrissy in time for dinner.

Classes for the second trimester started Monday, January 9. Toby preregistered for advanced studies in engineering, which steered his elective selection to mathematics. That night he and Chrissy celebrated his last trimester as a lower classman with a dinner out. When they came home, they climbed out on the roof to watch a spectacular total lunar eclipse. They nestled in a seam where two roof angles came together, Toby with one arm around Chrissy, and the other rubbing her swollen belly.

"I'll be glad when this is over," she murmured, as the golden moon glow started to yield to the earth-blocked sun.

"I'll bet. Won't be long now, and we'll both be up all night."

———— • ◆ • ————

A week later on Tuesday, January 15, shortly after Toby left for his first class of the day, Chrissy's water broke as she was putting a load of laundry in the dryer in the common area they shared with the other unit in the duplex. She called the administration offices in Tigert Hall to try to get a message to Toby, but not wanting to risk making a mistake, full of first-time jitters, she asked her neighbor to give her lift to the University hospital emergency room. She called her doctor as she was stuffing some personal items in a small duffel to use during her hospital stay, which she had been informed would be about five days.

While she was in the waiting room prior to being moved into the delivery room, Toby rushed through the double doors, flustered but with a big grin on his face. Fawning all over Chrissy, he was interrupted by a matronly nurse.

"Hold on there, cowboy. There's no reason to get excited. Nothing's going to happen for some time yet."

As forecast, Chrissy didn't get to see the delivery room until nearly midnight, and at one thirty the following morning, she gave birth to a healthy, seven-pound eight-ounce baby girl, who became known to her parents as Jennifer Irene Matthias.

By the weekend, Toby and Chrissy brought their little girl home. In an unexpected move, Chrissy's mom, Dorothy, volunteered a few weeks of her time to come to Gainesville to help out with her new granddaughter, the blessed event helping thaw the strained relations in the family.

The tiny kitchen became a mess of baby equipment and bottles. The additional assistance was needed just for the washing and cleaning. Fortunately the duplex had availability of a washing machine and dryer, although the neighbors were not crazy about sharing a washing machine with poopy diapers. A compromise was reached when everyone chipped in for a diaper service, which picked up and delivered stacks of cotton cloths twice weekly.

Toby and Dorothy took turns with nighttime feedings, which gave Chrissy a break for some needed rest after her ordeal. Tears flowed when Dorothy finally bid them farewell after a month. Toby joked with Chrissy that the tears were of joy that her mother didn't have to sleep on the rented cot that took up all the available space in the nursery, but the fact of the matter was that Dorothy really enjoyed having an excuse to be pleasant and accepting without having to acknowledge the tough-love stand she and Richard had taken after their advice had been overridden by two teenagers. She had come to realize that Toby was highly disciplined and deeply in love with her daughter.

Toby finished the semester with solid grades and decided to stay on schedule with a June '65 graduation, which enabled him to take June through August off to rebuild some of his cash reserves. Having no employer assistance, the hospital delivery and doctor fees had come to almost a thousand dollars. He was too proud to take advantage of his father-in-law's offer of financial assistance, relying instead on a gift from his grandfather, which he deemed a loan that he would pay back somehow, sometime.

Pop had also made the trek up to Gainesville, about a six and a half hour drive from Fort Lauderdale, almost all two-lane roads after he left the short piece of the Florida Turnpike that ran from North Miami to Fort Pierce. Holding his great-grandchild put a sparkle in his eyes that Toby was happy to see, the light having dimmed somewhat since the passing of Irene. The fixed base operation at the airport offered Toby employment for the summer, which kept aviation in his life, something that was missing since the birth of his daughter.

He learned to do light maintenance on piston aircraft in addition to handling fueling operations for Eastern Airlines, which provided regional service to the southeast out of Gainesville. He was allowed occasional use of the Cessna 172 that the outfit used for training, provided he cover the direct operating expenses.

Throughout the spring, Chrissy had worked hard at getting back in shape, and soon had the lean athletic figure she enjoyed before the pregnancy. Her life worked into a routine as she watched her little Jenny grow, putting on weight and getting longer. Toby remarked that Jenny wasn't much smaller than Phinney when he first met her, although that was not really the case. At six months, Phinney had been much bigger and more capable than his defenseless little girl, and his new responsibility weighed heavily on him.

The couple made friends with other student families. In a sort of club fashion, they shared one another's burdens, making management of necessary activities quite a bit easier. With encouragement from other young mothers, Chrissy decided to explore registering for classes in the fall, which would put her one trimester behind Toby. If she could handle the course load by taking the summer trimester next year, she could actually graduate with him in 1965, but she would have to see how things worked out. So far, the young mothers' club was able to help cover child-care requirements for the group, and the association gave Chrissy much-needed confidence and experience to look after Jenny's needs. She decided to explore the possibility for orienting her lower division courses toward a degree in nursing. Jenny was awakening care-giving instincts in her, and she thought it would be an interesting career to pursue.

Toby spent his free time at the airport where he learned as much about the aircraft services business as he could. He got to fly the training Cessna occasionally, working on his instrument rating when he could find a safety pilot to ride with him. Around midsummer, he took the written exam, passing with a respectable grade. By the end of the summer, he had met the requirements to take the flight exam.

His boss gave him permission to take the 172 down to Orlando's Herndon Field, where an FAA examiner gave him his check ride, which he passed without difficulty. He was now a qualified single-engine/multi-engine instrument rated pilot. He debated continuing his training to become a certified flight instructor, but the financial burden and time requirements were beyond his means. It would have been nice, however, to have been able to fly with other people paying for it, but students were not exactly beating down the door at the small Gainesville flight school for instruction, and they already had two qualified instructors available. He put that on a backburner for the time being.

Chrissy occupied her summer days trying to stay out of the oppressive heat, as there was not much breeze from the trade winds to cool her off this far north and so far inland. Jenny kept developing heat rashes, and she required a lot of attention on humid summer nights. She, Toby, and Jenny sought relief in air-conditioned restaurants whenever possible. The couple did not notice the gradual daily changes in their daughter, but she was in fact getting fatter and longer. She could mimic giggling, a constant source of amusement for Toby as he tried to help her spread some solid food around her high chair. He tried the airplane into the hangar routine without much success, as Jenny demonstrated she could spit mashed bananas farther than Toby could reach.

In the fall of 1963, Toby and Chrissy worked their schedules together so that they could both reenroll, she to prepare for a degree in nursing, and he to finish up the requisites for study in engineering. Somehow, with the help of the family club, they managed their schedules so that they had full coverage of their responsibilities for Jenny, and following Vernon's minimum everyday rule, they stayed on top of things resulting in A's and B's at the end of the term, which was December thanks to the conversion to the trimester system by the University.

———— •◆• ————

In November 1963, near the end of Toby's first term as an upperclassman, Chrissy and Toby joined the nation in shock and disbelief to learn that President Kennedy had been shot in Dallas. The couple spent the weekend of November 22 glued to their grainy fourteen-inch television, adjusting the rabbit ears every few minutes to maintain a clear enough signal, as they watched the events of the weekend unfold.

The talking heads speculated the possible scenarios that led up to the assassination and likely results into the wee hours. Tensions lessened slowly as the realization set in that the U.S. was not at war and that this was likely the random act of a madman. Conspiracy theorists expounded, but came up with no credible evidence of a more sinister plot against the United States. In the meantime, more military advisors were being sent every month to a place nobody ever heard of called Vietnam.

The Christmas break gave the new family a chance to see Toby's grandfather, who volunteered to come to Fort Lauderdale for the break, saving them the trouble of loading baby supplies and personal items on a cramped Chalk's Flying boat. The Mallens decided to spend the holidays in nearby Fort Lauderdale by the Sea, on the ocean just north of the apartment, to make it an expanded family celebration. It was the first time Dick Mallen had a chance to see his granddaughter, and the family soaked up the mild climate, wondering why they hadn't done this before.

Everyone returned home before the New Year, Chrissy politely declining her father's offer to bring Jenny to New York for a brief visit. In early January, fresh from a relaxing stay in the Fort Lauderdale apartment, Toby and Chrissy packed up the family station wagon and made their way back to Gainesville to start the second half of Toby's junior year.

In March 1964, the United States started sending combat marines to Vietnam to assist in the brewing conflict in Southeast Asia. In August, Toby got a letter from the local United States government selective service office requesting that he verify his personal information and status with the local draft board in Alachua County. He was relieved during his visit to find out that they just wanted to have a record of his local residence for notification purposes. Toby asked the gentleman at the office if this had any significance to him and was advised that most likely it did not. If the military considered him eligible for the draft, he would be exempt under president Kennedy's 1963 executive order that excluded married males aged eighteen to twenty-six from the draft, which was still in effect. In the unlikely event the order was reversed, his current status as a student would exempt him until such time as he graduated or dropped out of school.

They endured the heat of the summer without misadventure, marveling at the growth of their daughter, who was becoming quite a handful with her newfound mobility and her ability to mouth out meaningful words and phrases. Jenny was one and a half years old now with the evidence of her developing personality expressed daily. She was happy and bright, mostly cheerful, and very curious about her world. Her dress code was simple, consisting of sandals, training diapers, and tee shirts. She loved her raggedy stuffed animals and played well with others in the family club supervised children's activities. Toby was hired back by the fixed base operator as a "jack of all trades," which meant he did whatever needed to be done including washing rental cars, sweeping up, and occasionally fueling airplanes.

In August 1964, President Lyndon Johnson laid the groundwork for U.S. participation in the escalating war in Vietnam following the report of attacks on Navy ships patrolling the Gulf of Tonkin. The cadre of military advisors that had been stationed in Vietnam since the Kennedy administration began to double monthly. Over the next several months, the pressure for military trainees began to mount, resulting in the lifting of Executive Order 11119, exempting married males from the draft under the selective service system, but the exemption was still applicable to heads of households.

Toby was notified by the Alachua County draft board that his status had been updated to reflect his circumstances. Stories involving Vietnam had an ever-increasing presence in the news, and this was not lost on the young couple. One Sunday morning, after Chrissy and Toby watched *Meet the Press* highlighting the military escalation, Chrissy became concerned for Toby and her family.

"Honey, what are you thinking about a contingency plan if this mess gets worse? I remember neighborhood kids going away in the early fifties when the same kind of thing happened in Korea."

"I can't believe this will amount to anything, Chrissy. In any event, I still have a student deferment."

"Yeah, but what about after you graduate? What would we do then?"

"Let's cross that bridge when we come to it. This is just a local civil war; I'm sure it will be short lived."

Satisfied for the time being, Chrissy dropped the subject, but still it weighed on her from time to time.

———— •◆• ————

Toby entered his senior year at the University of Florida. His major was easy for him compared to the struggle Chrissy was having in the nursing school. The University hospital had merged with Shands Teaching Hospital shortly after the start of the new year. Requirements for nursing were reevaluated, which increased the requisites Chrissy would need for graduation. Even though she had picked up some course credit in the summer trimesters, it appeared she was not going to be able to graduate in June with her husband. She and Toby talked it over, and he agreed to spend another summer in Gainesville so that she could complete her degree, taking it wherever they decided to settle to begin their postgraduate lives.

At the end of 1964, they made the effort to visit the Bahamas for a holiday vacation with Pop. He greeted them on the wharf downtown, making a great fuss over Jenny, who was now only three weeks away from her second birthday. Jenny enjoyed the attention, sitting in her great-grandfather's lap at the controls of the Chris

Craft with her hands on the helm. This, her first trip to the Bahamas and the island, was unlike anything she had ever experienced before. Her inquisitive imagination began the staccato series of questions that were becoming familiar to her parents. As she noticed the new environment before her, she burst out with an excited series of observations.

"Daddy, water!" she pointed to the harbor entrance across from the city docks. "Blue!"

"Yes, Jenny, there's lots of blue water. There are lots of different blues. You'll see," Toby murmured gently as they eased out the channel.

As they cleared the jetty, Jenny craned her head around and noticed the beaches along Paradise Island, the newly renamed Hog Island. Pointing she said, "Beaches!" becoming more and more animated as they moved into deeper water. Pop throttled up to cover the short distance to the lagoon at Piper Cay, and Jenny, still in his lap, held tightly to his arms as the boat sped up. Toby shouted over the engine noise, "We have even prettier beaches at the inn where Pop lives! We can go swimming there!"

The Christmas of 1964 was a mix of beautiful and nasty weather, as a cold front passed through the islands just before the new year. The family made the best of the good weather, sailing, swimming, and making sand castles on the beach. Jenny had her own plastic pail and shovel to help move the sand around and pour water to make it malleable. She floated on beach toys, under the close supervision of her parents and Vernon, who now was known as "G Pop." Major and Herbert were favorites of hers by the end of the week.

Phinney was not in evidence, having moved to the shallow water of the Exumas for the winter. Toby felt a wave of nostalgia, saddened that he would not be able to introduce Jenny to his aquatic friend. When their short stay concluded, Chalk's brought them safely back to Fort Lauderdale. Jenny was intrigued that a boat could fly.

———— •◆• ————

Toby's last semester brought to light some realities that had not been front and center in his mind. The month of March was a huge employment recruiting week on the campus, as the larger of the nation's employers made camp in the University gym in elaborate booths and kiosks to woo the graduating class's employment prospects. The aerospace sector was well represented by companies like Honeywell, Allied Signal, Pratt & Whitney, and Grumman, all looking for engineers to help with their unprecedented expansion in the military-industrial complex.

Toby had a feeling that his interest lay in those areas, and he spent a lot of time with the recruiters. In the very week he started the interview process, the United States sent thirty-five hundred combat marines to Vietnam, as the country became formally engaged in the civil war in Southeast Asia.

It was soon apparent to Toby that his military service obligations were going to be an impediment to finding meaningful employment. The first question the recruiters asked was, how did he plan to meet his service obligations, should they arise? He was quickly disabused of his thought that his exemption as a married man with a child would relieve him of the requirement.

One recruiter candidly told Toby, "We are in the military machine manufacturing business, and I want to tell you we have a backlog of orders that will take us years to fill. Our government is sending thousands of troops to Vietnam every week. Our management tells us to expect troop levels to be nearly two hundred thousand by the end of the year. In what world do you think you are going to sidestep your participation?"

Toby was shaken by the thought that he and his family might

not move forward to the suburban home with the white picket fence he had vaguely envisioned. With most of the engineering employers telling him to come back when he had his service obligation out of the way, or at a minimum enlisting in an army reserve unit that would limit his exposure to the draft, they would be happy to make serious offers of employment, virtually guaranteeing him a good job.

He was so preoccupied on the way out of the gymnasium that he barely noticed the modest but colorful red, white, and blue kiosk near the entrance doors, manned by two young, tailored naval officers. The sign over the top said in bold letters: FLY NAVY. The job fair would go on the rest of the week, but for now, a troubled Toby headed across campus to talk to Chrissy, the only person who could help him get his head around things.

As the screen door banged shut behind him, he heard, "Daddy, Daddy, look!" Jenny held up a finger painting full of color and handprints.

"That's beautiful, honey." Toby got down on one knee and gave Jenny a big bear hug. Chrissy looked up from her studies.

"Welcome home. How'd the job interviews go?"

"Not so well, Chrissy." Toby proceeded to tell her what he had learned that afternoon. Feeling depressed, he asked if she had any ideas.

"You know the McCalls."

Buz and Pat McCall lived in Flavet Village, old military Quonset huts on campus that had been converted to student housing for veterans. A lot of the veterans who were going to school on the GI Bill lived there. Many, being older, were married and had families. Several of them formed the core of the family club that had taken Chrissy in and helped with the coverage of childcare for the last three years. Even though Toby and Chrissy were younger, they had been accepted by the group due to their circumstances. The

McCalls's maturity and experience had proven invaluable on numerous occasions.

"Why don't you give Buz a call and see if he can add any perspective."

Toby did exactly that. Buz volunteered, "If you buy us a beer, Pat and I will be right over, and I'll tell you everything I know. Lizzy can look after Jenny, and Brad can ride his trike in your driveway, so we won't be interrupted. In fact, you guys have a barbecue grill?"

"Yeah, we have that old rusty Weber out back," Toby replied.

"Great, I'll bring some burgers and we can make an evening out of it."

"Better bring some charcoal, too. I'm not sure we have any," Toby added.

Chrissy went out for another six-pack of beer and a bottle of inexpensive wine to share with Pat. Just having someone to talk to about the situation relieved Toby of some anxiety, and he looked forward to an evening with Buz and Pat to depressurize. It turned out to be just what the doctor ordered. Unfortunately, the information Buz had to share was not particularly encouraging.

Toby realized that the war in Southeast Asia was indeed escalating, and the fear of the draft was driving young men all over the country to look for solutions to avoid it. Buz related that he himself was completing a two-year army reserve requirement as part of his obligation to the United States Army where he had served two years on active military duty, mostly in the signal corps at Fort Bragg, North Carolina, after being drafted. He and Pat had married while he was still on active duty, and he had taken advantage of the opportunity to qualify for the GI Bill, which was paying for his education.

Buz explained that even after you serve two years of active duty, the total obligation is for six years, and that two additional years must be served in an army reserve unit, which met one weekend a month and two weeks in the summer. The remaining two-year obligation was only to be available in the event the country went to war and you were needed. This program kept the military response strength high without the cost of maintaining a full-time army of everyone who might be needed. Buz volunteered that there was an army reserve program that allowed someone who joins to serve only six months active duty, and then fill out the remainder of the five-and-a-half-year commitment in the active reserves.

"I'm still in the active reserves, now," Buz continued. "That's why you saw me in army fatigues at the grocery store last month. I had just gotten home from a weekend meeting."

Toby perked up. "So there is a reserve unit near here, then?"

"Actually there are two. I'm in the 221st garrison, and there is a small unit of infantry out on 441 as you head toward Ocala."

"Would I be able to get in one of those units? What's required?"

"That's the rub," Buz continued. "Six months ago, the unit would have welcomed you with open arms. We were never at a full complement of four hundred men. But this Vietnam thing has changed everything. Applicants have been arriving in droves. We are now totally full. What makes it worse, the unit commander has been given instructions not to accept additional reservists, because they are trying to make more young men available for the draft, where the military really needs them. Every reserve unit position available is one potential regular army recruit taken."

"Shit!" was all Toby could respond. "Could you do anything for me, put in a good word for me or something?"

"Sorry, buddy. It's out of my control. The government is trying to close up all the loopholes it can, for the very reason you want to get out of it. For what it's worth, much as I hated being drafted, it turns out it was the best thing for me. If I had gone to college, I probably would have flunked out, 'cause I was immature. My folks didn't have the money anyway. The army gave me a place to grow up, learn something about the world, and helps pay for my education through the GI Bill."

Chrissy moved over and sat on the floor next to Toby, putting her arm around him lovingly. She asked Buz, "Do you have any suggestions for us?"

Buz thought for a moment, and said, "Nothing really helpful. I think you guys should consider that military service is in your future, whether you like it or not. I would try to take charge of the situation and get the obligation out of the way on your terms, so that you do not have to go to a war zone, like Vietnam. We're in combat now, and Americans are getting killed. See if you can get in with training in an MOS like snow shoveling; that will keep you away from the action."

Although Buz had delivered his words with sarcasm, the concept had merit, thought Toby. By the time they finished exploring the options, the kids had all fallen asleep in comfortable lumps around the living room. Pat and Chrissy washed the dishes while Toby cleaned the grill and Buz pretended to help. With sleeping children in their arms, Buz and Pat made their way to their station wagon for the trip home.

On the way to the car Buz suggested, speaking quietly over his shoulder, "Chris, why don't you go with Toby to the Job fair tomorrow. Maybe the sight of the whole family will make enough of an impression on the recruiters to make an exception and risk offering you something. But you still have to deal with the military obligation somehow. It won't take long for your local draft board, wherever that ends up being, to find you."

"That will probably be here until the end of the summer," Toby said. "Chrissy needs to finish her degree, and she won't graduate until the end of the summer trimester. I agreed we'd stay until she finishes."

Chrissy and Toby said their goodbyes and went back inside. Jenny was asleep on the floor with her blankie wrapped around her and her Raggedy Ann doll firmly in her arms. Toby lifted her and placed her on her bed in the sitting room, carefully so as not to wake her. Chrissy raised her mustard-stained sundress over her shoulders, wiggled her into an oversized tee shirt, and took off her remaining sandal while Toby searched the living room for its mate. After cleaning up the evidence of the impromptu barbecue, they sat down together and shared a beer while mulling over the conclusions from the evening's conversation.

"Toby, if it's all right with you, I would like to come to the gym with you tomorrow to get a feel for the process. Maybe Buz's right about the recruiters seeing the whole family."

"I don't think it will make much difference. From their points of view, those companies don't want to take on the investment of training a new employee who might be drafted in the next year. There is no upside in it for them. They don't even have a guarantee that an employee would even come back to them after military service. Hell! He might not even come back at all."

"Don't even joke about that, Toby!" Chrissy was genuinely upset with his inference.

"Okay. Sure, let's go together tomorrow. There are a lot of opportunities to choose from. I think you'll be impressed. Absent the military thing, it looks like my skills are in high demand."

The next morning with a reluctant Jenny in tow, they walked the three blocks to the University gym. Chrissy was impressed by the organization of dozens of ten-by-ten kiosks lining the floor of the basketball stadium. She saw the banners of mostly familiar names from corporate America. The booths were manned pretty much by identical-looking young men all dressed in dark suits with narrow ties on button-down shirts. Even with the air conditioning blasting, a lot of humidity spread throughout the gym, as the main entrance doors were propped open. Toby stopped by the larger aerospace employers and introduced them to his family.

Most remembered him from his visit the previous day. They cooed at Jenny and said all the right things about his beautiful family, but the end result was that they strongly urged him to make some arrangement for his upcoming military obligation before wasting a lot of time on the interview process. His grades were exemplary, and they were looking for engineers, but not if the near-term employment was most likely temporary.

Discouraged, they made the rounds as Jenny pointed out all the pretty colors on the signage; she seemed impressed by the officialness of it all. As they made their way out of the hall, it was Jenny who noticed the men in uniform at the booth that had a big banner above that said: FLY NAVY.

"Look, Daddy! Airplane!" Jenny pointed with her free hand at the silhouette of a Navy fighter on the back wall of the kiosk. She caught the attention of two young officers manning the booth who acknowledged her declaration with broad smiles, which encouraged her to tug on Toby's hand as she pulled him toward the booth.

Chrissy moved alongside as the three approached the smiling officers. As they neared, the shorter of the two young men decked out in dress khakis and spit-shined shoes offered his hand.

"How's the job search going? Are you graduating this year?"

Toby frowned. "Not so good. No one wants to invest in an engineering major who hasn't taken care of his military service obligation."

At the mention of the engineering degree, both sailors perked up. "Well, we can certainly accommodate your difficulty. Have you considered serving your country aboard an air-conditioned ship?" The taller one smiled. "It's a lot better than a rice paddy, and while you're serving your country, you can learn how to fly."

Chrissy looked up at Toby, wild and conflicting thoughts going through her head.

"I already know how to fly," said Toby nonchalantly.

Now he had the interest of the two recruiters. "Really! What kind of flying do you do?" asked the shorter and obviously more senior of the two.

"I'm just a recreational pilot, mostly. I have multi-engine instrument ratings, and I fly other people's airplanes when I have the opportunity. I have about five hundred total hours."

Toby was exaggerating a little, as he had made liberal use of ink when filling out his logbooks. Clement always joked with him that he should log as flight time the duration from when he decided to go flying to when he got home from the trip. Although that was extreme, Toby did pad his flight time a few tenths each flight, as did most other pilots he knew. He *really* had the attention of the Navy recruiters, now.

"I am Lieutenant Callander, and this is Ensign Cuthbertson. Is this your family?" asked the shorter man, nodding to Chrissy and smiling at Jenny, who was fascinated that men in uniform were talking to her dad.

They all shook hands as Toby introduced his wife and daughter to the officers.

Callander continued, "I'm serious about the Navy. It's no secret what's happening in Southeast Asia, and the job hunting will only become more problematic as this war escalates, at least until it is resolved. Unless you are unhealthy, you will need to make some provision for military service before anyone hiring will take your application seriously. We can do that for you, and give you an invaluable skill while you are doing it. Would you spend a few minutes with us and let us explain the Aviation Reserve Officer Candidate program? You would make an ideal match for what we offer."

Chrissy and Jenny listened in for a while, but when Jenny started to get fidgety, her mother took her home for an afternoon nap. Toby listened cautiously to what the recruiters had to say. It all sounded too good, except for the part where Toby would be away from his family for extended periods of time, but he figured, hell, he would be away if he got drafted anyway.

The lieutenant explained the difference between a career Navy officer and a reserve Navy officer. The program of interest to Toby, as explained by Lieutenant Callander, would be the reserve officer program. The Navy would put Toby through a three-month training program, after which he would receive a commission as an officer in the United States Navy, or during which, if he didn't like the program, he could exercise his right to withdraw, called a DOR, or drop on request. He was cautioned that if he dropped out, he would undoubtedly be drafted shortly thereafter. Following a physical to be sure he met the requirements, he would be guaranteed a position in flight training as a Naval Aviation Cadet, and thereafter be assigned a squadron for deployment somewhere in the world, most likely Southeast Asia.

"Your flying experience will undoubtedly guarantee you a slot in flight training as you will be way ahead of the other candidates who you are competing with."

That seemed logical to Toby. In addition, serving his time in the military as an officer aboard an air-conditioned ship sure beat the prospect of an infantryman. The idea of flying jets was also very appealing.

Toby arrived home after several hours loaded with brochures highlighting the glory of Navy fighter pilots, feeling good about things for the first time in a while. Anticipating this, Chrissy had invited Buz and Pat over for a beer, so her husband could bounce what he had learned off a veteran. Buz listened to Toby's understanding of the recruiters' portrayal of AVROC and made his feelings clear.

"Toby, the military officer programs are not furry bunnies and lollipops. You can tell when a recruiter is lying, because his lips are moving. Don't believe anything they tell you about guaranteed assignments or getting out if you don't like the way they treat you. They will tell you anything to get you to sign up. Their performance is based solely on meeting quotas, and they know they will never have to see you again after you commit."

Deflated somewhat, Toby said, "But they seemed like such nice guys; I can't believe they would just lie to me like that."

"When you go back there, ask them to put all the promises in writing, and then decide. You do make a lot of good points, even if you don't end up flying airplanes. There is always the possibility that you won't be sent to a war zone, and if you are, probably nobody is going to be shooting at you on a battleship!"

———— •◆• ————

Toby returned the next day without the euphoria and asked some hard questions. The lieutenant's response was, "We can't put anything in writing because we are not authorized. We can only tell you what Navy policy is and what others have experienced. Your friend is correct in that you will have to compete for pilot slots, but with your considerable experience, it is unlikely you won't make the short list. As for the DOR, we can show you that in writing, and you will find that you will be tested and encouraged to drop out in your training for a commission, just to see what you are made of."

Toby returned home to Chrissy to have a serious discussion about the possibility of his joining the Navy. They made the obligated call to Pop to get his take on everything.

"Son, it sounds like you and Chrissy are asking all the right questions, and I can't help, nor do I want the responsibility of making your decision. Seems to me like you have to choose among some not too attractive alternatives. But I agree wholeheartedly with you that doing nothing is the worst option, and I will feel a lot better about your well-being if you are on a ship as opposed to humping around in the bush in Vietnam getting shot at. I know how much you love to fly, but I'm not sure I'm excited about you landing jet fighters on boats and getting shot at while you are flying. Personally, I am lacking in experience. With the luck of my age, I was not high on the draft priority during my wars, so I can't help you there."

After a lot of deliberation and planning, Toby and Chrissy decided that the officer's program in the Navy was the best among poor options. How long could this war continue anyway? Vietnam was a tiny country, so the U.S. involvement couldn't last too long. Toby might never see a war theater, anyway. The AVROC program offered Toby some flexibility with his timing, which would make it possible for him to spend the summer helping Chrissy with Jenny while she finished her requirements for her nursing degree.

The next day he drove to Jacksonville to the main Navy recruiting center and signed the requisite paperwork. He was told to expect orders to report to Pensacola at the end of August where he would enter the officer candidate class 3465, to be known as a ninety-day wonder when he received his commission in the United States Navy a few weeks before Christmas.

———— • ◆ • ————

Finishing up the trimester proved routine, Toby's degree in engineering all but guaranteed at this point. In celebration of the event, Chrissy threw a big party at the house the night before graduation, inviting Toby's close friends. Vernon drove up from Fort Lauderdale for the graduation ceremony in the University gym, where just two months before Toby had tried to find a job and ended up talking to the Navy recruiters for two days.

Vernon beamed with pride as Toby walked across the makeshift stage and received his diploma from Dr. Reitz, president of the University of Florida. The jubilant graduates milled around the Plaza of the Americas in the middle of the campus for an hour before moving off with their families to start new lives. Toby, Chrissy, Jenny, and Pop strolled arm in arm back to the small wood-frame duplex.

"I really miss Grandma, Pop," Toby mused.

"I do, too, son. I miss her every day, but I know one thing; she would be really proud to be here today to see what a fine young man you turned into and what a beautiful family you have. Do you think you might have time to come back to the islands for a visit? I know everyone would like to see you."

"I don't think so right now, Pop. I have a lot of things to clean up here before I report to Pensacola, and we have to get things organized and settled for Chrissy when she graduates and I'm gone."

Later in the evening in the screened in porch, they continued their conversation. Vernon was not eager to go to bed on the cot in Jenny's room, so the three of them sat up and enjoyed a beer as they listened to the Florida insects sing their evening songs outside.

"Chrissy, you know you can always have a place with us at Piper Cay while Toby's away? And, Toby, if you can squeeze in a trip, I know there is someone special who will want to see you. Phinney used to come by regularly, but I think she's figured out that you have moved on. Doesn't come by so much anymore. Last time I saw her, she was fully grown, must have been seven or eight feet long and about six hundred pounds. She always comes by alone, though, splashed up a storm off the end of the dock. One of us waves to her, but we're not who she wants to see."

Toby's heart felt heavy, full of sadness. He hadn't seen Phinney since his wedding, several years earlier. He imagined what she must look like, now fully grown. He regretted that he had not made the time to get back to the island during the warmer months these past few years. He wished Phinney well and hoped she didn't think he had forgotten her.

CHAPTER ELEVEN

Phinney always included the cove at Piper Cay in her hunting circuit, which started around Rose Island, moving east and south through the Yellow Bank, then reversing across the north side of the big island to pass around the entrance to the harbor at Nassau, which put her minutes away from the cove.

Before heading out to the deeper water in the sound and the reefs that protected the barrier islands, she would swing by the dock and look for signs of Boy, to no avail. Phinney enjoyed the days she spent with Boy and Girl after the big gathering at the buildings where Boy and his family lived. She even grew to like Girl, who now obviously held the place of closeness to Boy she once held, but the feelings of jealousy were subsiding as Phinney realized that she wasn't really being replaced.

As time went on after they said their goodbyes, she came to understand that this was going to be one of the long separations that happened during the annual cycle. As the days shortened, she only occasionally visited the cove. Often the dark-skinned human would see her from the dock and wave, showing his big teeth. If he had a hose nearby, he would playfully spray her with the bitter-tasting water. Boy's older family sometimes whistled for her to come by the beach where he would wade in and talk to her softly in human sounds as she rubbed around his legs, emitting a soft highly pitched sound in acknowledgment.

After a whole cycle of the moon, Phinney curtailed her visits, deciding rather than frustrating herself with passes through the cove, she would wait for Boy to ring. The days moved along to the shortest of the year, and Phinney's pod started to move off in groups to the southeast. The water was just a little cooler, but noticeably so; reef fish migrated to shallower water, which was warmer, and the dolphin followed.

Phinney loved the shallow banks of the smaller islands to the southeast with their bleached white sandy bottoms that went on endlessly. Similar to the coral heads on the Yellow Bank outside of the town on the big island, there were stretches of beautiful reef in the shallow water, separate from the reefs on the sound side of the island. The pod traveled in smaller groups, never far away from each other, resulting in packs of dolphin becoming socially close to one another.

Phinney was seven years old now, almost fully grown, weighing in at around five hundred pounds. Although she had not been sexually active, she had drawn the attention of males in the pod who made it clear to her that they would be willing partners when she was ready. When she was younger, her mother would intervene when young males became excited in their playfulness, but her mother was not around now as she had been years ago. She had more calves of her own to deal with, and Phinney was pretty much on her own. In fact, she had made this migration with about a dozen of her pod, unaccompanied by her mother.

Spending so much time with a smaller group of dolphin heightened Phinney's social skills. She loved to play with the males and *females, jumping in rotation as they moved through the waves. To an observer, their antics were circus-like and very orchestrated. Her favorite exercise was with her friends in the bow wave of a growling boat, the bigger the better. Matching speed with the boat, they would alternate taking the lead, as first the one on the left would jump over the lead dolphin, becoming the new lead for one jump while being crossed by a dolphin jumping from the opposite side as they dived into the next wave. Their pattern resembled a child's braided pigtail.*

A group could keep this up for long periods of time, alternating back and forth between which would be lead and which would jump. Looking up they could often see humans peering down from the bow rails of the boats shouting their excitement. Getting a human response made the exercise all the more fun. The whining sound of propellers always got the group's attention, as they gauged the speed and distance of an approaching boat, deciding whether it was worth the chase relative to whatever else they might have been doing at the moment. Sometimes they just took turns jumping and turning summersaults, often in competition with one another to see who could go the highest. Phinney and her friends were all playful, and they took advantage of it at every opportunity.

This particular low sun season, Phinney found the males in the group were more playful than other times. They often swam near to her, even touching as they swam in the shallow water. They cut in and around each other, moving for position to rub against her, but she just didn't feel ready for a sexual encounter. Although the males often got quite aggressive with their penises extended from their lower bellies, they always respected her wishes, seemingly enjoying the foreplay as much as what came next.

Phinney had spent so much of her time with Boy, this attention was somewhat unexpected, and she enjoyed being with her traveling companions. Because Phinney was so accustomed to humans, she showed no hesitation when her group occasioned upon the infrequent human diver to sneak up behind and startle the human with a nudge on his torso. The reaction was often enthusiastic, causing the human to thrash about in the funny way Phinney had seen Boy do so many times in the past. When the humans realized Phinney meant no harm, they invariably calmed down. The group also learned that putting on a jumping show for a stopped boat full of fisherman often resulted in baitfish being tossed to them as a reward.

Time passed as the sun rose higher each day. The shallow water became very warm, telling the group that it was time to move back to the big island and the reefs and islands surrounding it. Back in familiar waters, Phinney listened for the distant ring of the bell, but she heard nothing resembling the sound. Frustrated at no sign of Boy, she paid the island where she was born another visit, and then another, and then another.

Finally the older human called for her from the pier as she swam over the bar, motioning for her to join him in the shallow water by the beach. She crossed over as he moved slowly into waist-deep water and kneeled on his skinny legs. Phinney pushed against him as he spoke softly to her and rubbed her brow. She sensed that the older human missed Boy as much as she did, and he sat with her for some time, something he had never done before. They shared the moments until he finally stood and waved his skinny arm to her, bidding farewell. As she passed the end of the dock, the dark-skinned human threw some fish heads to her, which she caught midair and swallowed before the assembly of nurse sharks below were even aware.

The next low sun season brought a new set of adventures for Phinney. Back on the smooth white sands of the shallow bank of the islands to the southeast, she swam and played with her smaller group. This time the young males were more insistent in their pursuit of her. After prolonged periods of foreplay, a large young male enticed her to swim on her side, opening herself to his belly. She could feel his erect penis rub along her lower belly as they moved in unison, their undersides aligned. In a blink of an eye, he penetrated her and began thrusting. Just as she was getting the hang of the simultaneous motion required to keep the two paired, he withdrew and moved off to join the others.

Phinney was well aware of what had just happened, but it was over so fast she didn't know what to think about it. As she was going over the experience in her mind, she was approached by another male who had the same thing on his mind. She tried to focus and pay attention, but again it was over so fast she didn't really have a grasp of it. She felt no emotion, but the physical connection wasn't unpleasant, and by the third time, she found she was quite adept at it, although the social part of the act was all in the foreplay. She vowed to herself that she would make an extended foreplay a requisite.

Her sexual activity seemed to have an effect on the whole group, as dolphins paired and even quartered together moving in unison, touching in every which way, front to back, belly to belly, nibbling on each other's dorsals, then separating and repairing. The water was warm and shallow, and the agitated sand reduced visibility, as the randy mammals choreographed their ballets impromptu among the coral heads.

The days reached their shortest and began the process of lengthening again. When the sun was past its highest, the season brought two savage storms to the great bank. The winds and waves grew steadily. In the night when it was dark Phinney could see the surface of the turbulent water glow with phosphorus excited by the wave action, causing curtains of light to wash among the coral and reflect off the white sand bottom. Of course the storms had no direct effect on her other than making the hunt more difficult as the reef fish scattered to find refuge deep in the rocks forming the reefs at the edge of the sound. The noise was annoying to her as she listened to the heavy surf crashing on exposed parts of the reefs, but the tides were higher than normal, giving her more safety nearer the surface, the prospect of current or waves pushing her against rock or coral minimized.

By the time the sun moved further north, Phinney and her friends moved back to the deeper water near the big island. The thought of Boy drove her to make a pass by the cove, but again she only saw activity on the windward beaches, humans playing at the water's edge, or sailing on one of the tiny boats with white sails. In the lagoon she saw the nurse sharks lazing on the bottom under the pier, waiting for someone to toss fish remains to them from above, but there was no one at the cleaning table. It was early in the day, probably too early for fishermen to have returned from the deep water to clean their fish.

Phinney loitered in the calm water of the cove, tail smacked a mullet over by the barge where her mother had been trapped so long ago, and suddenly developing an appetite, looked for more to eat. She reflected that she was feeding much more than was normal for her. Slowly she began connecting the dots. She was always hungry, her nipples in her mammary slits were tender—in fact, she was tender across the whole area between her pectoral fins—and she felt bloated. Phinney was going to be a mother! She knew it had only been a season or so that she had been sexually active, but the idea that life was growing inside of her gave her a renewed sense of excitement.

She began socializing with other females in the pod around Rose Island, evaluating and selecting one who would be a good birthing companion. They would spend their days together bonding closely, so that Phinney could rely on her companion when the time came for her to deliver her calf. She hoped the calf would arrive before the pod moved south for the low sun season. Of course she could not travel great distances in her condition, but she felt comfortable that her companion would stay with her. The companion she selected was a little older and had already given birth to two, one of which was still young and stayed in the vicinity of her spotted mother. Phinney had already decided that she would deliver her calf in the same lagoon where she was born. She and her spotted companion made familiarization trips to the cove with the young calf in trail. The companion was confused by the apparent relationship Phinney had with some of the humans on land, particularly when she jumped and screeched at the end of the pier and interacted with the humans. She even watched from a distance as Phinney moved into the corner of the lagoon and rested in the shallow water by the crescent beach with the older human and seemingly communicated with him, showing affection. The spotted one would have no part of that, but she was here to help, which she would, but she would keep her distance from them.

Phinney cruised the reefs throughout the high sun days, passing by the cove only very occasionally. As she put on weight with the baby, covering distances was more of a chore for her. As her lower torso filled, she became more and more uncomfortable. As the days grew shorter, seasonal storms moved in earlier than usual and most of her group began the migration southeast without her.

Phinney's spotted companion stayed by her side along with the two-year-old calf, who was not quite ready to be off on his own. Hunting was easy without so much competition for food. As the water became noticeably cooler, the rest of the pod moved out in smaller social groups. As uncomfortable as she was, feeling as though her belly would burst, Phinney actually gained some relief from the lowering water temperatures.

When the days grew very short, Phinney knew her time was near. To make the trek to the cove easier, the threesome moved their center of operations to Salt Cay, cutting the distance to the cove in half. The reefs there were less substantial, but provided more than enough food for them. It was late one night that Phinney felt the need to void herself, which was followed by a cramp, and she knew it was time. Phinney and her spotted companion and calf made their way to the island where Phinney was born, crossed the bar, and entered the cove, moving to the corner by the barge where the water was less gradually shallow. As Phinney kicked, she could feel the calf inside her reposition to her lower midsection, so she continued her kicking motion, pushing her back against the sloping sand when at last she felt the tail flukes emerge. Her companion engaged and tried tugging on the tail until at last the newborn was clear of his mother.

They took turns pushing the little one to the surface while he convulsed reflexively until his blowhole was clear and he began taking in deep gulps of air. Even in his exhaustion, his tail flukes began to move instinctively to help raise himself to the surface. He could not stay submerged for more than a minute before taking in fresh air. Phinney and the spotted dolphin nudged the newborn's pectorals to help keep him on the surface. An exhausted Phinney finally rested and looked over at her calf struggling to breathe and marveled at the thought that she was now a mother with a family of her own to care and provide for.

Phinney raised her calf, a male, just as she herself had been raised. First was a lot of attention to learning to swim and breathe. She nursed the newborn as she had been nursed. As the newborn progressed through the life cycle and began to grow little sharp teeth, Phinney winced as her nipples suffered when the calf suckled with excitement; even though he accessed his mother's milk by curling his tongue around her nipples, sometimes his tiny, new teeth just got in the way. He experimented with solid food, which at first Phinney mushed in her mouth before passing it on to the babe. In time, as the sun cycles came and went, the calf grew stronger and bigger; after two complete sun cycles, the calf was old enough to accompany his mother on the seasonal migration to the white sandy banks of the islands further south.

Phinney identified with a different group, now socializing with other cows and their calves. The young ones kept the older females busy, and there was little opportunity for interaction with libido-driven males.

Phinney devoted herself to her calf for several more seasons and companioned for two other pregnant cows for two more seasons after that. Her first calf was now four years old and quite capable of taking care of himself. Unlike Phinney, he did not seem to have an interest in things human, leaving Phinney to herself for most social activities, including the occasional visit to the cove.

There had been no sign of Boy for many sun cycles, and she had come to accept that he was a part of her growing up from which he had moved on. She rarely visited the cove, having now found out that she was the social center of the young male dolphins once again, not having the continual diversion of newborns and calves to hide behind. Life was good for her.

The memories of Boy were so distant that they became foreign to her. Just occasionally she would come across a young skinny human diving on the reefs around the big island, and she would remember wistfully the days in the sun with her Boy, lying on the warm white sand on her belly, Boy's legs akimbo around her, caressing her, tracing the outline around her snout or rubbing her brow, cupped water cascading over her forehead, speaking to her in those soft low tones. She would watch wistfully from afar just to be certain it was not he.

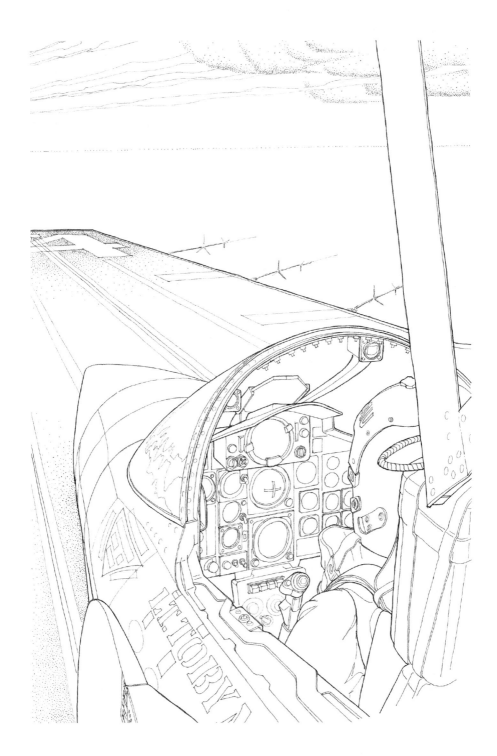

CHAPTER TWELVE

Toby sat with his harness loosened, shoulders hunched over a little to relieve the pain in his lower back from hours of sitting in the cramped cockpit of his F-4B Phantom, on ready three, the catapult dedicated to launch him into combat if required. He wondered to himself how the hell he had gotten there. He had not been assigned a sortie today, but sections of his squadron had launched earlier for a routine bombing mission on Route Pack 3, trying to disrupt troop movement down the Ho Chi Minh trail supplying munitions to the Viet Cong in the south.

It was his turn in the barrel, which meant designated fighter aircraft had to be left behind to defend the carrier group from possible attack or provide other assistance if necessary. It usually meant waiting hours in a ready-to-go position fragged with appropriate missiles for such a defense, with a ground power unit hooked up to supply electricity to the busses powering the instruments and a huffer cart to supply air pressure to spin the J79 engine turbines to sufficient speed for an engine start.

243

Ahead, Toby could see ocean spray kicking up off of the waves carried by a heavy wind from squall lines that were passing through, but none high enough to get over the deep flair of the topsides of the USS *Constellation,* or the "Connie" as the Kitty Hawk class aircraft carrier was known. "Connie" or CV64 was the latest and greatest of the flagships in this battle group, and the officers who were assigned to the Connie felt honored to be included in her company.

Toby was dry, except for the sweat running down his back and between his legs from all the gear he was wearing. He looked at his watch, an hour to go before some other sucker got to take his place in the barrel.

Where's the air conditioning now?! he thought to himself as he remembered the options outlined to him by the Navy recruiters in Gainesville just three and a half years earlier. Upon reflection, they were right about most things. Most of Toby's and Chrissy's friends who graduated with him were now about two hundred miles to the west, shlubbing around in rice paddies and getting shot at to boot.

As planned, Toby had stayed with Chrissy in Gainesville while she finished her nursing degree. The last time he saw Pop was when he made the trip for her graduation and to see his granddaughter, Jenny, then two and a half years old. Chrissy had considered all of her options and finally settled on a position at Shands, the new medical center created out of the University medical school. She had friends and a support base from their years of living in Gainesville. This choice won out over following Toby around for the training portion of his Navy obligation, most of which would preclude her being with him anyway.

Toby had reported to Pensacola at the end of August for admission as a Naval Aviation Officer Candidate. The first two weeks were known as "hell week," during which he was quickly disabused of any thoughts that he was some kind of special wonder boy who was already a qualified pilot, pretty much guaranteed a spot flying jet aircraft. True, he could "Drop On Request," but the next step was an early draft notice. He learned that less than fifty percent got to continue in flight training after they received their commissions, only half of those got to fly jets, and less than twenty percent of those got to fly fighters. Fair enough; Buz and Pat had warned him that if a recruiter's lips were moving he was probably lying.

The treatment was brutal at times, trying to take the individual initiative out of the candidate, so as to instill a team-focused orientation. Ironically, that training had to be reversed later when Toby was entrusted with a twenty-million-dollar piece of machinery for which he was solely responsible. He did endure, however, and in mid-December, he received his commission as an ensign in the United States Navy. He was further comforted to find out he had been selected for flight training.

Toby was given leave for the Christmas holiday after which he reported to Saufley Field, adjacent to Naval Air Station Pensacola, where he spent another four months being trained to fly from scratch, the Navy way, in T-34B Mentors, which were basically Beechcraft Bonanzas with a tandem cockpit and controls and instruments configured as a fighter's would be. He was taught to fly all over again, but to a different standard. His instructor pilots demanded perfection. "You fly plus or minus zero!" one curmudgeon had rasped at him, meaning that if his airspeed was to indicate 130 knots, it meant 130, not 129 or 131.

If Toby performed a maneuver below the acceptable standard, he would often be rewarded with a jab on the back of his flight helmet from his instructor, who could remove his stick controller from the aft cockpit and use it as a weapon. Only later did Toby figure out that this was really a compliment, in that without the stick, the instructor had no means to recover a departure from controlled flight initiated by Toby, should that happen. The instructor pilot would have to have sufficient confidence in his student to remove a required tool of salvation from his arsenal.

Toby learned to fly the Navy way, precisely under stress. He also learned the basics of formation flying. This was a real wake-up call for him the first time he tried to follow a flight lead and maintain a specific reference point off his wing. When he was put in position and given control of the aircraft, suddenly his flight lead started moving erratically up and down.

"Why doesn't he stay in one place?" complained Toby to his instructor over the intercom.

"You're a moron, Matthias! He's flying straight and level. You're the dumb fuck who's moving all over the place. Figure it out or we're retuning to base to let some other schmuck have a crack at being a Navy pilot."

This got Toby's attention. Sure enough, if he took his hand off the stick for a second, the oscillations stopped, but now he was changing positions relative to the flight lead. He started making miniscule adjustments. Eventually he found that if he just kept stirring the stick in minute circular motions he could hold his aircraft steady. Eventually it became second nature.

Toby completed his basic air training in about four months. His experience in flying gave him an edge over the other trainees, not to be a better pilot, but so that he could focus on the finer points of instruction without having to get bogged down in the early stages of the learning curve. When combined with his natural ability to fly, he was more precise and skilled than his peers. He was rewarded with his wings and a slot training in jet fighters.

After a short leave, he was reassigned to Naval Air Station Meridian, training squadron VT-9, where he would begin his introduction to jet aircraft. The Navy trainer was the T-2 Buckeye, a straight-winged jet trainer that was not particularly pleasing to the eye, but a real jet, nonetheless. At Meridian he learned to apply his flying skills to an airplane powered by a turbine engine, capable of speeds far greater than he had experienced before. The engines spooled up slowly, meaning that power was not immediately available for making adjustments, as it was in propeller-driven airplanes. This was compounded by the speeds being so much faster, which meant that the pilot had far less time to prepare for what was coming at him, and a lot of stuff could arrive at the same time in a hurry. Toby learned how to think way ahead of the airplane, so that he could anticipate well enough in advance to deal with situations in an orderly fashion as they arose.

Formation flying became second nature to Toby as he gained seat time. Section takeoffs, where he followed the head nod of the lead pilot for brake release, accelerating alongside and a little behind, were fun for him, and he felt comfortable flying in close proximity to others. The most fun for Toby was the aerobatic and unusual attitudes portion of his training. In the practice area over by Greenwood, Mississippi, the planted fields gave great reference for positioning his aircraft in loops, barrel rolls, split S's, and Immelmanns, starting and ending his maneuvers on corresponding section lines where the varying crops grew. Once, at the top of a loop, Toby ran out of airspeed, because he entered the maneuver too slowly. Inverted, looking down at the rows of corn sixteen thousand feet below him, the Buckeye began to shake violently as the aircraft started to stall. The stick and rudders became mushy, and Toby realized he had no control over the plane as it departed controlled flight.

"Holy shit! What do I do now, Lieutenant?" Toby's voice showed the first lack of confidence, as the plane rolled off on one wing, inverted.

"You got yourself in this mess, so figure it out. I won't be sitting here when you're flying a real fighter next year. You are passing eleven thousand descending at four thousand feet a minute. We're out of here at six," said his instructor pilot abruptly, referring to the mandatory minimum altitude for ejection, "and you're out of a flying job in the Navy."

After another half minute of unsuccessful control adjustments, Toby became really nervous. His instructor volunteered, "Just put your hands on the canopy. You're only making the problem worse."

Toby did as he was told; passing eight thousand feet, the nose dropped and the aircraft rotation slowed, airspeed building. As the plane steadied, Toby resumed his authority over the controls, and things returned to normal just before he reached the mandatory ejection altitude.

"The airplane wants to fly, you moron," came over the intercom. "Sometimes you just get in the way. But let me give you a piece of advice. Have more respect for your airspeed when you start flying high-performance swept wing fighters. They are not at all as forgiving as the Buckeye. You learned a good lesson today. Remember it."

"Yes, sir," was Toby's humble reply.

———— • ◆ • ————

In the heat of the following summer, Toby found himself in Kingsville, Texas, getting his advanced training in high-speed jets. Toby had a little more free time during this period, and Chrissy was able to make several trips to Texas during the fifteen weeks he was there flying the Grumman TF-9 Cougars, a variant of a real Navy fighter.

He learned more of the bombing and air combat side of flying during his time there, and he became carrier qualified. Toby was beginning to experience the humiliation of being judged publically on his flying abilities. Every carrier landing was evaluated by the LSO, the landing signal officer, and his performance was posted showing his ranking against all of the others in his unit. It motivated him to do better and better, but unfortunately, it did the same for the others. To stay the same was to move backward, and he benefited from the precision it brought to his flying. He was constantly reminded of his original instructor's mantra, "Plus or minus nuthin'!"

His next stop was a Replacement Air Group that moved him to the west coast to Miramar, California, where he trained in the McDonnell Douglas F-4B Phantom, the fighter he would take into battle.

Who couldn't like Miramar?

Toby thought he had found heaven. Chrissy took a leave from Shands, and brought Jenny to Southern California. They found an apartment, not much larger than the duplex in Gainesville, and the family spent as much time as they could together. Toby left early every morning for classes on weapons systems and ground school. When the flying began, Toby was not prepared for the power he had to manage, but in time, he adjusted to the speeds and began to out-think the airplane. He did not find the transition to a front-line fighter as difficult as he had imagined. The plane had all the same parts doing the same things as the others he had flown, and transitioning up to higher speeds was an adjustment he already knew how to make.

However, what he did not anticipate was the difficulty of transitioning as a member of a two-man flight crew, wherein he and the radar intercept officer, a non-pilot who operated the airplane's sophisticated navigation and radar systems from the rear seat, pulled together as a team to handle the mission workload of air engagements. At first the arrangement fought against all of Toby's training, which was to act alone and be responsible for his own decisions. In time he learned how to use the additional crewmember as a resource, and he developed an appreciation for the complexities the two of them could handle together that he alone could not.

Following his final four months at Miramar, Toby was assigned to his new squadron, VF-142, shortly after the squadron returned from its first cruise in Vietnam. He would continue his residence in Miramar until the *Constellation* received orders for its next deployment to Southeast Asia, which was anticipated to be in the late spring. He was given the squadron responsibility as airframe maintenance records officer, wherein he was responsible for all of the logbook entries for all of the aircraft in his squadron, making sure they were current and that all required inspections were complied with to ensure that each Phantom was mission ready at all times.

During the next several months he got to know his fellow pilots and support personnel as they initiated him into the fraternity. His associations prepared him for what he could expect aboard ship after his tour started. As his fellow pilots got to know and accept him in their ranks as a nugget, or new member, the subject of a call sign was discussed. After learning that he grew up on an Out Island in the Bahamas, it took no time for the squadron leaders to settle in on "Nassau" as his new call sign, replacing his training call sign, "Trademark," which was derived from his initials. It reminded Toby of his years at Flagler, and he kind of liked it.

In May 1967, Toby shipped out to the *Constellation* at Yankee Station in the South China Sea and began flying missions in Vietnam. Midway through his cruise, his squadron was informed that the tour was going to be extended another four months. Toby hoped he would be home in time for Christmas; it would be close.

Now as the holiday approached, Toby reflected on the blur of his last three years. He and all of the other pilots in his squadron would never say it aloud, but each felt he was a shit-hot fighter pilot, the fiercest of modern-day warriors. All of the confidence notwithstanding, all any of them could think of after giving a thumbs up and salute to the catapult officer, head back against the seat restraint, throttles full forward waiting for the force of the steam launch was, *Dear Lord, please don't let me fuck up!*

"Nassau, your duty time is almost up. Wingnut is coming out to relieve you," cackled over the earphones in his helmet. Toby looked up and spotted Cunningham and Burkman crossing the flight deck toward the airplane.

"Boomer, you copy?" Toby asked his back-seater over the intercom.

"I'm already unhooked," came the reply.

Toby signaled for the ground crew to pull the boarding extension struts so they could climb down to the flight deck. As they walked over to do that, Toby disconnected his oxygen, belts, and restraints and stood carefully on his seat, stretching his back, which was aching from the upright position he had been maintaining for the last several hours. After he replaced all six pins in his ejection seat, tied together on a single red chord, he put the red "REMOVE BEFORE FLIGHT" placard on the side of the headrest.

As they climbed over the canopy rails and placed their feet in the footholds, beginning the climb eight feet down to the deck, sections of their squadron began circling overhead for the recovery operation about to commence. Toby and Boomer exchanged friendly vulgarities with Cunningham and Burkman as they climbed aboard to replace them, reversing the process.

Toby and Bruce Holecek, his radar intercept officer, stowed their gear in the locker room and joined the returning pilots in the ready room for the debrief. It was not required of him, but showed a sign of respect for the aviators who had been in harm's way. Toby was of the opinion that he learned more in the debrief than any other segment of a sortie. The debrief was the venue for each of the pilots to come clean and volunteer any contributions he may have made to a screw-up, before it was brought to his attention by anybody else.

Seldom did a pilot have to be told of a mistake. If it happened more than once or twice, that person had a problem with the rest of his squadron. Pilots who flew in combat in pairs had to have complete trust in one another, and there was no room for a pilot who couldn't own up to his own shortcomings. Today had been a typical mission, considered by operations a successful one. They had skillfully dropped a lot of bombs on some trees and "suspected" truck parks along the border with Laos and provided some air cover for some A-6's returning from another bombing mission.

"Anybody see any MiGs?" was always asked by someone in the room. None had been seen, which was not uncommon. The pilots were all eager to bag a MiG, not thinking that it might be the other way around.

The debrief finished with a caution that intel indicated a squadron of new MiG-21's had been sent to the North Vietnamese by the Russians, possibly even flown by Russian pilots. Any such sightings were to be formally reported at any debrief.

When Toby got in side discussions with other fighter pilots about "bagging a MiG," all he thought about was killing another person. The idea of the competition against another airplane did get his adrenaline flowing. Air-combat maneuvers were his favorite training activity. If he was attacked, then that was something else again. Afterward, he worked his way to the forward mess for a cup of coffee, and then crossed back to the hangar deck to review maintenance records. He was working long days, sometimes sixteen hours, and tomorrow he was scheduled to fly two sorties, and he still had a bunch of paperwork to catch up on.

———— • ◆ • ————

It was still dark when Toby awakened to the banging and rattling of the steam catapults. He dressed in his flight suit, got some breakfast in the forward mess, grabbed his flight gear, and settled in his chair in the ready room just as the others arrived. He was briefed on two missions for the day. He would have to recover aboard the carrier, hot fuel, which meant refueling without shutting down the engines, and launch for the second sortie without a break. The first was a combat air patrol over the western shore of the gulf that concluded without incident. No enemy aircraft that could pose a threat to the fleet were sighted or seen on radar. The second proved a little more exhilarating.

Two sections were tasked with providing air support to a group of A-6 attack aircraft assigned a bombing mission in route pack 6B, surrounding Haiphong Harbor, which was heavily defended by surface-to-air missiles and triple A, antiaircraft fire, as well as air cover provided by MiGs. Toby's job was to precede the attacking bombers to clear the airspace of the threat of any MiGs, and attempt to destroy SAM sites that were foolish enough to try to radar lock the incoming attackers. He was the wingman in the lead element; as such, he would provide cover for his flight lead as well as backup to defend against any MiGs that would attempt pursuit of his flight lead.

They flew at twenty-seven thousand feet, or angels ten, meaning ten thousand feet above the prearranged coded base altitude of the day, which was seventeen thousand feet. This confused enemy eavesdroppers as to what altitude an operation was using when U.S. communications were intercepted by the North Vietnamese.

Toby and his flight lead, call sign Buick, flew in a "loose deuce" separated about a thousand yards, Toby higher and a little behind as they crossed the shoreline over the harbor.

"Feet dry," Buick announced. As they began a wide arc around the target area at three hundred knots indicated, the A-6's began their bombing runs into a thin undercast developing from the moist air moving in off the cooler water of the harbor.

"Two," Toby acknowledged. As the A-6's began their bombing runs beneath them, Toby could see the explosions of antiaircraft fire below him, as the A-6's peeled off from their echelon formations to align with their targets. He could see them jink left and right to make it more difficult for the antiaircraft gunners to anticipate their positions. It wasn't terribly effective as a defense, but better than lining up like fairground target ducks.

Boomer's voice came over the intercom and element frequency. "I've got one ten o'clock, ten miles climbing, closing fast," he called to Toby and Buick.

Scanning the horizon ahead, Toby saw the flash of morning sun off a metal fuselage as it climbed through the thin stratus layer of cloud below them. "I have a visual."

"Tally," Buick chimed in. "Can you identify the model?"

"He's closing fast, about ten miles a minute. He'll be behind us by the time he gets up here."

As the MiG neared the formation, Toby moved behind a little, and he had a better position to keep the visual contact. Straining in his belts, he craned his neck to the fullest, just getting a good view as the MiG climbed behind and initiated a turn toward them. He saw the distinctive delta wing and long narrow fuselage, accented by the cone in the front of the engine intake. There was no question about it. "It's a twenty-one, for sure, Buick."

"Okay. He's got altitude and he is going to turn in on us. Let's be patient and see which one he goes after. I'm going to break left. If he is smart he will follow you. You know the routine."

Buick broke hard left, while Toby pitched up and started a less abrupt turn to keep the MiG in sight. The MiG pilot made a poor decision to turn very tightly to follow Buick, who was in a hard turn away from them. The MiG tried to out turn Buick, another mistake, which allowed Toby to pitch up and barrel roll, reversing direction. As the horizon came into view, he was above and behind the MiG. His altitude gave him an energy advantage, whereas the MiG was bleeding off speed rapidly pulling Gs in his turn. Even with the tactical advantage, Toby was impressed with the MiG-21's agility and turning radius, and its power enabling it to keep its speed up far better than Buick's Phantom with the ever-increasing G load.

"Talk to me, Nassau!" came Buick's strained voice, breathing hard from the Gs. "I'm in the blind here."

"He's trying to out turn you. Succeeding. I've got a firing solution. Fox two!" With that Toby selected his Sidewinder, heat-seeking missile. He looked away as it dropped from the left-wing pylon, expecting to avoid the sight-limiting flash as the rocket ignited. There was no flash. Toby looked down over the canopy rail to see the missile tumble harmlessly down and away from the aircraft. "Mother fucker! It's a dud!"

Boomer saw this, too. "I knew this was going too well," he said over the intercom.

Toby reselected and got a tone that his other Sidewinder had a lock. He loosed it. "Fox two." This time he watched it drop and, to his relief, ignite, streaking ahead toward the MiG. In seconds he watched the smoke trail track the unsuspecting MiG and fly right up its tailpipe. The MiGs fuselage seemed to swell momentarily at impact, almost like a balloon, and then erupt into a fireball. There was no ejection or parachute, as the whole of the airplane was consumed in the explosion. Toby and Boomer watched as the debris plunged earthward and disappeared through the undercast.

"You're clear, Buick," Toby radioed.

"Roger, Nassau. Good work. Buick has the lead, right turn rejoin, Angels fifteen."

Toby started a turn to the right, inside of Buick, and slowed to three hundred fifty knots for the rejoin. Back on Buick's wing, Toby saw the lead Phantom yaw, so he moved out to a loose tactical position, as they moved back over the harbor to continue providing cover for the returning A-6's.

As Toby approached the Connie for the overhead approach, he

noticed that his legs were shaking from the knees, and his heart was pounding from adrenaline. It took all his concentration to align the landing position lights, and he felt like he was all over the place with varying speed and position. He was greatly relieved when the LSO didn't wave him off, and he barely managed to snag the four wire, not to his standards but safely aboard. He followed his shutdown procedure and just sat in the cockpit, trying to settle his nerves before climbing down to the deck.

Word traveled quickly around the squadron. Everyone was high-fiving Toby to congratulate him on bagging his first MiG. He couldn't enter a room on the ship without receiving a standing ovation. He was treated as though he had just won a popularity contest, but that didn't match the melancholy he felt as he recalled the fireball engulfing the aircraft he had just shot down and realized that the pilot had not been able to eject safely.

He was proud of his performance, that he had followed his training protocol to textbook perfection. If the bogey follows the lead, the wingman moves in behind, if he follows the wingman, the plan is reversed for the lead to turn in on the bogey. His head knew he had done well, but his heart thought it was too easy, not deserved.

His squadron commander promoted him to flight lead for the remainder of the cruise, which was only another month or so. Toby was no longer considered a nugget, and he was valued as an experienced combat veteran with almost six hundred missions in his first tour.

During the last month of his cruise, the sorties were limited to bombing and ground support below the twentieth parallel by order of Lyndon Johnson, the President of the United States. Toby found the missions were becoming routine. On advice of his commanding officer, he stepped up his vigilance, so as not to fall into complacency with the resulting consequences of becoming a statistic of the war. The Connie had flown more than eleven thousand missions and dropped over twenty thousand tons of ordinance, losing fifteen aircraft, none of which were due to enemy action. Six flying crewmembers had been lost, and three had fallen into enemy hands. Toby had no intention of becoming one of those unfortunates due to letting down his guard just because he was not flying as far north as he had earlier in his tour. At the end of January, the Connie received orders to leave the operating theater for San Diego for refit, and Toby was on his way home.

———— •◆• ————

About two hundred miles off the Southern California coast, Toby's squadron left the carrier for the last time, returning to Miramar. He was now an accomplished combat veteran entitled to shore leave. Chrissy got another leave from Shands, where she was now an experienced ICU nurse, and surprised him at the base when he arrived. They had three weeks together, so Chrissy suggested a family cross-country trip in her new Chevy convertible, finishing in Florida where they could visit Pop before Toby had to head back to his squadron.

Jenny, now quite the young lady having just turned six, was enthusiastic about the chance to miss some classes at the University-run grammar school. The first night they spent in the trendy local motel near the base. After burgers at the local diner, Jenny watched some TV in the room while Toby and Chrissy squeezed in a padded lounge chair by the pool.

"She's gotten so big," Toby remarked when they snuggled together, arms around each other. As they caressed, Toby began trying to work out the arrangements in his mind, not liking the conclusions he was coming to. "Why didn't you get her her own room, Kiki?"

"She's only six!" she replied. "She'll be fine on the pullout."

"How soon will she fall asleep?" Toby asked, starting to get aroused as his hips pushed against her.

They continued necking and caressing for a while, when Chrissy volunteered, "We'll work it out, don't worry."

Relieved that they were on the same page, Toby relaxed and enjoyed the moment holding his precious wife in his arms. They repositioned themselves more comfortably and gazed at the Milky Way above them.

Toby thought for a moment and spoke. "You know, dear, sometimes on a night like this at high altitude when I am not busy making war, I turn off all the ambient light in the cockpit, instruments and everything, and surrounded by blackness I look up at the stars. You couldn't imagine the sight from above most of earth's atmosphere. The stars are soooo bright, ten times what we see in the Bahamas, even. I wish you could be there to see it."

Chrissy planted a wet erotic kiss on him and, holding him fiercely close, whispered in his ear, "I think we have been out here long enough. I'm sure Jenny is asleep by now, and she sleeps like the dead."

The two moved off the lounge and ambled arm in arm to the first-floor room; their lips never parted.

They left in the morning with the top down, enjoying the sunny day. It got cooler in the mountains, so the top of the convertible was exercised constantly as warranted. They took four days of leisurely travel to reach the panhandle of Florida where Toby had started officer candidate school over three years ago. Pensacola looked unchanged as they passed through.

Nearing the barn, Toby assumed most of the driving responsibilities as they sped, top up for relief from the wind, down the length of the state to Fort Lauderdale where Vernon was waiting at the apartment to greet them. As they walked across the loggia by the pool at Pop's co-op, he spotted them and came out to welcome them.

Toby was shocked to see the toll the last few years had taken on his grandfather. Vernon had lost a lot of weight, almost all of his hair, but not his warm smile. He came forward and wrapped his huge arms around Toby and gave him the bear hug of his life. "What a stud you turned out to be, young man." Vernon would not release his hold. Toby felt his grandfather's shoulders shake, and he knew the embrace was concealing his anguish and emotion from exposing his weakening condition to his grandson. "My God; I'm almost bald, and I still have more hair than you have," he said referring to Toby's "wash and wear" buzz cut and trying to deflect attention from his display of emotion.

As his grandfather relaxed his hold, Toby averted his eyes, so that Pop could not see the shock on his face. He turned to Chrissy to help her with a small bag, and remarked over his shoulder, "But at least I can grow mine back out," giving back some of the sarcasm he had learned over the years. The awkwardness of the moment passed in the blink of an eye.

"Get your things inside and let's sit down and catch up. Jenny, sweetheart, you can swim in the pool if you want. Chrissy, love, take the guestroom. I have the convertible sofa in the living room made up for Jenny. Come, come, come inside!" he urged them along.

After Toby got what they needed out of the car, they all settled in the living room, Toby and Pop with beers and Chrissy with an iced tea. Toby couldn't help noticing that his grandfather's legs looked a little swollen, and he had a blister on his foot where his flip-flop had been rubbing.

Toby had always been direct with his grandparents, and his candor was only hardened by his time in Vietnam where communication was so important and failure to achieve it can cost lives. "What's going on with you, Pop? I hear you're not spending as much time at the inn as you used to. Are you all right?"

"Things are as they appear, Toby. I have been diagnosed with a pulmonary heart condition. My heart is not as efficient as it should be to remove fluids from my body. That's why my legs swell up. The doctors feel I should not be too far away from medical care, so I spend a majority of my time here. I do need to keep it to less than one hundred eighty days, depending on who's asking, for tax reasons."

"Forget the taxes, Pop. Are you at risk?" Toby asked.

"I'm seventy-seven with a weak heart. What do you think? Of course I'm at risk, but I get by."

"I just worry about you, s'all."

"I'm sure you do. You think I didn't worry about you in Vietnam? Give me a break!" Vernon snapped.

"Hey, gents; we're here to reconnect, remember," Chrissy admonished. "I'm just glad we can all be together again. If you feel up to it, I have a great idea. Jenny would love to see the floor show at the Mai Kai, and so would I. Toby, you never took me there, and I know you've been. What do you say, Pop? Could you handle one of those mystery drinks?"

"Not a bad idea, Chrissy. The alcohol would make a good diuretic, don't you think? What's your professional opinion? I'll even be traveling in the company of a hot, professional nurse. How could you beat that?"

Later at the Mai Kai, Jenny watched the dancers perform with sharp blades and fire, and when it came time for picking some poor slob out of the audience to join the hula dancers onstage for a humiliating exhibition, Vernon became the obvious choice thanks to his proximity to the stage. He had slipped the maître d' twenty dollars for a good table, so he could impress his great-granddaughter. He was none too reticent after more than his fair share of the famous mystery drink that he ordered for the table, for medicinal purposes, of course.

———— •◆• ————

After two weeks of showing Jenny touristy things and reminiscing, which, once again, included embarrassing moments from

Toby's younger years, the four Matthiases gathered for a farewell in the parking lot in front of the apartment building. Toby and his grandfather embraced for the longest time; Vernon was unable to release his hold on Toby. His shoulders shook as before. "I can't tell you how proud I am of you, your choices, and the way you have conducted your life. God bless you and your beautiful family. I think of you every day." He finally let go.

Toby could see the dampness on Pop's cheeks. He knew better than to devalue his grandfather's emotion by saying something trite, that they would get together again soon, or some other such cliché. Toby knew in his heart that it was possible he would never see Pop again, and it pained him to his core. He turned his head away as they climbed in the car, Chrissy driving while Toby took Jenny in his lap, hiding behind her so as not to reveal his tears for his grandfather to see.

Chrissy backed out of the parallel spaces silently, taking Oakland Park to A1A and turning south toward the airport where Toby would take connecting flights back to San Diego. Halfway she asked, "When will you know your separation date?"

Toby reflected for a minute. "They will tell me when I get back. The Connie won't go back to Vietnam for probably six months. My obligation for active duty is finished before I have to start another cruise, so if they want me back in Vietnam, they will have to reassign me to another squadron, which is unlikely. What usually happens is a reassignment to an active reserve unit while I am finishing my stateside rotation."

"So, you don't have to go back?" Chrissy asked for clarity.

"Probably not."

"I think Jenny and I should stay in Gainesville until you know what your future plans are, so we don't have to uproot her twice. Is that okay with you?"

"Yes, I think it's best." agreed Toby.

"I'm sorry about Pop," she volunteered. "I'll keep checking on him while you're at Miramar."

"I appreciate that, honey." Toby found it difficult to carry on the conversation any further.

They pulled up to the curb at National Airlines. Amid the construction of a new terminal, the family pulled together for a group hug, kisses, and goodbyes. Toby waved from the Jetway stairs as he climbed to the airplane door, and blew kisses to Chrissy and Jenny, whose distorted face he could see pressed against the departure lounge window in caricature fashion, tongue and nose flattened comically. He sat in his seat on a half-full airplane and again when he changed in Dallas for Southern California. Most of the trip was spent in quiet contemplation about his grandfather, frustrated that there was nothing he could do to help. He sensed that Pop would be heading to the islands before long to await the inevitable at Piper Cay where he called home and where the love of his life smiled from the depths as curtains of wavy light danced on her memorial through a hole in the reef.

———— •◆• ————

Toby settled in with his routine in a stateside-based squadron. He still flew regularly in training at the fighter weapons school where he was brought up to date with the latest technology and findings from what had been learned in the Vietnam conflict. His reputation as a shit-hot jock followed him to Miramar. He was one of only four who had shot down a MiG in Southeast Asia, and the only one to have brought down a MiG-21 from the carrier USS *Constellation*.

Toby was informed that his scheduled separation date was being moved up to May, or about halfway through his stateside tour. As the date approached, Toby was asked to report to CAG, the former commander of his air group. At fourteen hundred hours, he arrived promptly at Commander Hodgson's office curious as to what he had done wrong, the usual reason for a request of an audience.

"Sit down, Lieutenant," the expressionless air boss offered.

"Thank you, sir," Toby responded.

"Don't worry, son," the commander continued, sizing up the young fighter pilot seated before him, carefully watching how Toby reacted to being called to his office. "You're not in trouble. Quite the contrary."

"Oh?"

"You joined the Navy as a ninety-day wonder, probably to meet your military obligation, I presume, correct?"

"Yes, sir. Job offers when I got out of college were not forthcoming to people like me."

"Your record while on active duty has been exemplary, as I'm sure you're aware."

Toby amended, "I've applied myself to my responsibility with good results, I think."

The commander appreciated that Toby wasn't full of false modesty; he liked that. "I think you know that, so here's the deal. We have been watching you, evaluating your leadership skills as well as your talent as a pilot. So, I have a proposition for you. We would like to offer you a career position in the Navy. We are starting a new program here at Miramar, separate from the fighter weapons school, to be known as Top Gun. The new program is designed to train our more skilled and experienced pilots in the lessons we have learned in Vietnam by putting them through an intense flying program. The bigger plan is for these pilots to take the skills they develop here back to their squadrons to improve the overall effectiveness in air-to-air combat. As you know, we have suffered far more losses pro rata in Vietnam than we did in Korea, and we in the Navy feel it is attributable to training, not equipment. What's your take on that?"

"As a Phantom pilot, sir, I would generally agree, except for the obvious problem with the rules of engagement that prohibit us from using the missile technology we have to our advantage, and the need for guns in the Phantom, which we lack. We outperform all of the older Russian equipment, except for the MiG-21, which we can outrun. I personally think that if our pilots can learn to use more vertical maneuvering as opposed to trying to out turn a more agile airplane, we can still achieve superiority."

"That's exactly what we believe. We would like to offer you a position in that school as an instructor pilot. You would be up for lieutenant commander within two years."

"Sir, I'm flattered. I have not given a career any consideration prior to this. Could I have some time to think about it, talk it over with my family and such?"

"You have until your separation to make a decision, but the sooner the better. Once you become a reservist, this option is no longer available."

"I understand, sir. Thank you for the opportunity. Frankly, I don't know how I was going to give up flying fighters. I don't fancy flying for an airline." Toby stood, saluted, and shook hands.

As he walked out the door of Hodgson's office, the senior officer felt confident he had Toby hooked.

Toby got in his VW Bug, and headed off to the bachelor officers' quarters. On the way to his room he picked up his mail and sat down to think about the issues that had been placed before him. He decided to call Chrissy in the evening when she got off work to discuss his new development. He reached the nanny on the first couple of calls, leaving word that he would try later. This was not uncommon. Chrissy's shifts did not always end on schedule, her father being kind enough to supplement their income for a nanny, so that Chrissy's schedule wouldn't make her a slave to Jenny's needs.

With the absence of Toby, mother and daughter were extremely close, spending much of their free time together. Jenny was beginning to socialize more regularly with friends her age now that she had started first grade. In any event, the family was reassured that Jenny would always have a secure place to come home after her day's activities. The nanny was a married graduate student in the nursing college, so she was reliable and valued the opportunity to work with children.

Toby made his calls from the payphone in the BOQ, not the most private place on the base, but others made allowances to officers who were engaged in domestic conversations, allowing an environment for intimacy when required.

He finally got through around four o'clock. Chrissy was excited to hear from him, but Toby could tell she was distracted, not really focused on the details of the offer extended to him earlier in the day.

Finally she interrupted him. "Honey, I had a call at work from the nanny just after you called. She said Herbert was trying to reach you from Piper Cay, saying it was important. I didn't know how to reach you; the base said you were in a meeting, but that you had left. I tried to call him, but I wasn't able to get through. I know Pop went back there last week. I hope it's not bad news."

"Oh, no. Let's finish this conversation later. It's almost seven thirty there now, and the lines won't be as busy. I'll try him from here, and let you know what I find out. Love you!"

"Love you, too. I'll give Jenny a hug from you. Goodbye."

Toby was embarrassed that he didn't think of his daughter; he always asked about her when he called home, but this business of a call from the island left him unsettled, and he feared the worst. He got the operator on the line and placed a third-party call to the inn. It was easier than fumbling for quarters he didn't have at hand. He couldn't imagine his phone bill at home with all the charges to it. The department of the Navy didn't take kindly to personal use of the base phone system; however, Chrissy never mentioned it in their conversations. He finally got through after 8:00 p.m. Bahamian time. A staff person Toby didn't recognize fumbled the phone when he announced who he was. After a shuffle and delay, Herbert came on the line. There was some static, but the heaviness of his voice was clear.

"Toby, I'm so, so sorry, buddy. Your grandfather passed this afternoon. He was sitting peacefully in a chaise on the veranda, sipping an iced tea, looking out over the lagoon, and he just fell asleep. We didn't know anything was wrong until my mom tried to wake him for dinner. Guests passed by him and didn't even notice; he was that peaceful. No sign of a struggle or anything. I don't know what to say." Herbert broke down in sobs. "He was so good to me and my family. Hell, we *were* family! I am so sorry for you."

Toby was just stunned. He felt sadness, of course, but his overriding emotion gave way to the clinical. What kind of service was planned and when? Would he and Chrissy be able to make it? Who was in charge of the operations of the inn, looking after guests, etc.? Could he get leave, and what was the process? All these things were running through his mind, as he realized there was nothing he could do now, as it was five in the afternoon and eight on the east coast. He would have all night to deal with his emotions, with no answers for his questions until morning.

He called Chrissy back to give her the news. It was when he said the actual words that the tidal wave overtook him. His shoulders slumped and he pressed his forehead on the wall by the payphone, trying to shut out the world around him as he blubbered what he could manage to his wife. Doors opened up and down the hallway with faces peering out and retreating as Toby's fellow officers witnessed his pain. Those close to him knew a little about the circumstances, and from the bits they overheard, it wasn't too hard to connect the dots.

Word spread quickly around the base. Chrissy volunteered to act as an intermediary, following up with Herbert. She suggested that since they were the only remaining family, they could make whatever arrangements they wanted. Toby agreed and asked her to use her best judgment to work out the details with Herbert. He said he would try to arrange leave in the morning.

Toby was up early to get to his office in the maintenance records facility where he would have access to a phone and make contact with the administrative offices, which could tell him what he had to do to apply for a hardship leave. When he got to his desk, there was a message waiting for him to report to his commanding officer, Lieutenant Commander Brubaker, a career man who started flying Banshees in the Korean conflict.

He welcomed Toby with a sympathetic smile. "I figured you would be wanting to see me this morning, so I thought I would save you the trouble. I'm sorry to learn of your loss. I know your grandparents played a significant role in your upbringing. Let me know what you need in terms of leave, and I'll make it happen for you."

Toby was surprised that word had gotten around so fast. He hadn't spoken with anyone last night, preferring instead to be alone in his room examining his feelings. He guessed correctly that he had been observed on the phone. His closer shipmates knew of his grandfather's failing condition, so it all made sense. He received permission to use the base phones to make some calls to family.

Toby started with Chrissy, who was at home, having swapped shifts so she could get engaged in the planning. Toby became emotional again as soon as he heard her voice. They agreed that they would need to rely on Herbert to make funeral arrangements; otherwise, the family would have to make preparations to ship Pop's body home, since he was still an American citizen. Vernon had always made it clear that he wanted to be cremated and his ashes spread in the same waters as his beloved Irene. Herbert joined in an operator-assisted conference call and confirmed that Sawyer's Funeral Home could handle the arrangements in about three days after Mr. Matthias's passport could be located and surrendered for diplomatic paperwork requirements.

This was Wednesday, April 9, 1969. Herbert estimated that he could get notice out for a service to be held on the island the following Sunday, if Toby felt he could be at Piper Cay by that time. Toby said he was confident he could. Toby said he had talked to Mr. Tylander, Vernon's attorney in Nassau, who would be available to go over legal matters in the days after the service. Herbert said he would make the arrangements for all of Vernon's friends in the area to receive notice of his passing and an invitation to attend a small memorial service at the inn on Sunday. Chrissy had already been in touch with a few acquaintances she was aware of, particularly Clement, who said he was at their disposal to help with transportation.

Herbert took a minute to ask Toby to begin consideration of his plans for the inn, as he felt sure that Vernon would have left the decision in his hands. He assured Toby that everything was under control for the time being. All guests' needs and expectations were being met. Naturally the staff needed some guidance so they could make their own plans for the future.

Toby said he would be thinking about it. They agreed to talk again later in the day. Toby requested an audience with Commander Brubaker, and requested two weeks to attend the funeral and make arrangements for dealing with matters of his grandfather's estate. He was asked if he had made a decision regarding the position he had been offered.

"Not yet, sir. As you can imagine, this turn of events changes everything for me, and I need to see what I am getting into when I get home before I can make an informed decision."

Brubaker gave Toby a compassionate look. "Let me make this simple for you. I am going to put a request in for an early separation from active military service. When you get back in two weeks, you will only have a month until your scheduled release. The morning report will reflect that you are relieved of your duty assignment effective midnight tonight. Take your two weeks. If you decide the Navy is your future, report back to me on the twenty-fourth of the month. If I don't see you, I will take that as your answer. I don't need to tell you a lot of people have gone out of their way to make this opportunity available to you. We think you are good career material. If you decide it is not for you, we wish you the best for your future. The Navy thanks you for your service."

They shook hands, and Toby left to make plans to return home.

CHAPTER THIRTEEN

Toby sat on the end of the pier, his legs dangling over the edge as he finished telling Jenny about his adventures with Phinney.

Jenny was enthralled, as she always was, to hear about the dolphin her daddy grew up with after saving its mom. "Did I ever get to meet Phinney?" she asked, knowing already that the answer was no.

"No, honey. You know you didn't, but you've heard the story so many times before that it might feel like you met her."

"I remember you told me the last time you saw Phinney was when you and Mom got married."

"That's right; we spent most of our honeymoon together. She has been back in the cove, though. G Pop and Major used to see her from time to time when she visited, probably looking for me. Hasn't been by in a few years, I'm told. You were at the island when you were a baby, but Phinney had moved south for the winter, so we didn't see her. . . . Come on, Punkin'; it's time to go inside and join the others."

"Okay, Daddy, but can we ring the bell tomorrow and see if Phinney comes?"

"Sure thing, darlin'," Toby responded, knowing that the probability was remote at best.

He pulled his legs under him and stood, knees crunching at the effort. He and Jenny moved down the dock to the solemn gathering on the veranda. Earlier, Toby had led a moving service for his friends and family. He spoke of the strength he had gained from his grandfather, Chrissy spoke of the kind and welcoming man who took her in when others in her family were less than accepting of her choices, and Herbert spoke of a man who treated him like family, seeing that he got an education, so he could make a place for himself in the world.

After the ceremony, those attending approached Toby and Chrissy individually to express their sadness upon learning that Vernon had left them. The mood was somber, but before long, the guests began remembering stories from years past, and the room filled with occasional outbursts of laughter.

At first there was some discomfort until Toby laughed heartily at a story about his grandfather dumping his grandmother in the ocean when he took off on the powerboat before Irene could secure the dinghy line to the cleat on the back of the cruiser. She knew she couldn't hold on, but she didn't want to suffer Vern's wrath by just letting the thing go, so she jumped in the water with it. It proved a tension breaker for everyone.

As the sun set, Toby offered cottages to those who wanted to spend the night, while Major and Herbert took the others in to the city docks in Nassau. Bob Tylander, Vernon's attorney, agreed to stay the night so that they could begin a discussion of estate matters in the morning. Everyone on the island went to bed early in preparation for a busy day tomorrow.

———— • ◆ • ————

Toby was up early, before the sun. He sat on the beach on the windward side of the island among the sun lounges and umbrella stands. Chrissy heard him stirring and joined him, entwining arms with his as they sat on the chilled sand and watched the brilliant red globe emerge above the horizon. Slowly it revealed itself as a round ball, seemingly many times the size it appeared during the day. Toby never tired of watching the circle form perfectly still touching the horizon, until it separated with an almost audible pop as a small tear stayed behind and disappeared. Slowly the globe ascended, turning more brightly white as it seemed to shrink perceptibly with each degree of elevation. When it established itself firmly in the sky, they kissed and smiled at each other.

"What are you thinking?" Chrissy asked.

"I'm thinking I miss this, I love you and Jenny, and I love these islands. I'm thinking that the thought of staying here is selfish," replied Toby.

"What do you mean?"

"Well, you know, it's crossed my mind. I'm sure Bob Tylander is about to tell us that Pop left all this to me, and if he did that, it must have been on his mind for me to keep this operation going."

Chrissy thought a moment, then said, "You don't know that at all; you haven't a clue what would have been on his mind. Why would it matter, anyway? So what if he did?"

"That it's not fair to you or Jenny. These islands are changing. They will probably be independent in the next few years. A sovereign nation, you know, and who knows what that will bring, with the lack of ties to Mother England. Even Pop figured out it was no place to raise me; that's why he shipped me off to Flagler."

Chrissy feigned offense and punched him hard in the shoulder. "You're suggesting that didn't work out so well for you, are you?"

"You very well know what I mean. And ow! That really hurt!"

"Good!" Chrissy smiled.

"This is a real opportunity, once in a lifetime, in the Navy. We would get to live in a home, settled for a change, and I would get to keep flying, only without anyone shooting at me. I would be able to retire in my mid-forties."

"Slow down, Mario. I think it's a little early to start thinking about retirement. Let's just wait and see what the next few days bring. I think by this time next week, our path will be clear to us. It will be based on what we know, and not what we think we know."

Toby pondered this for a moment. "You know, Kiki, sometimes I get really sick of your sensible good judgment. Let's go in for breakfast and see what Tylander has to say."

Toby and Chrissy stood and walked back to the inn and the dining room where they were joined by the few who stayed over. After breakfast they said their goodbyes at the dock. Those who hadn't brought their own transportation boarded the Chris Craft to be taken to the big island by Herbert.

Bob Tylander suggested they assemble at 9:30 in the library where they could have some privacy. On schedule, Ossie brought a pot of fresh coffee and cups stacked on a tray to the library room, which was really just a glorified reading lounge overlooking the beach. It was a cozy room with green-and-white floral print fabrics on white lacquered wicker furniture. She set the tray on the large coffee table centered in the room. At Tylander's suggestion, Herbert was asked to join them. Bob began with a preamble.

———— • ◆ • ————

While the family was engaged in family matters in the library, Jenny set about figuring how to find Phinney if she was still around. She got a produce box from the kitchen and set it on the dock next to the piling under the brass ship's bell. When she climbed up on it, she could reach inside and feel the clapper and the shaft attaching it to the pin inside the bell at the top. She could not get the clapper to move, so corroded was it from years of salt air and lack of use.

Major watched her from the seawall as she explored the inner workings of the bell. He was fascinated with her determination. He walked out to her on the dock.

"Miss Jenny, can I be of help to you?" he offered.

"I want to ring the bell. I want to call Phinney, but I can't get the ringer to move," she whined in frustration. "Can we put oil on it or something?"

Major decided to humor her and got an oil tin from the tool room behind the kitchen.

"Can I do that for you, Miss Jenny?" he asked when he returned.

"No thank you, Major. I want to do it myself. Show me how to do it."

Major showed Jenny how to press the bottom of the oilcan to push oil out the end of the spout. After he showed her how to put oil on the pin from the outside of the bell, she covered the area lavishly.

"The problem, Miss Jenny, is dat most of the corrosion is on da inside, but you can't put da oil there without taking it down, 'cause da oil won't squirt up. Try to work the ringer back and forth and see if it will loosen up."

Major let her work the clapper for a few minutes. She was successful in getting it to move back and forth, but not free enough to ring the bell. Major watched her struggle. Finally realizing she was not going to give up, he volunteered.

"You know, Miss Jenny, there's more than one way to make dat bell ring."

"What other way is there?"

"You could try a hammer."

"Good idea, Major. Do you have a hammer?"

"I know where dere is one. I'll get it foh ya." Major ambled off to the tool room to get a hammer and returned with a medium-sized ball peen. He handed it to her and helped her back up on the box.

"Use two hands and hit the bell right in the middle as hard as you can. If dat girl's around here, she gonna hear it."

———— •◆• ————

The interested parties assembled, and Bob Tylander began, "Before we get into your granddad's will, Toby, I need to set some ground rules for what we can talk about. This situation is complicated in that your grandfather was a U.S. citizen, and therefore subject to some U.S. legislation, estate taxes being the primary example, although he was essentially exempt from income taxes there because he resided outside of the country. He is also considered a resident of the Bahamas for our purposes locally, which provides him some protection from U.S. inquiry, for all intents and purposes. The bottom line is that I am representing you as to your Bahamian obligations and rights. You may have different circumstances to deal with in the States that are your responsibility. I can, however, advise you as to what my past experience with situations such as yours have resulted in. Is this clear to you, Toby?"

"I guess you are telling me that I have tax advantages here that I don't have in the States, and that I have to behave carefully if I want to take advantage of that. You, on the other hand, are being careful to avoid giving me advice that might get you or me in trouble in the United States. Is that about it?"

"Exactly," Tylander replied.

Over the next two hours the attorney and confidant of Toby's grandfather covered the essentials of the estate. After a number of specific bequests to long-term and faithful members of the staff at the inn, Vernon left the entirety of the remainder of his estate to Toby, which included Piper Cay and all of the real estate situated there. In addition, he had established numerous trusts under Bahamian and Commonwealth law that had quasi ownership, which would be passed on to designated beneficiaries through directives outlined in the trust indentures. These trusts owned sizable investments in marketable securities and real estate investment partnerships, most of which were managed by Clement Mills in Palm Beach.

In all, the estate was worth tens of millions of dollars, most of which was now under Toby's direct control, and available to him if he so chose, but not perceivable by authorities in the United States, except for the assets that were situate there, such as the co-op in Fort Lauderdale and the land partnerships located in the Orlando area. Toby took a minute for this to sink in.

"No shit! The old codger really knew what he was doing, didn't he?" he said at last.

"You think?" Chrissy chimed in, wide-eyed with astonishment.

Toby was thoughtful for a moment, and then he leaned forward. "Could you guys give Chrissy and me a moment?" he asked.

"Surely."

The others left the room quietly to give Toby and Chrissy some privacy.

"What do you think?" Chrissy asked earnestly.

"I think this is a far bigger decision with so many, many moving parts that I can't get my head around it. I'm trying to do what I did in Vietnam when I had multiple problems coming at me at the same time, like enemy fighters showing up on radar at the same time I was lining up for a bombing run, while missile threat alerts filled my ears, all while I had warning panel lights glowing in my face indicating I had an equipment malfunction. We need to find the lynchpin to the decision tree, and prioritize the rest, working on them one at a time. First would be, do we take advantage of the tax benefits of keeping our Bahamian business separate and offshore? That decision will affect our flexibility in the other decisions we have to make."

The two sat opposite each other and methodically worked through the alternatives. Chrissy repeated what she had said on the beach this morning. "If we work through this carefully, our path will be made clear to us."

In the midst of their discussion, they heard the distinctive clanging of the bell on the dock. It rang ten, twenty, and more times, sometimes a little muffled, and sometimes, particularly toward the end, loudly and clearly. They rushed through the veranda to look out at the dock, where they witnessed Jenny raising a hammer with two hands and repeatedly striking the brass bell, occasionally with the assistance of Major, who wrapped his big mitts over Jenny's tiny hands and helped her guide the blows.

"What on earth are you doing, Jenny?" Toby yelled.

"I'm calling Phinney, Daddy!" she explained.

"Honey, I think you can stop now. If she's going to come, I think she heard you already."

"What do we have to do now?" Jenny asked.

"All you have to do is wait. If Phinney is still in the area, she will hear you. It takes her about twenty-five minutes to get here from Rose Island, where she and her pod usually hang out. But remember, sweetie, I haven't seen her in years. I would suspect she has moved on by now. Don't get your hopes up."

Jenny crossed her arms in defiance. With a glaring stare, she said, "I'm going to wait right here!"

Toby and Chrissy returned to the library to continue their deliberations. He hoped Jenny wouldn't be too disappointed if Phinney didn't show up. After a while, they called for Mr. Tylander to join them to answer more questions. Their conversation ran on into late morning. Toby hadn't figured on the delay a calf would add to the travel time from Rose Island.

Phinney and her newborn are moving along the edge of the reef. Her second calf is just beginning to grow in his first set of conical teeth.

He is nourished predominantly by his mother's milk, but he is being introduced to the rudiments of foraging around the shallow reefs on the inside of Rose Island. He is already comfortable with swimming and traveling short distances to keep up with his mother and her companion. He is able to breathe and sleep on his own. He nurses at his mother's slits about eight or nine times a day, and his mother is always nearby.

At first Phinney is not even really aware of the distant, muffled tone of the bell. The clangs come regularly at first, blending in with the ambient noise of the water surging around and through the reef. Finally the distinctive sound brings a memory to the forefront of her brain, and she begins to pay more attention.

She is distracted by her calf, who is poking his snout among the rocks in an imitation of what mother does, but without any specific purpose. That's how he learns the basics of hunting. Every few minutes or so he has to return to the surface for a breath, and it is at this time when Phinney has the most concern, when the top of the reef is exposed at low tide, and her calf is at risk of catching a wave wrong and stranding himself on the sharp coral. Phinney always keeps an eye out for her young male, which is why she does not notice the ringing at first.

There it goes again! Phinney nudges her calf away from the edge of the reef on his next descent where she can devote her attention to the sounds coming from the sea. "Claaang, claaang, claaang." Sometimes crisper, sometimes softer, but definitely there. Her calf lifts his head in concentration. He hears it, too. Silence for a moment, and then again, "Claaang, claaang, claaang, claaang."

Phinney is flooded with memories from her past, images of Boy with his skinny arms diving with her for fish and lobster among the reefs of the area, following him in his boat with the big white sail, especially the intimate moments she shared with him lying between his skinny legs on the sand in the shallow water of the cove or a beach. She remembers how he spoke to her softly and how he cried when he was sad. Mostly, she remembers the laughter when they frolicked together anywhere on the water, his joy when he watched her jump and tail walk for his friends, screeching and clicking acknowledgment of their approval.

She feels the need to head for the cove at Boy's island, but what to do with her calf? He can only kick at a fraction of her speed, and her companion is off foraging with the rest of the pod. Having no choice, she nudges the calf and signals for him to follow. The two set out for Piper Cay at a pace the calf can maintain, Phinney sometimes leading, sometimes urging from behind. The calf definitely has the message; they are going someplace specific, and they are in a hurry. Slowly they make their way along the south side of Rose Island where the going was easier in flat water sheltered from a wind that was blowing out of the northeast. In her excitement, Phinney sometimes draws ahead, only to slow for her calf.

The minutes pass slowly, but they make progress, slowing a little in the rougher water before Salt Cay. Finally in the lee of Salt Cay, they slow and cruise at an easier pace. With each kick, the excitement within Phinney grows. For a while the clanging becomes louder, as they swim in a direct line to Boy's island, but after the longest time it stopped. Phinney becomes anxious, as she fears that Boy will not wait, but she knows she cannot leave her newborn. Her thoughts switch to her firstborn, now nearly fully grown, living independently with the pod. He did not stay with his mother for long, preferring instead the companionship of the group. He was not in evidence when Phinney gave birth to her second calf just six months previous, so Phinney had to rely on her companion for help during the difficult period after the male calf was born.

Passing the end of Salt Cay, the waves build again, and Phinney encourages her calf forward. When Phinney clears the water for a breath, she can see the casuarinas on the spit of the island forming the shelter for the cove at the ocean side. Her calf catches a second wind and kicks faster, picking up speed as he senses the urgency to complete the journey. Finally, the island is in sight and the calf can see his goal. Knowing he is near urges him faster. His heart is pounding from exertion as they drift over the bar into the protected water of the cove.

So is Phinney's, but not from the effort. Her anticipation of seeing Boy again pumps adrenaline throughout her system. She moves ahead of her calf, heading straight for the end of the pier, ignoring the lazing nurse sharks at the base of the pilings. Off the end, she kicks herself up on her tail and lets out a streak of screeches as she tail walks off the end of the dock. All she sees on the end of the dock is a dark-skinned human, one she had seen before, and a human immature female with curly blond hair and skinny arms and legs. As Phinney watches, she hears the girl call out her name.

"Phinney, Phinney, Phinney!" and then some unintelligible human talk as she claps her skinny arms, making popping noises. Then she turns, running down the dock toward the building, shouting all the way. After a few moments of watching the dark-skinned human smile at her with his big white teeth, the small girl returns jumping and shouting and pointing at Phinney with one of her long, skinny arms. Behind her, walking slowly, then faster, finally running down the dock is Boy. She is sure of it. Behind him runs Girl. Boy is wearing pants, not something Phinney remembers seeing much, and Girl is wearing a dress.

Boy waves his arms in excitement and jumps off the end of the dock, almost landing on Phinney, who has moved closer to get a better look. Her calf keeps his distance, unable to decipher the turmoil, unsure of himself. Phinney swims to Boy and pushes her snout in his midsection as a greeting. Boy reaches around her to grab her pectoral fins. Hanging alongside, Phinney starts to circle with Boy in tow. Boy is laughing now, waving his arms and pointing to the calf.

He moves toward him, and the calf backs away, shifting closer to the protection of his mother. Girl stands on the edge of the dock with her arms around the small child, as they point and shout Phinney's name.

Boy surveys the situation and swims to the shallow water by the curve of the beach next to the pier, motioning for all to follow. Girl and the young human run down the dock and cross the crescent beach to meet Boy in waist-deep water. Phinney's heart pounds with excitement as she encourages her newborn to follow her to the beach and join them.

Toby, Chrissy, and Bob Tylander are just finishing up when they hear Jenny shouting at the top of her lungs, getting louder as she reaches the veranda and crosses to the library. "Daddy! Daddy! Daddy! She's here. Phinney came! She's here! Come, Daddy, quick! Come see Phinney; she's here! And she has a baby with her!"

Toby and Chrissy stand, as Toby takes Jenny's outstretched hand and trots after her across the veranda to the dock. With all the new developments, he has forgotten all about Phinney for the time being, and hearing her name awakens his feelings for her in an instant.

Chrissy follows behind as they run out to the dock. Upon seeing Phinney standing on her tail, he cannot restrain himself. Leaving a trail of upended patio furniture in his wake, Toby almost knocks Major over as he jumps fully clothed into the water, almost landing on his best friend from childhood. Phinney gives him a good nudge in his stomach as he reaches around her to grab her fins for a ride around the lagoon. It is then that he notices the baby dolphin, barely two feet long, holding position nearby.

He releases his hold on Phinney, who is now so big he cannot get his arms around her and moves toward the tiny dolphin. He senses immediately this is a mistake, as the baby backs away and seeks protection from his mother. Toby surveys the situation and shouts up to the dock for Chrissy and Jenny to meet him in the shallower water of the beach. They run down the dock and cross the beach to Toby and wade out into the water.

Phinney moves in toward Toby and leaps at him as he sits down in the water, forgetting for a moment that she is now almost four times heavier than he. She crashes on his chest, pinning him under the water until he can roll out from underneath her. Partially beached, she wriggles her way backward until she is buoyant again, settling in her familiar place between his legs with her stomach resting on the warm sand.

Chrissy gives them the moment, knowing how special it is for each of them, but Jenny has other ideas. She wades over to Phinney and rubs her back above the dorsal. The calf edges ever closer to her mother, gaining confidence by the minute. Chrissy moves into the deeper water, and Phinney gives her a belly nudge of affection. Then, backing away a few feet, the dolphin focuses on Chrissy's midsection, and begins rolling her head in circles and clicking loudly.

This is not lost on Toby, as he remembers the similar reaction when Phinney "saw" something in his grandmother. Chrissy and Toby lock eyes, as big grins spread across both their faces. Chrissy is expecting.

"Is there something you've been meaning to tell me?" Toby asks.

"I'm not sure, but I think so," Chrissy replies sheepishly. "I wanted to wait until after everyone had gone; you have so much on your mind." She sits next to Toby, and gives him a gentle kiss.

"Jenny, sit down next to us, and see if her calf will come closer." Jenny kneels, as the water is too deep for her to sit. "Move closer to me and Phinney, so the baby won't be afraid."

As Jenny kneels next to her father, the calf ever so tentatively moves closer and lets Jenny put a hand on his brow. He begins making quiet squeaking noises to accompany his mother's soft clicking.

Chrissy moves closer now, and the two families share the space in the warm sand together. Toby takes Chrissy's hand and smiles at her. Chrissy gives his hand a squeeze, as a small tear forms in the corner of one of her beautiful blue eyes. "As always, dear, you are right. Our path has been made clear to us."

THE END

AFTERWORD

This effort is my first successful completion of a work of fiction. It has been a joy for me to write; if you have gotten this far, I hope you enjoyed it as well. Several of my friends have had a chance to read the manuscript in various stages, resulting in questions about the topic. Upon reflection it occurred to me that other readers may share the same curiosities, so I thought a few paragraphs might be in order to try to answer questions that have come up. First, please remember, this is a work of fiction. I have no special insight into the workings of the minds of bottlenose dolphin other than my imagination and what is available to anyone on the Internet.

The original idea for the story came to me about twelve years ago, and I have never been able to get the idea for it out of my mind. I wrote a few pages to test my motivation for completing the story and consolidated my plan in a chapter outline. It was only after I received encouragement from close friends that I was able to make the commitment to complete the task.

Armed with a story, I drew heavily on my own experiences to make the circumstances as real as possible. I learned to sail when I was eight years old, which gave me a foundation in those aspects of the book. Wherever I could draw upon my own experience to make references in the book more accurate, I have done so. Dates and events of public record should, for the most part, stand up to scrutiny of any readers who shared them, and I have tried to be true to the geography, as well, except for the creation of the imaginary Piper Cay outside of Nassau harbor. The other islands and waters surrounding them should be reasonably correct.

I feel compelled to discuss the naming of some of the characters to avoid any confusion. I realized early on in the process of writing that the introduction of characters would require associating them with names. For an amateur, keeping track of new personalities as they progressed through the manuscript became problematic for me, and so I took the easy way out, naming new characters after people I have known in my life, just so I could keep track. My plan was to change them at the end of the process to names unknown to me, so as not to embarrass anyone, but then it occurred to me that the new names would belong to somebody in the reading public, so what's the difference? I eventually decided to leave them as they were originally written.

Again, please remember, this is a work of fiction, and none of the characters portrayed have any connection to people I have known. The personalities are the unique property of the characters who are all of my own creation. If you are known to me and your name appears in this book, please do not be offended by the way your character has been portrayed. Conversely, if you are known to me and your name does not appear, please do not feel slighted. I just ran out of story.

I have so many people to thank for assistance in the creation of this book, I cannot mention you all. I must acknowledge my good friend Doris Kearns Goodwin, who convinced me that this was an endeavor worth pursuing. Her encouragement pushed me over the edge. Coleman Absher and his Navy fighter pilot friends helped me fill gaps in my flying background, as well as Flip Cuthbertson (who's name is in the book, no connection), Sam Baker, and others who flew in Vietnam. I find it oddly interesting that I could download the entire operating handbook for the F-4B Phantom from the Internet, so detailed is it that I am confident I can fly one. I must acknowledge my wife, Barbara, an international best-selling author in her own right, and my son, David, and daughter, Michelle, for their support while I shut myself away to write. They were eager early victims for story vetting. I also want to thank my cousin, Dale Raymond, who is responsible for the illustrations, and Carol Rosenberg for her copy-edit recommendations. As well, thank you, Whitney Anderson and Karen Krumholtz, for laughing and crying with me as this story came to life.

ABOUT THE AUTHOR

Dick Schmidt is a lifelong resident of Florida with a background in banking, real estate development, and aviation. His time is filled with philanthropic endeavors, which he spearheads with his wife, Barbara, an international bestselling author. He has two grown children and resides in Boca Raton, Florida.

CPSIA information can be obtained
at www.ICGtesting.com
Printed in the USA
LVOW01*1958030516

486535LV00005B/5/P

9 780997 501018